Chaos Vault

By

Allisha

McAdoo

AF603762

Copyright © Allisha McAdoo 2022/2023 This book may not be reproduced or used in any manner without the publisher's express written permission except for brief quotations in a book review in the United States of America. The characters are purely fictitious. Any likeness to persons living or dead is coincidental.

First Printing, 2022/2023

My other paperbacks are:

1. Dark Desires (a collaboration with Thomas J Kline)
2. Playthings with the devil (a short story collection)
3. Mr. Nice Guy (My first novel)
4. Your dirty secret (two of Mr. Rumple's stories.)
5. Night Terrors (A short story collaboration with J.M

Swiger

6. Forever together (a vampire novel)
7. Yours for a price (Origin story of Mr. Rumple)
8. Twisted sideways (Asylum short story collection that ties all stories together)

9.T//Error404 (A revenge story)

10. Absurd witch (a comedy for teenagers under the pen name Allysha McAdoo)

11. Corpse Prison (a collection of stories that star Mr. Rumple)

12.No loose ends (The last story of Mr. Rumple)

13. Rumple Chronicles (The complete collection of Mr. Rumple stories)

14. Fatal Tales(a collaboration with Howard Carlyle)

15. Severed Dick Chili(a godless exclusive only story)

16. Absurd Witch 2(A sequel to Absurd witch under the pen name Allysha

McAdoo)
17. Absurd 1 & 2 (A book with both stories of absurd witches under the pen name of Allysha McAdoo
18. I'm Cursed(an extreme horror story)
19. I know your secrets (An extreme horror short story collection)
20. Picture Perfect (A godless only exclusive)
21. Spiders, Toasters, Rootbeer, and other prompts (My first ever prompt book)
22. Bibliophobia Fear of books (A godless only exclusive)
23. Book of fear (A godless only exclusive)
24. Naughty List (A godless only exclusive)
25. The wrong door (An extreme horror story)
26. Friends Forever (An extreme horror story)
27. Play Hearts (A godless exclusive

story)
28. Luckier than you (An extreme horror anthology)
29. The pen (An extreme horror story)
30. Alura (A godless exclusive)
31. Beauty and Mr.Rumple (A sequel to Rumple
Chronicles)
32. I eat people (An extreme short story collection)
33. Cryptid Carnage (An anthology with my story Wendigo)
34. Heart of the Mavka (A collaboration with Jack Presby)
35. Painted smiles (An extreme horror story)
36. Revenge (A collection of revenge stories)
37. Twisted Images (A collaboration with Jack Presby)
38. Pillow Talk (A godless exclusive)
39. Twisted Images (A pubshare exclusive collaboration with Jack Presby)

40. Mama and Mavka (A sequel collaboration with Jack Presby)
41. Mavka Collection (Both Mavka collaborations with Jack Presby)
42. Demons (A godless exclusive)
43. Chaos Vault

Coming Soon

Mr. Yoinks (YA comedy with the pen name of Allysha McAdoo)

Beast and Mr. Rumple (Book 3 in my Rumple series)

12 Shadows of Christmas (An extreme horror short story collaboration with Jack Presby)

My group
https://www.facebook.com/groups/1718802991696554/
My Facebook author page
https://www.facebook.com/allishamcadooauthor/
My amazon page (Where you can find my other ebooks on kindle and Goodreads)
https://www.amazon.com/s/ref=nb_sb_ss_i_4_6?url=search-alias

%3Daps&field-keywords=allisha +mcadoo&sprefix=allish%2Caps %2C205&crid=1XQBXSJGNHP0
My author central page
amazon.com/author/allishamcadoo
My Godless.com page
https://godless.com/search?q=allisha +mcadoo
My Tiktok name is allishamcadoo
My Instagram is mcadooallisha

About the Author:
I started writing at a young age and have madly fallen in love with it. I have paperbacks on Amazon and ebooks on Godless, Pubshare, Nook, Kobo, Google Play, Apple Books, Goodreads, Smashwords, and Kindle. I have been published since 2017 and don't plan on slowing down anytime soon.

Welcome to my vault! Within this book contains all my short stories from the year 2022 that didn't make it into a paperback book. I kept the covers, and author notes with each story. I hope you enjoy them all.

Demons

Author's note

Warning This story may contain graphic materials that some may not find suitable. Read at your own risk. In no way shape or form, am I making fun of any religion. This is a short story collection I wrote over the years. These are stories that are from my nightmares and have no real depiction of religion in any way. If this offends you, please go read a Dr. Suess, because this book won't be for you. You have been warned.

"I call to mind flatness and dampness; and then all is madness - the madness of a

memory which busies itself among forbidden things."
~Edgar Allan Poe~

Prologue

For thousands of years, there has been a battle of good vs. evil. Millions of people have died thinking they had served some vengeful God. The Earth is littered with bad history and has stained any future where good prevails.

My name is Abatha, although no one calls me that. Generally, people tend to call me Abby. I don't know why my mother chose the name she did; everyone thinks it's a typo from Agatha. I've always hated it. I never met either of my parents. I was raised in an orphanage with a local church. I was highly religious until I reached the age of 12. I had too many questions that God never answered. The nuns that raised me thought me being disruptive and made it their personal mission to whip me into shape.

I used to pretend I was dumb and hated books so my punishments would land me in the library. They didn't know that I actually loved to read. I was very intelligent for my age and could solve math problems the college students were doing. As I got older, I found it was easier to deceive everyone around me. I left the orphanage at the age of 16 with a family. The Andersons were not looking for another mouth to feed. So we struck a deal with each other about 80 miles away from the orphanage. I would be on my own, and they would say they adopted me so they could collect the checks from the state. The deal was they could collect on me until I reached the age of 19, then they could arrange a fake funeral for me. I would fake my death and start over brand new.

For the most part, the deal lasted for about six months before they died horribly in a car crash, along with the other kids they had in their care. I desperately needed money and didn't want to return to the orphanage, so I did something evil. I snuck into the building that kept all of the state's birth certificates. I found mine after a few hours and erased it. I created another birth certificate naming myself a twin. I was no longer going to be Abatha but my twin Abernathy. I would keep the nickname Abby. I didn't just stop there. I created a whole life for myself and even gave myself rich relatives. I created a whole new family tree just to make sure I inherited Uncle Max's wealth, whoever he was. I never stopped questioning God. I lived a pretty good life until I met Cody. Cody was the leader of a satanic cult called Morningstar Embassy. Not an original name if you ask me, but for some reason, I felt like I belonged there. All the bad things I had done in order to survive and escape those hateful nuns seemed like it all led me to this path.

The nuns raged war against us once they discovered what I had done. They blamed me for the Anderson's death. Late one night, they set fire to the entire compound that I had claimed as my home. About 85% of us didn't make it, including Cody. Everyone else fled and left me behind. I was lost in a world I no longer understood. That's when the nightmares started. If Cody were alive, he would tell me to investigate each nightmare. That they were calling me to find the people in them for some reason. However, Cody is not alive, and nothing makes sense to me anymore. Instead of doing what he wanted me to do, I wrote them all down. I suppose I should have burned them, but I didn't. Now I only have a few days left before I am claimed by Death. I am dying from a mysterious illness that no one can diagnose. I guess that is my punishment after all that I have done. This book will find someone who was just as lost as I was when I was alive. Maybe it will shed light or start something born from chaos and viciousness.

If you are reading this, I can't guarantee that this book will give you the answers you want. I don't know if anything I wrote held any sort of truth or if it was just my fevered mind. Do with this book as you wish. If it turns out that my nightmares have truth in them, then I am sorry for not doing anything about it. There are things in this world that can't be explained or controlled. I hope you find the strength to stop them all.

Dream # 1
NOKOMIS

Nokomis Irene walked slowly down the street with her head bent down. Small crystal-like tears fell silently down her pale face. The night was foggy and damp, filled with silence. The fog made it to where Nokomis could walk without sticking to the shadows. She was a nocturnal creature of fair beauty, but the sight of people always made her panic. No one had gazed upon her face in decades, and she liked to keep it that way. The last person who gazed upon her face was her love, Nakieto, and that was decades ago. She pushed the thought of him out of her head and slowly trudged to the lake that surrounded the city. She sat there in the fog, by the water's edge, crying silently. The modern times were rough on her, and tried her best to adapt to it. Her stomach rumbled a bit loudly as she wiped her tears away. She hadn't eaten anything in almost three weeks, and the stomach pains had become unbearable. The fog seemed to envelop her, and she screamed out her rage to the sky within her head. She had the worst luck in the world and was barely surviving.

It all started a few weeks back as she walked home from her library job. It was a late stormy night, with the full moon held up high. She walked, enjoying the storm ducking only when flashes of lightning seemed too close for comfort. However, the storm became fierce, and soon she was flung into a building. Her slender body fell right thru a wall, and she lay there trying to ignore the pain while the rain pounded at her face. While the storm raged on, she did her best to pick herself off the ground, but suddenly there was a green flash, and the darkened room was suddenly aglow. She felt an eerie tingling sensation and felt herself transform into her true demonic form. She walked further into the room, unsure what could cause the form she had hidden for many decades to come out. Suddenly all went black, and she felt a sharp prick on the back of her neck; her body went back into her human form. Her body crumpled to the ground like a wet tissue, and soon she passed out. When she had awoken, she was back in her own condo lying in her own bed. For a while, she wondered if it was a dream, but after a couple of hours of pondering it, she left her condo to start her shift at work. The back of her neck pulsed and throbbed with great pain. By the time she got to the library, her world had turned upside down. The pain in her neck had become unbearable, and with each step she took, she could feel her knees knocking against themselves. That day she lost her job, her condo, and everything she had held dear to her heart.

Nokomis couldn't remember what terrible events had happened to make her lose everything, and each day the pain in her neck increased. At night she could get some peace from it all when she came to the lake. At night came the serenity of peace from the pain, but soon her human form seemed to fade away slowly. Whatever had happened to her that night was killing off her human side, forcing ill luck to follow her no matter where she went. She knew she wouldn't be safe much more longer, for her demonic side was transforming, and pretty soon, her human form would die. She had no idea what she was becoming, and it frightened her. She sat there trying not to move, to blend in with the fog. From behind her, she heard footsteps, soft and slow, like someone was sneaking up behind her. She wiped away her tears and sat there, trying to will her demonic side to stay dormant.

From out of the fog, a lone figure stood beside her, and a hoarse whisper cackled in her ear, " Do not be afraid, Nokomis, I am a friend sent here to help." A gnarled hand rested on her shoulder making her feel uneasy. The woman sat down beside her and looked Nokomis deeply in the eyes. Nokomis soon became lost in her eyes and saw images appear in the old woman's eyes. She watched intently as the story of her destiny played. Long ago, there was a war that raged on the Earth that never met the human eye. Demons and angels fought to get the upper hand over the humans. The war became brutal, and many were massacred. Humans walked past, unaware that they were stepping on demonic guts and angel wings that lay in ruin heaps on the ground. She saw her demon standing alone, unaffected by the war. She raised her hands and clapped them, forming a green light around herself like a poisonous gas. She screamed, and all went silent, stilling all that was around her. Time seemed to have stopped for a brief moment as the green glow around her danced and swirled, growing larger.

Suddenly just as it had begun, the war stopped. The demons returned to hell while the angels flew off. The mangled bodies that lay on the ground vanished, and there was no evidence that there had ever been any violence. Nokomis watched the images unblinking as she watched her demonic side kiss passionately a male angel of tremendous beauty. He reminded her of Nakieto, and tears formed in her eyes as she watched his wings being stripped from his back. Blood poured onto his perfect body, yet he still stood kissing her deeply. Soon both were engulfed in flames melting their beings that once stood there. Nokomis blinked, aware that she was crying hard, and whispered, "What does all this mean?" The old woman whispered, " Your demonic side fell in love with the forbidden angel. A love like that could destroy the world as we all know it. Both were destroyed ages ago but were given the chance to be with each other as humans for the reward of stopping the war. However, when you crashed into the building, your demonic side was enveloped with his love. You were right to think of him as Nakieto, for he is the angel from your past. However, humans have altered you now, and your human side will die. Once you become your demonic self fully, the war will commence this time to stop you from getting to Nakieto and being with him.

The sharp pain in the back of your neck is the human's curse to take away your outer shell, your beauty, your luck, and even make your heart black. The lake eases your pain because it's pure, and this lake was formed by Nakieto's tears. The humans have captured Nakieto and have been experimenting on him, breaking his spirit. The only way to stop the war is to save him and disappear from the plane that holds humans. I must go now, Nokomis; humans are approaching. Follow your heart to him, and go to the plane that's unknown to all." With the last words whispered, the woman seemed to vanish. Nokomis felt strange as she got up from the water's edge and dived into the lake. She swam to the very bottom of it, hiding herself from whatever dangers lay upon the surface. The deeper she went, the faster her human side died. Once again, she was engulfed with the green glow the pain in her neck was gone, and all she could think of was Nakieto. She swam deeper to the bottom, watching her flesh melt away; soon all that was left was her demonic side. She screamed with rage that she would be denied her love once more and shot up from the water. She cloaked herself and walked amongst the humans that were throwing rocks into the water, turning the water a rusty red color. Wings red and black as darkened blood shot out of her back, ripping clear thru the muscles. She winced in pain as her black blood poured freely down her back.

She closed her eyes and thought of Nakieto, a brief smile playing on her face. Soon she shot up into the sky and flew with her eyes closed, searching the terrain below for Nakieto's scent. No human saw her flying, and no machine came close to her, but she was far from feeling at ease. She could feel Nakieto's pain and heartache with such an extremity that it almost doubled her over in pain.

Soon corrupted and fallen angels surrounded her slicing her skin with their fiery swords. Nakieto screamed inside her head, and she powered up. She refused to kill those who were hurting her, so she just disappeared into the clouds. She knew then that the search for Nakieto would not be an easy task, but she was prepared to walk thru the Earth and hell just to gaze at his face once more. She cursed herself for letting him walk out of her life decades ago, being young and stupid was turning out to be the biggest mistake of her life. She kept to the clouds that swirled around her with angry fury as she concentrated on Nakieto. During the day, she cloaked herself and walked amongst humans as a human. Her rage grew with each lonely day she had to spend alone; soon, even humans kept their distance from her. She walked with darkened eyes, never stopping to rest. She walked intently, listening to Nakieto's pain and torment, fighting in the streets as the others tried to rip her apart. Her wounds poured with blood, yet she didn't feel it. At night she took to the skies, flying with a rage that could tear apart any plane that dared to cross her. As she neared the mountains, she could feel Nakieto once more, almost tasting him.

Nakieto's screams got louder when Nokomis reached a darkened compound. She touched down flames shooting up her body, leaving a trail of blood and fire behind her as she walked toward the compound. Nokomis screamed in fury as the fallen angels swooped down from the sky, cutting her demonic body deeply. Tears of blood ran down her face as she fought herself free from them. Their swords sliced thru her with a force that she started to fall down trying to fight, and her vision blurred. Suddenly Nokomis shot into the sky once more and crashed into a window on the compound's roof, cloaking herself as a human. Her wounds became horrendous, and it hurt her to walk. Limping badly, she did her best to stop her bleeding following the sounds of Nakieto. Nakieto's pale body lay on a metal table, hooked to various machines. Nokomis growled softly and unhooked him from the machines. She cradled him against her as she did her best to shield him from the blows of the swords she was enduring. Nakieto opened his eyes, and her heart swelled with love and pride. Slowly she unfurled her wings and shot up into the sky with him in her arms. Ducking the flaming arrows and swords that attacked her savagely. Below, hell opened its gates and flooded Earth's plane with demonic armies. The heavens above her swept her with a torrent of raging storms and angels. She held onto Nakieto as best as possible, fighting with every inch of her life.

The strongest of angels sliced thru her demonic wings, causing her to fall mercilessly to the ground below. She braced her body for the impact so that Nakieto couldn't feel it. She grabbed a fallen sword and tried to slay the millions of demons charging her. Nakieto saw Nokomis from his blurry vision and realized she had come to save him. Swords flew all around him and her, whizzing past them with hatred. All the decades just melted away as he took her face into his hands and lovingly kissed her. They stood there, fighting and kissing as the demons tried to tear them apart. Nokomis fell against Nakieto, and both kept each other up by the strength of the other. Hell's fires licked at their bodies, causing them to scream. Nokomis cried and screamed to Nakieto, " No matter what they do to us, I'll always love you, and no matter what life we decide to live in, I'll find you. We may be eternally denied, but I'll never stop trying." Nakieto cried with Nokomis and held her close as he did his best to whisper, "Always and forever, I remain yours." Nokomis and Nakieto both screamed their rage, transforming their bodies. They fought, slaying all that stood in their way, linked hands, and felt only love for each other. Angels screamed in their ears, deafening them with their roars, and the demons clawed out their eyes. Still, they stood together, refusing to give up. The humans walked past, unaware of the massive battle that was being held on their grounds.

The war raged on for centuries, mutilating their bodies beyond repair. Nokomis and Nakieto died in each other's arms from wounds pouring blood onto the ground in a massive, crimson, and dark river. Today, where their bodies lay for centuries has become the most beautiful landmark the human eyes have ever seen. For in death, Nokomis and Nakieto merged their souls so they would never be apart again, living their afterlife in purgatory. Their love defied all laws, leaving them outcasts for all eternity. Sometimes late at night, you can still hear their screams of rage as time flies by, unaware of their existence. Unable to ever get the chance to be together in a physical form again. Every once in a while, a massacre will happen at that very spot. The most beautiful landmark in the world has a strange effect on people, as it should since it’s the death place of two powerful beings.

Dream # 2
Nayleon

It's hard to figure out where to begin, especially since things are muddled and blurry inside my head. You might say that this story is the writing of someone insane or hyped up on drugs. I am neither of those things; I am, in fact, perfectly sane and off drugs. The story I am about to tell is beyond the bounds of reality. I must write it even though it pains me to. Otherwise, this story will haunt me forever.

My name is Nayleon, and I don't have much time to write. The demons after my soul are closing in fast, and I must keep moving to survive. My best friend, my love, Arlina, had warned me that this would happen, and like an idiot, I had laughed at her. Now I am alone, fighting to save mankind and keep the demons from tearing my soul apart.

Arlina was into the supernatural, and every time she had a vision, she would
warn me of what was to come. On the other hand, I called her crazy and eventually started to avoid her. Now I wish I had listened to her; if I could go back in time, I would have chained her to my side and kept her warnings at my heart. But I am getting ahead of myself; let me start from the beginning.

I had met Arlina way back in elementary school, and one day she saved me from getting my ass kicked by bullies. Since that day, we became best friends, and in high school, I realized that I was deeply in love with her but was too shy to ask her out. In high school, Arlina realized that she had special abilities and powers. She started to concentrate more on that than our friendship. She would come running up to me, warning me of some unforeseen danger. At first, I thought it was cute that she cared, but I grew tired of hearing it all after a while. In the end, I distanced myself away from her to the point that she no longer came running up to me, warning me.

One night I had a very disturbing dream and

decided I needed Arlina's help. She was cold to me when I finally got her on the phone, but never -the-less she was able to help me with my dream. After telling me what my dream meant, she became super worried about me. She made me a necklace that held a small crystal, and to make her happy; I wore it. She asked to meet me in the local library to do some research. At first, I tried to blow her off, but after several minutes, I realized I wasn't getting out of it.

When I got to the library, Arlina was standing outside looking beautiful, and she took my breath away. I smiled at her, and we went into the library without saying a word to each other. She quickly found the books she was looking for and sat me down at a table. "Your dream isn't a good one, these are called demons, and this is called the sword of destruction. Now, in your dream, you held the sword of destruction and were slaying demons. If you look closely at the pictures, you will find the exact demon that was in your dreams. Once we figure out which demon was in your dream, we can truly analyze the danger you may or may not be in." Arlina quietly said as she handed me the very heavy and old book. I glanced at her eyes and realized that they were bottomless; I felt that she could see into my soul. Very curious, I started to thumb thru the book. One particular page leapt out at me; it startled me, and I fell out of my chair. Laughing quietly, Arlina picked me up off the floor and looked at the picture. Her beautiful eyes widened, and she looked at me worriedly. "You're kidding, right? THIS was the demon in your dreams?" Arlina said without looking away from the page.

I lifted up her chin to where she was looking me directly in the eyes, "Arlina, I am not in any danger. It was just a dream, probably brought on by something I ate." I winced as she looked at me with a hardened look. Very quietly and coldly, she said, "You're wrong, Nayleon. There are many different forms of danger. You may think I am crazy, but I am just looking out for you. There will be a day when you will have to use all this info. and I may not be around to help you out. The time is coming for you to train your body, mind, and powers to their full potential. One of these days in the near future, you will have to make a choice. If you fall into the darkness, you will be lost forever, but if you listen to me, you will fight to save mankind."

I didn't say anything, her voice had chilled me to the bone, and I started to look thru the books again. I spent the next 2 hours listening to her explain all sorts of things about demons and my destiny. After I had left her, I began to feel uneasy and kept looking over my shoulder. Night had come while I was in the library and with it brought a chilly wind that seemed to slice right thru me. I wasn't one to admit it, but Arlina had scared me.

I wasn't sure I believed anything she had said, but her eyes kept catching me off guard. I had felt her inside my head, which made me beyond uneasy.

The night plagued me with nightmares, and I woke up sweating and shaking. I took a long drive with my music blaring, hoping it would clear my head. I avoided Arlina more than ever once I got back to school. After about a week, I got a panicked message on my cell phone from Arlina. I listened intently as hysteria crept into her
voice, "Nayleon.... I think I am in trouble...please believe...." static had cut the rest message off. Worried, I jumped into my car and drove to her place. No one was home, so I let myself in the back door with the key she had given me when we were little kids. I went up to her room and gasped at the sight I saw. There was blood everywhere, and her room was trashed. On the bed was the pendant she wore that matched the one I had. I picked it up, cradling it with my hands, then putting
it around my neck. On her desk was a small vile of the latest potion she was working on. I picked it up along with her written notes and pocketed them. I searched for her laptop and found it shoved under her bed. I unplugged it and put it under my arm. If she were in trouble, she would need these things.

I quietly let myself out of the house and locked the back door. I drove to the spot where we used to run to get away from everyday life. I hadn't been there for months, but I could tell Arlina had been living there off and on. I went in and plugged in her laptop as I started to read over her notes. They were detailed and in-depth about what the potion was and what it could do. I set it down and lit a cigarette; my head was wheeling. This potion was a very serious thing, and I was a little afraid to touch it. Nevertheless, I strung it up with the two crystal pendants, all the while thinking to myself that these three items were the most important.

I hid her written notes in our safe that only we had the combination to. Then I went to her laptop; there was a voice and picture message waiting to be read. I pressed the button and watched in horror as Arlina started to speak in a low, hurried voice. "Nayleon, if you are watching this, then I am either dead or captured. I stumbled onto a potion that gives people magical powers. I took one vile for myself, and I hope that you have found the other vile. Whether or not you believe you are in danger that potion will help you. Keep it with you at all times. You must destroy everything on this computer; you know the password. It's the same as the safe. If I am right about my visions, then by the time you see this, I may have run to the safe house in Maine. The one out in the country, where we hid that one time from both of our parents. Nayleon, you and I don't have much time, so please open your eyes and do what I say. The demons you saw in your dreams are real, and they are coming after you and me. My suggestion is to make your way to the safe house in Maine. In the safe, you will find money; I have been saving up for a while, just in case. Be careful and keep a low profile. One more thing, Nayleon, I never told you this but.... I love you." The last three words sang to my heart, I would do anything for her, and if it turned out she was crazy, I would help her thru it.

I wiped her computer clean, took out the hard drive, and shot it full of holes. Then I put the entire computer in a huge barrel and set it on fire. In the safe, under some bundles of things we viewed as valuable, I found the money she had stored. I looked at the vile that was around my neck, and I felt the power inside it. It caught my attention and caught my breath in my chest. I unscrewed the cork and drank the vile down; instantly, I felt more powerful than I had ever felt. I finally understood what she had been saying all these years. It was time for my journey to begin.

I took the money she had left in the safe and climbed into my car. I filled up my tank and called everyone I knew, and told them a story about how I was going to go college hunting for a few days. I drove halfway to Maine without stopping for rest, my back ached, and my eyes burned. The only thing I could think about was Arlina, and I had hoped that I could make it to her soon. I pulled off

the side of the road
and slept in my car for a couple of hours. Every time I closed my eyes, I could feel Arlina screaming at me.

It got to the point where I didn't want to rest; her screams in my ears were almost deafening. I would down as much caffeine and no dos pills as I possibly could. Finally, after a day or so of driving, I arrived at the safe house. Arlina's screams in my head had intensified, and I knew she was hurt badly. I felt connected to her on a stronger level. I hurried inside and checked the safe that we had hidden when we were kids. I found more money in the safe and was shocked to see how much she had saved up.
There was a little note taped to it that read as follows "Nayleon, I am glad you made it here safely. I got taken to the haunted castle in Ireland. It has a spiritual nexus at the bottom of it, and I am being kept prisoner by the demons who have crossed over to this plane. My knowledge is what is keeping me alive, but you must hurry; I am running out of time. I love you, and keep to the shadows."
Tears rose in my eyes, and I held her note close to my heart. I whispered to her to stay strong; I was on my way to her. I was heading out of the safe house to go to the airport when I found a sword handle sticking up from the backyard.

It was the sword Arlina had bought at a fairgrounds festival when we were kids, and I had sunk it into the ground by accident. When I looked closely at it, I realized it was the sword from my dream.

Suddenly everything made sense to me; I grabbed the sword and read the inscription on the handle. The powers inside me surged, and the sword gleamed until suddenly, I felt like I had armor on me. I felt super strong, and I jumped up in the air picturing Arlina in my mind. Before I knew it, the sword had brought me to the haunted castle and from deep inside, I could feel her screams. The power inside me surged and I punched thru the outer wall. The demons were after me trying to claw at me and rip me apart. The sword seemed to come alive and fight them off. I made my way to Arlina's screams, and as I got closer, they seemed to hurt my head.

She was chained to a wall and badly hurt, with a bloody outline of her body on the wall. I fought like hell till I got to her and kissed her on the lips for the first time. "I love you Arlina." I unchained her and held her in my arms. Her cold limp body felt heavy in my arms. She was dead. Because I was an idiot and laughed at her, I couldn't save her. Demons screeched loudly at me, as she was ripped from my arms.

I was not going to make it out alive. I had messed up so much and the demons were going to take over the plane of the living. I lifted up my sword one last time and plunged it hard into a demon's chest. Right before I got ripped apart I could see it's fiery heart stop. "I'm sorry Arlina, I failed." I whispered as everything went into darkness.

Dream # 3
Maila

I was born from evil and greed. I never was apologetic for it. Why should I be sorry for being born, no matter how it happened? I didn't ask to be born, and I didn't ask to stay alive all this time. I made the best of the situations I lived through. I lived with my grandmother, Beebee. Beebee was not a kind woman and made sure she was strict with everything she did to raise me. She would even count the rice for dinner to make sure I wasn't being a glutton. She was a crazy God fanatic. She believed that God would visit her late at night in her room. Truth is, she was addicted to porn, and that wasn't God that was visiting her.

From a young age, I refused to give in to anything she wanted. I didn't believe I should try to be a better person, so I didn't bother. I didn't belong anywhere and spent my life entirely alone with the shadows to keep me company. I stumbled across a necklace in a closing store that changed my life. The store was fairly new, but the owners suddenly got ill and couldn't keep the store open anymore. Everything was discounted to an insane percentage. The store was a mess; I remember seeing dirt and grime smeared all over the floors. I had no money, so originally, I was just window shopping.

I must have spent an hour going through the shelves looking at all the crap the store was trying to give away. That's when I found the necklace. It was made from glass and cut my finger. I was about to throw it to the floor when I noticed its unique design. The pendant was a sharp cube but inside the cube was a green holographic eyeball. The eyeball seemed to follow me no matter where I held it up. I stuffed the necklace in my pocket and causally walked out of the store. As soon as I stepped onto the street, the entire store went up in flames. I took the necklace out of my pocket and put it around my neck. The chain was flimsy, but for some reason, I felt different wearing it. I ignored the fire trucks and screaming people as I walked home. Beebee was in the living room watching a show about a preacher pretending to heal people. I ignored her and went into my tiny room in the basement. The basement was always cold because Beebee didn't believe in turning on the heater during the winter. My room consisted of multiple blankets and anything I could find to keep me warm. After covering up with about six blankets, I dug out the tiny jewelry box I had stolen from the neighbor.

I dug out a thicker chain that held a cross on it. I tossed the cross in a corner that had Beebee's failed projects. The pendant I stole from the store looked amazing on the new chain. I didn't care if people asked me where I got it; I was going to wear it all the time. I fell asleep last night dreaming of a man with long horns on his forehead. I couldn't tell you what the dream was about, but when I woke up, I knew I was no longer the same person I was when I went to bed. Beebee started the morning bitching at me about my grades. "You are so lazy! You better get better grades, or you will end up flipping burgers at the burger shack for the rest of your life." She yelled at me. I touched the pendant and smiled. "As long as I don't turn into you," I said quietly.

Her mouth widened in surprise, and I turned around to leave the house. I had no intentions of going to school, but I wasn't going to stay there and listen to her bitch at me anymore. I held the pendant in my hand and made my way down the driveway. The house exploded just like the store did. I could hear Beebee screaming inside. I ran down the street and didn't look back. I didn't care if she made it or not. Let her God save her. For the first time in my life, I couldn't care less about anything or anyone. I was happy not to be freezing in that fucking basement anymore. Somehow, I made my way to Florida. The heat was intense, but I still felt cold. I didn't care where I lived as long as it could warm me up. The more places I searched, the colder I felt.

I felt like I was trapped in an ice cavern, even when the sun was beating down on me. As I grew up, I didn't feel any sort of attachment to anyone. I enjoyed being alone. I enjoyed not having to say anything to anyone. There are millions of people in the world who can't handle the silence or being alone. I was luckily not one of them. I didn't finish school; what was the point? There was nothing in school that could be taught in real life. I didn't find myself a job. I found ways to get what I wanted without having to slave away. People were so gullible. In most places, it was easy to steal. I never went back home, fuck that place.

I never took off that pendant, and I felt like I was living my best life. Until one night when I lost it. I met a man in an alley who decided it was time for me to learn how to fight. I could smell the booze on his breath and the fact that he hadn't showered in a long time. He grabbed me by the waist and thought he could overpower me. He threw me against the dumpster, all the while muttering to himself. Something deep inside of me snapped, and I felt a rage that I had never felt before. It gave me warmth for just a brief moment. I grabbed him by the throat and twisted his head until I could feel his spine crack loudly against my hands. The feeling as his body went limp made my entire body feel alive. I felt like I had stuck my entire body into an electrical current.

I shoved the man deep down inside the dumpster. He smelled like he crawled out of one, so he probably wouldn't be noticed right away. I didn't care if he was discovered, however. I didn't care that I just took someone's life. I felt nothing except warmth for once in my life. By the time I got home, it was raining, but I still felt like I was on fire. I changed out of my wet clothes and ran a bath with the hottest water I could find in the house. I never used cold water for anything. I turned up the water heater to full blast and waited for the steamy water to burn welts on my skin as I climbed into the tub. I didn't mind the welts. For a few minutes, until the water cooled down, I felt warm. By the next morning, the welts had always disappeared.

When I climbed out of the tub, I realized that the necklace that I had worn around my neck for the last 20 years was no longer there. Panicky, I dressed and ran back to the alleyway. I searched all over the alley and didn't find it. I searched the dead body and the entire dumpster to come up empty-handed. I was soaked head to toe and reeked of death. I kept my eyes on the ground as I walked home, hoping to find it lying in the grass. I didn't find it. I woke up the next morning sick. I had never been sick in my entire life. I could barely stand up, and my head felt like it had been soaking underwater for a long time. My ears were ringing painfully, and my eyes would not stop watering.

Thick green snot oozed out of my nose no matter how many times I blew my nose. My entire body ached, and I looked deathly pale. What do people do when they are sick? I asked my phone for advice, but it fell out of my weak hands. It clattered loudly to the floor, and when I picked it up, I realized it was severely damaged.

The room spun around dangerously as I felt my body give out. I crumpled to the floor like a wet napkin. My stomach muscles hurt, and I barely crawled to the bathroom before I started to vomit. I couldn't tell if I was making it to the toilet as I vomited. Everything was blurry, and I had no strength left. I could feel my body lose consciousness. The man from my dream many years ago was sitting beside me when I woke up. He was severely chiseled with a body that only could have come from a porn site. I couldn't help but gaze at it because he was entirely naked.

"Hello, Maila." He said in a raspy voice. I looked at his face and realized that I could see no color in his eyes. Where his eyes were, there was nothing but black pools. "How did you know my name?" I asked but instantly felt stupid for doing so. There sitting in my dried vomit, was the man I dreamt of when I first found the necklace. He still had the horns on his head, but they looked smaller than before. He didn't bother to answer me. I didn't think he would. He smiled at me. The smile was sinister and made my entire body shiver. "Want me to help you feel better?" He asked quietly. I didn't care what he was implying; I just knew I couldn't handle being sick any longer. "Yes. What do I have to do?" I coughed. I couldn't think my head hurt so bad it felt like a rave party was happening.

"Well, it will be painful." He said, smiling even bigger. I noticed that his teeth were not white or straight. They were black and sharpened to points. His tongue was black, as well as his gums. "Whatever, I don't care. Just do it." I said, making sure I didn't break eye contact. He reached to the top of his head and broke off his horns with his massive hands. His forehead was gushing with dark red blood that looked almost black. I could see bone in the holes the horns made. He grabbed me by my wrists and dragged me closer to him. His horns were digging into my skin, and his smile was getting bigger by the second. He kissed me in a passionate way that should have revolted me, but I couldn't stop myself. I had never been kissed before, and I never thought that my first kiss would be with a man that had horns.

I closed my eyes for a split second, enjoying the moment, and I felt something sharp hit me in the chest. My eyes flew open in surprise, and I saw that he had stabbed both of his horns in my chest. Blood was gushing out of the wounds and splashing loudly onto the ground. "What?" was all I could ask before I could feel my lungs filling up with my blood. "You found my necklace, which means you are my betrothed. You took off the necklace to signal that you were finally ready to be my wife. "I lost it." I managed to say in between gasps. He laughed and put something around my neck. It was my necklace that I had lost. "You are lucky I found it and no one else." His smile now stretched to both ears.

I didn't understand what was happening because my chest pain had gotten worse. I looked down to see the hole where the horns were sticking out getting bigger. The man watched me in fascination as I struggled to breathe. It seemed like an eternity before my body slumped to the floor. It only took seconds for me to bleed out. Suddenly, I was no longer in my body but standing beside it. The man stood up and grabbed me by the hand. The bathroom slowly disappeared, and it became a beautiful garden of fire. I felt warm, and for the first time, I felt happy. I glanced at the man who looked different in the garden. He was more handsome, more human-like than before. I threw caution into the wind and took his hand. At least I was finally warm.

I never saw his horns again, and he never changed his appearance from that of the garden. I was happy, and for the first time in my life, I was in love. That is, until the war broke out. I wasn't sure what caused the war, but the humans I left behind raged in a war that affected both sides. Both in Heaven and Hell, everything was dying.

The man I married was injured and succumbed to his injuries. Right as he took his last breath, I took his eyeball out from his head. I put it into a glass cube and sent it to the land of the living. This time when I found the necklace, I would do things right. I looked around what I remembered as my home one last time and put my necklace around my husband's neck. I stepped into the rift humans created and found myself back in time. Right before the rift closed on me, I realized I had done something wrong. I could see my home collapsing on itself and fire consuming everything I loved. My necklace was like a bomb and made everything explode like it was made from glass. The rift closed behind me as a shard hit me in the head.

I was a different person with a different life and couldn't remember why I was standing in front of a closing store. Was I going to go in? Something deep inside of me was nagging me to go inside and take a look around. Instead, I turned around and continued on my way to work. It was the last day of winter, and I needed to ensure the water park would be ready to open within a few days. I turned around and glanced at the store once more before moving on. Whatever was in that store, I am sure it had nothing in it for me.

I couldn't get the store out of my mind and kept looking back at it. Finally, I made it to work. Surely, nothing would happen for me not going to the store.....

The End

Revenge
By
Allisha McAdoo

Table of Contents:

Malina
Halloween
Malina
Bullies
Malina

Warning
This story contains graphic materials that some may not find suitable. Read at your own risk.

"Words have no power to impress the mind without the exquisite horror of

their reality." - Edgar Allan Poe.

Malina

I was sent to the principal's office today for fighting. It wasn't my fault; it was my best friend Angie's fault. Angie started spreading rumors that I was sleeping with another friend Katy's boyfriend. I had never met the guy, but Angie slept with him instead. She lied and said it was me because I was the stronger fighter. The next thing I know, it's lunchtime, and I am putting my retainer back in my mouth when Katy comes up behind me. She grabbed me by the waist and punched me in the back of my head. My ears were ringing from the amount of force she used to punch me in the back of the head.

My retainer fell out of my hands and into the trash can. I whirled around to stand face to face with Katy. "What the fuck are you doing?" I asked, trying to keep my voice down. "You slut!" Katy screamed at me. She hit me a couple more times in the face, then stopped as I stood there staring at her. Her punches hurt, but I wasn't about to show her that. I smiled even though tears were stinging in my eyes. "My turn," I said simply. She wound her fist up in the air to hit me, and I kicked her hard in the knee cap. She dropped to the ground with a heavy thud and a scream that seemed to echo the hallways. I grabbed her by her hair and made her look me in the eyes. "Next time, you should get your story straight before you start punching people!" I yelled. I hit her one more time, then stood up. Everyone was silent and watching me. "I didn't sleep with her boyfriend. I have never met her boyfriend. I don't care about her boyfriend. I am not the villain here; Angie is!" I knew I was throwing my best friend under the bus, but I was tired of getting beat up because she had to sleep with everyone's boyfriend.

Katy was wailing on the floor, and someone had run to fetch the principal. Nobody moved, and the minute the principal saw me, he immediately ordered me to his office. I tried to explain to him that I wasn't the only one fighting, nor had I caused the fight, but he didn't listen. The cops came and escorted Katy to the hospital. The principal closed the school for the rest of the day and called my mom. Katy needed surgery to fix her knee cap that I busted with my kick.

I told the cops what had happened repeatedly. No one seemed to believe me. Eventually, they told me to wait in the counselor's office until they could prove I was telling the truth. The counselor's office was cold, and the light kept dimming. I had never been to this office before; it was newly built over the summer. I had never seen the counselor either. The room was bare except for a desk, two chairs, and a heavy book. There was nothing personal in the room at all.

Sighing loudly, I hugged my legs tighter to my chest. I was shivering, and my teeth were chattering loudly. I didn't see a clock in the room, so I had no idea what time it was. I was starting to get hungry and hoped the cops would return soon. I just wanted to go home and finish my homework to go to bed. I picked up the book, and a smaller book fell onto the desk. The heavy book was a math book, but the smaller book looked worn. It had a faded red cover on it, and the lettering was faded.

I flipped through the pages to find the book's title, Revenge. I thought it was weird that a school counselor would have such a book. I settled into the chair and did my best to keep warm. I began to read slowly. After reading several paragraphs, I realized this wasn't a self-help book. This book was the most twisted book I had ever picked up to read. I couldn't stop reading it. There was something about the book that made me stop shivering. The book felt warm in my hands, and with each word I read, it felt alive.

I could have sworn that the book would breathe every time I turned a page. I ran my finger over the title of the first story. Halloween. It sent a shiver down my spine.

Halloween

I grew up never afraid of anything or anyone. For some reason, nothing scared me, even when I dipped into the darker side of everything. I saw many things I couldn't explain and still can't to this day. I still feared nothing. One night I went to the park to think. I couldn't sleep like every other night since I was 7. Hunters Park was so beautiful at 2 am. No one ever played at the park and left it abandoned for no real reason. Slowly I started to swing, gazing down at the ground. My nightshirt clung to my body, and my feet dangled as I picked up speed. Suddenly I heard a noise in front of me that startled me and caused me to whip my head up. Two kids in my college class stood directly in front of me. "No one knows the true story about Aimee Milner. Two men were hanging beside her lifeless body on this very swing." The taller one said to the other. I waved my hand in front of them, but they acted like they didn't see me. The shorter one grabbed the chains of the swing and ran his finger right over my hand. It sent a chill down my body. "That's a sad fucked story." He whispered to the taller one. I stood up, swinging the swing back, and it crashed into his kneecaps.

"Let's get out of here! I can't believe you talked me into coming here. Especially since it's the 20th anniversary of Aimee Milner's death!" The smaller one grabbed, the taller one's arm, and both ran off. I stood there watching them run. I had no idea what kind of prank they were pulling. I didn't die. I was going to let them have it at school on Monday. I walked home with my long hair sticking to the back of my neck. Ugh, I hated the heat; why was it always so hot? I couldn't remember the last time it got cold or snowed. It was almost like I was stuck in hell. I got home and switched on the lights. My sister screamed as she jumped off the couch. Curious, I looked at her; I didn't remember her sleeping at my place.

"I'm sorry I didn't do anything to save you, Aimee. It was 20 years ago when these carnies kidnapped you when I was busy making out with my boyfriend. Twenty years ago when they found your body. I'm so sorry. Please stop haunting me!" She broke down sobbing, holding the necklace I wore every day close to her heart. Suddenly it all came crashing back to me. I was in hell. I had died from those two carnies who had hurt me. I tricked them into hanging themselves, and as a result, this was my hell. I wanted to comfort my sister but turned off the light instead and returned to the park.

I felt terrible for my sister; I didn't mean to haunt her. On most nights, I couldn't remember that I had died. Once the carnies had hung themselves, a demon popped from the ground underneath the tree. He looked like a normal person, except he had glowing red eyes. “Tsk, tsk, tsk, Aimee Milner. Now you must face the consequences. You made my two top men hang themselves. They kept Hell alive with the souls they would collect.” He said in a weird voice. The voice didn’t match his face at all. It was too deep and sounded off.

I couldn’t remember if I had spoken to him, but I knew I had kicked him in the balls. He grabbed my arm and cut me in a weird design with a knife bigger than his hand. I didn’t feel it much. It was like a searing pain that lasted only for a few seconds. The cut took my memory of the fact that I had died. I went to school every single day. I always thought it was weird I had all math classes. Math was the subject I always hated and did poorly every year. It would seem that every

Halloween, I would get my memory back for a short time. Did I hear those kids right? I had been dead for twenty years. What was I supposed to do? Just roam the Earth doing math all day? Surely, that wasn't the whole reason why that demon marked me. Why was I the one punished when those carnies hurt me? I felt rage boil up inside of me. That was complete and utter bullshit! I was going to go to that spot where the carnies died and give that demon a piece of my mind.

It was a long walk, and the heat made sweat pour down my entire body. The heat made me angrier. Once I got to the tree where both carnies died, I started to yell as loud as possible. "Hey! Demon! Get your ass out here now!" The hot wind picked up around me as the ground seeped with red. He once again appeared under the tree, this time smoking a cigarette. "Why am I being punished? Those guys of yours hurt me! They killed me! I only made them hang themselves after I was dead. How come I have to endure this shit? Where are the two guys?" I was angrily shouting and panting because I had run out of breath. "You are getting punished for tricking my top men into hanging themselves. That's the ultimate sin for a demon. Their souls vanquished like a squished grape. You possessed their bodies until they were hanging themselves. I am still not sure why a simple dead human with nothing special about her was able to control both men to the point of their undoing. I spent the last 20 years finding out why you could do such things. Why aren't you in Hell and free to roam around like a lost puppy."

He tossed the cigarette aside and laughed as the leaves caught fire. "Why can't I leave?" I asked, afraid to hear the answer. "Because it turns out you are special. You have an extraordinary lineage. It turns out you are the daughter of the devil himself. You are the result of the devil having a one-night stand with someone he thought was a human. Your mother was a siren, luring him in. Your blood would have made you royalty. You can't move on, nor can you be cast to Hell. How about you come work for me?" He said as he pulled out a flask from his jacket pocket. He took a long swing of something that smelled like whiskey. "Why would I work for you?" I asked, pulling my long wet hair into a ponytail. I was getting beyond pissed off. "You just said I can't leave and can't be dragged to Hell. So what's the point of working for you? I don't remember my name more than half of the time."

I turned around to leave when he appeared in front of me. He grabbed the scar on my arm until it started to pulsate with pain. “I own you. I won’t make you collect souls, but you must pay.” He began to hurt my arm, so I let out a yelp. He put his mouth over the top of mine and kissed me. His breath smelled like something had rotted away. I pulled away and spat in disgust. “What the fuck is wrong with you?” I hit him hard enough to make him fall back. “What I did was give you your punishment. You will be alive now, a brand new life. However, no human food will sustain you in any way. You have to eat people. That’s right; you heard right. You are now a human, not a spirit. You won’t look like you used to; that girl died long ago. You will be nameless, and you will be a cannibal. I’ll let you die once you have eaten enough people to pay for taking away my two best men.”

I couldn’t hold back the vomit

anymore. The smell of his breath was making my stomach churn. I started to vomit harder than I ever had in my entire life. I was panting and out of breath when he patted me on the back. "Have fun!" He laughed, then he vanished back into the ground. I had thrown up all over my nightshirt. It wasn't normal vomit; it was thick and clumpy. It looked like the blood that had been congealing for many years. Clumsily, I stood up, trying to get the strength to walk. Did he mean I was alive once more? What did I look like now? I had no place to go, so I broke into the motel by the highway. They never locked their doors, and most doors no longer had keys.

I showered and then looked at myself in the cracked mirror. I had long jet-black hair with red streaks that looked like blood in my hair. My eyes were no longer blue but the darkest shade of green I had ever seen in my life. I was no longer tanned but so pale I could see my veins. My lips were a dark blood-red color. I had long fingernails that looked like black talons. The first thing I wanted to do was trim them; I always hated long nails. I found a fingernail clipper on the table beside the bed. I sanitized them as best as possible with the hand sanitizer I found in the bathroom. It looked pretty new and was still sealed in its package. I tried to clip my fingernails but couldn't even make a dent. They were rock solid.

I was not digging my new look at all. There were a couple of outfits that people had left in the tiny, dirty closet. At least I wouldn't be naked when I went outside. The clothes smelled, but at least they seemed to fit okay. I checked under the mattress and was happy to find some money. At least I will be able to get some decent clothes. I put the money in my pocket after I counted it. There was a little over 5k that had been stuffed inside the mattress. Lucky me. Taking it would probably get someone killed, but at this point, I needed it to survive.

I was happy I no longer had to take math classes, but I had died without finishing high school. I was only 16 when I died. I had no skills to survive. I walked to the store and bought a few new outfits, toiletries, and a burner phone. I went back to the hotel in a different but cleaner room. I barricaded myself in the room so no one could enter. I first tried to cut my long hair but found that nothing could cut it. Frustrated, I decided to embrace the new look. I spent a couple of hours trying out different makeup styles until I found one that suited my new look best. I missed my old body and my old life.

I waited until the sun rose and hid at my sister's house in the bushes. I followed her around everywhere she went. Eventually, I was sitting across from her at her job. "I need a job," I said simply. My sister rubbed her eyes; she looked tired. "Ok, what's your name?" She asked as she was filling out a form. Fuck! I had forgotten to pick out a new name. I shifted uncomfortably in my seat. "My name?" I started to look around to see if anyone was watching me.

I felt like I couldn't breathe. "You ok?" My sister asked me as she poured me a glass of water. I held the cup with shaking hands. Time had not been my sister's friend. She had worry wrinkles all over her face. Her hair was long when we were kids, but it was cut short and looked messy. "Uh-" I couldn't get the words to form out of my mouth. "Hey, come with me." my sister said gently. She brought me to a bigger, more private office and closed all the blinds. "My name is Tina, and if you are in danger or escaping from something bad, I can help you. If you don't want to use your name, you are welcome to choose another name. Are you in a dangerous situation?" She asked while pouring me a glass of water. Her eyes were so piercing I couldn't look at her in the eyes. I had missed my sister but seeing her alive just broke my heart. "I- uh," I still couldn't say anything. I looked around the office and could see my sister's face in everything in the office. Not only did she help people find jobs, but she helped kidnapped victims and families who lost their kids. She lived in our old house; our parents had died when we were both young. She had raised me and kept us from going to foster care. I could tell she still blamed herself for what had happened to me. She was a force to reckoned with; somehow, my disappearance and death made her a woman made of steel. "Are you in a dangerous situation?" She asked again.

"No," I whispered. I tried to smooth out my hair and sit up straight. "I need a job, ma'am. I don't have much schooling. I am shy and not very strong. But, I'll work hard," I managed to whisper. She looked at me and looked like she didn't believe me. She was furiously typing away, and her brow deepened. "Honestly, I'm not lying, Tina." I crossed my heart in the shape of an X with my finger. She gasped slightly. Fuck! I had forgotten I was no longer my old self. I had no name. "I'm sorry. Did I do something wrong?" I asked, hating the fact that my voice was quivering.

"No, it's ok. My sister used always to do that to show me how sincere she was. Unfortunately, she died over 20 years ago. I miss her." She quickly wiped away a tear. I wanted to hug her, but I knew I had to be someone else for right now. My stomach was growling loudly. I hugged myself tightly, hoping my sister didn't hear it. "My name is Amber," I whispered. My stomach was growling so much it was starting to become super painful. "I can set you up with a night shift as a cleaning woman for the hotel. They can give you a free room if you need it. It's not the scary one that never locks. It's the nice one they built by the new highway." She gave me the address and some paperwork to fill out. I quickly wrote out what I could, lying about everything. I thanked her and then hurried out of the office.

I ran back to the motel. My stomach was convulsing against itself. I grabbed all my stuff and walked slowly to the motel I would be working at. It was over nine miles. I wasn't going to turn to eating people. I couldn't do it. Let him come for me; I whispered as my eyes narrowed. I hugged my jacket closer to my body and snaked my arm around my stomach. The job was easy, and I kept eating hamburgers. It didn't help with the hunger pains. It didn't make my stomach hurt less. The other employees wrote me off as a meth head going through withdrawals. I didn't talk to anyone and kept my head down. Finally, the stomach growling got worse, and people started to speak.

Months later, the demon woke me rather rudely while I was sleeping. "Why aren't you eating, people?" He sat down, smoking a cigarette. "Put out that nasty shit." I snapped at him. My stomach growled loudly. I was exhausted. I had been working so many hours because I couldn't stand the sound my stomach was making. "I don't answer you. Now get the hell out of my room. I must get at least two hours of sleep before my next shift!" He stood up and put his cigarette out on top of the scar he had created. I didn't bother to flinch. I was used to the scar throbbing constantly. I pushed him out of my room and locked the door. I flopped back down on the bed, only for him to grab my leg and throw me onto the floor. "You will consume people. You hear me?" He spit as he yelled in my face. "Or what? Are you going to drag me to hell? Punish me?" I laughed. "You going to give me a spanking because you are a big mean scary demon?" I said in a mockingly sweet voice. I almost couldn't hear myself over the growling of my stomach. He screamed and opened the floor of the motel room. The hot searing heat blasted me in the face. Sure enough, he was dragging me to Hell. I smiled as the hot rocks embedded into my legs. The demon was strong. I was starting to think he was going to rip off my arms. Slivers of my flesh kept getting caught on the rocks.

"Why are you like that? Get up and fucking walk!" I could barely hear him over the roar of flames that surrounded me. "Fuck you, you want me here, drag me bitch." I screamed. I didn't care if that pissed him off. Judging by how he tightened his jaw and started to stomp faster, I could see his anger building up. In Hell, there was no way I could ignore my stomach pains. Then an idea hit me. I would just eat him and everyone else that was part of the carnival. I remembered every carnie's face from when they kidnapped me. After so many years of wandering around, my memory of that night came rushing back. As she said, Tina was making out with her boyfriend in her room. She didn't hear me sneaking out to go to the carnival. I had planned to return before her boyfriend left so she wouldn't have noticed me gone.

The guy in the ticket booth smiled at me as I tried to peek inside the metal fence they put around the carnival. He smiled and whispered in my ear that I could go in and just tell no one I didn't have a ticket. I remember him saying something on the phone as I passed through the gates. All the carnie's let me have free prizes and free food. I got to play all the games and was having so much fun until they lured me into a room that held a single cage. Somehow, I tripped over something on the floor and landed face-first in the cage. They locked the cage door and refused to let me out.

I couldn't tell you how long I was in the cage. They all took turns whipping me with horse whips and breaking bones. My eyes had matted from the crying and blood, so I could never defend myself. They had played creepy music on the speakers loudly 24/7 until I thought my eardrums were going to burst from the sheer noise of it all. They sealed the cage up entirely once I stopped crying out. I was no longer fun to them. I just lay in the cage corner, letting them do whatever they wanted from me. I had no strength to fight back, and my bones never healed. If anything looked like they had started to heal, the carnies would break it all over again. Finally, they threw the sealed-up cage into the local lake by the school playground.

Water had rushed in from the bottom of the cage, and still, I lay there. There was no point in trying to fight to save my life. There was no way I was going to be able to break free from that cage. They found my body in the cage almost a year later as it was washed up by the swings at school. I had found myself wandering by the carnival shortly after I died, and it was easy to jump into the two carnie's bodies. It was so easy to hang them.

I let the demon drag me until he stopped in a big room. The room looked exactly as the carnival did all those years ago. They even played the same music. He probably thought I would sink to my knees and start sobbing once I recognized the place. Instead, I stood up slowly and picked out the smaller rocks that had embedded into my joints. I clapped my hands loudly and started to laugh. "Thank you for bringing me here!" I shouted. Everyone stopped what they were doing and looked at me with curiosity. Unfortunately, all I could hear was the roar of the fire and my stomach growling. I didn't bother to elaborate on why I was thanking them; I sprang into action. I was so hungry that I could bite through demons' throats with two bites. Soon, there was nothing but a pile of bodies strung over the floor.

Once everyone had died, I sat happily on the floor, crunching loudly on the bones. I could see black smoke lingering around, so I started to stab at them with the bones that I hadn't eaten. The smoke made a weird puncture sound like a balloon with a small leak. I took as many deep breaths as possible to inhale all the smoke. "Thanks, guys, for such a great meal. I was so fucking hungry." I laughed as I continued to eat. Looking around, I felt at home. The heat wasn't so bad. I could stay here and never worry about my stomach ever hurting again. I didn't have to eat any people, I got to see my sister one last time, and I got revenge on the fuckers who were hurting people. I could feel the smoke bubbling inside, so I laid down on the wet, squishy mess I had made on the floor. Closing my eyes, I could hear the soul's scream, which brought a smile.

The End

Malina

I sighed loudly again. That story was intense! How could the counselor have a such graphic story among her things? I didn't know but the cops were taking their time and I was starting to feel cold again. I always hated the cold. There was a time when I was a little girl where I got trapped outside in the cold. It had started to rain when I was walking home from school by the time I got home, it had started to snow. It was snowing heavily with big flakes and my hair was matted to the back of my neck. The house was locked and I didn't have a house key. I waited on the front porch for hours until someone came home with the housekey. By that time, my fingers had started to turn blue.

I had gotten in trouble that day for waiting so long in the snow. I explained to my mom that I had no where else to go and never had a key. She tossed a key at me and it cut me just below my eye. I had never seen my mom so angry before and I wasn't sure that she was actually angry at me. I found myself stuffing my bookbag with jackets and gloves just in case I was ever caught in the snow again.

I was dreading my mom coming to the school. She was going to be so pissed off that she had to leave work just to deal with this issue. I'm sure the cops had already called her and she was waiting til the restraurant was no longer so busy to come to the school.

I picked up the book once more. It felt so warm that it felt comforting. I didn't know why the book felt warm, but I may as well read the next story while I waited. I carefully turned the pages until I came up with the next story. I had a feeling this story was going to be worse than the last one I read.

I took a deep breath and mentally prepared myself for the next story. When I felt like I had prepared enough, I slowly began to read. The book once more felt alive, each page throbbing like a heart beat again.

Bullies

When I was in school, I got bullied a lot. In elementary school, it was because I was skinny and intelligent. My teachers didn't help. They wanted to say how smart I was in front of everyone. "Oh, look how well Maggie is doing!" My teachers would say it all day long. On my long walk home, the kids who were made to feel stupid would throw rocks at me the entire way home. "Maggie is so smart!" They would taunt. By the time I got home, I would be bleeding from all the rocks chucked at me. The house would be empty, silent, and cold when I got home. My mom usually worked 18-hour shifts, and my dad had run off when I was a baby. So I was used to

coming home and being by myself for hours. I cooked for myself, cleaned up after myself, and then made sure I got up in time to get to school. I rarely saw my mother, even on the weekends. When I did see her, she usually spent the night cradling a bottle of whiskey. It was like I didn't exist with her.

She never asked why I was always covered in bruises and cuts. She never asked if I had eaten anything. Whenever I got an award, I would hang them on the refrigerator. They would be in the trash by the following day. When the teachers decided to bump me up a grade, I wrote a little note to my mom and put it on the fridge once more. She wrote back on it with the words, "I don't care." That was the last thing I ever shared with my mom again. I moved again in the grade, but things did not get easier. Middle school was rough and filled with mean kids who did anything to see someone cry. They upgraded from rocks as well. Now it was dull swiss army knives. “Hey, smart Maggie,” They would taunt and jab me with the dull swiss army knives until they broke the skin.

By the time I was in 8th grade, I was 13 years old and didn’t have a friend in the world. Spending so much time alone was not healthy for a normal teenager. The teachers no longer praised me. But, it didn’t stop the bullying. By the time 9th grade hit, I was ready to run away from it all. Highschool was a different ballgame. Then, I met Norris, which turned things around for a little bit. Norris was the distraction I needed. Finally, it felt like someone had cared about me. I didn’t know it back then, but Norris was the king of bullies. He was best friends with the people who loved to hurt me. He had me fooled, though. I thought he was my protector. I didn't know that he was egging on his friends to pick on me.

I graduated high school with the hopes that it would end my being bullied. I got accepted into a college and moved out of my mother's house without saying goodbye. I doubt she noticed. When I moved out, she was heavy into drugs and drinking. I didn't qualify for financial aid because I had already worked two jobs. I didn't get a scholarship; I was on my own. I couldn't stay in the dorms because I didn't qualify. It wasn't an out-of-state college, so the locals had to find places to live. Norris suggested that I live with him. At first, I was hesitant, but as I said, I had been fooled. I moved all my things that fit into two suitcases into Norris's home. He had inherited it from his parents when they died from a drunk driving car accident.

Things were great for a couple of months. Norris was sweet and had gotten a job at a local factory. That was what he had told me. However, the bills started to come in, saying we still owed them. How could we owe bills when he was paying? I called each company, sticking to that story. However, by the time I called everyone, I realized they all had said the same thing. The entire time Norris supposedly worked at the factory, none of the bills were paid. One night I decided to follow him.

He drove past the factory and to an abandoned farmhouse outside of town. I could hear laughter and loud music coming from behind the house. Once he went inside, I quietly got out of my car. What in the fuck was going on? Once inside, it became clear that I was in trouble. The farmhouse had been turned into a fetish party house.

Dominatrixes, BDSM, orgies, and so many drugs littered the house. No one was paying attention to me as I followed Norris quietly upstairs. He went into a room with a black door painted with the number 666 on it. Everything inside of me told me to run. Instead, I opened the door and went inside. Norris and every single bully were completely naked and were staring at me. "Babe! Welcome to the party!" Norris said as he dragged me over to a filthy bed. The bed had no bedding and was stained with what looked to be blood and cum.

"Time to strip!" One of my school buddies shouted. They all started to do a shot of something on fire in a glass. I took a step back and tried to run to the door. "Where are you going, love?" Norris said in a voice I didn't recognize. He grabbed my arm, so I punched him as hard as possible into his ribs. Norris laughed, and the next thing I knew, he was on top of me, ripping off my clothes. I kept fighting; I knew what was going to happen to me if I didn't. He broke my arm and a few of my ribs with ease. I kept fighting. His buddies were standing patiently in a half-circle around the bed. I thought I was making some sort of progress and that I would escape. Then Norris hit me over the head with a hammer, and everything went black. I could hear their cruel laughter as I gave into the darkness.

Darkness swirled around me as I floated inside of my head. I didn't care if I ever woke up. Eventually, I did wake up. I couldn't tell how long I was unconscious. I was in pretty bad shape, and I noticed that my blood had congealed into thick jello in some places. It looked like I had maggots eating my flesh around the broken bones in my arm. Ok, so judging how my body looks, I had been unconscious for quite some time. How was I still alive? I didn't hear any music or noise in the house. The house was eerily quiet, and I could see the light coming from the slats from the boarded-up windows. I sat up slowly, not looking at what had been done to my body. Norris must have thought he killed me. The door had been boarded up from the inside as well. It was clear that I wasn't meant to leave this room. Well, that was going to change.

I couldn't stand both of my ankles had been smashed to bloated oblivion. Spending all that time alone growing up, I learned a few tricks that I was happy for now. I had made a special friend from the shadows and the emptiness I felt during that time. At first, my creation was so I wouldn't have to eat alone. It was someone to listen to my problems as I solved them myself. I hadn't had to call him in a while; I hoped he was still lingering around in the shadows.

My throat was dry, and it hurt to take a deep breath, but I was determined. I let out a scream that came from the bottom of my stomach. "My Demon!" I repeatedly screamed until my throat felt raw. Finally, the sun went down, and I was plunged into darkness. I saw My Demon's red eyes and gasped in relief. "I once made you so I wouldn't feel alone, but now I need you for more. My physical body is in the worst shape I have ever seen. I need revenge." I said as My Demon grabbed my hand. I could see him smile, baring his fangs. "Yes, Miss." His distorted voice rang out in the darkness. Those two words seemed to breathe life into the room. "I will set you free once this is done," I said, offering my broken arm to him.

He took a bite out of my arm, and I could feel his entire being slowly entering my body through the bite. Fuck being average and going to school to get some bullshit degree. This world takes survival. The room exploded with a red light from inside my body. I could see the maggots being fired out of my body like they were made from fireworks. My bones snapped loudly as they healed themselves back inside my body where they belonged. I could see that there was no blood circulating in my body; it was just a thick sludge that lay dormant in my veins. Within minutes, I could heal up all my wounds and stand up. I pried off the boards across the door like they were made from butter. Unfortunately, the house was left filthy, and it looked like everyone panicked and ran out.

I was able to locate Norris and

his party quite quickly. This time, however, they were all fully clothed. They were sitting in a room whispering about my death. I walked into the house they had moved the party to. No one paid attention to me, but it didn't matter; I ripped everyone to shreds before I went upstairs. Each person felt made from silly putty, and I was surprised by how easy it was to tear them to shreds. Piles of body and mangled flesh painted such a pretty picture. It was time to deal with Norris. As soon as I entered the room, they all grew silent. They stared at me in complete horror. I didn't bother to put any clothes on, and you could see all the damage that had been healed.

"Hello, I am glad I found you all in the same place," I said in a voice that sounded like it was a strangled cat. Norris stood up and tried to make a run for the door. "Tsk, tsk, tsk, do you think it's going to be as easy as that to escape?" I admit I was disappointed that he thought it would be that easy. I guess I had always thought he was more intelligent than that. I threw boards over the windows and doors from the ceiling. Then I threw steel plates over it all. "Welcome to your final resting place. You fuckers did nothing but hurt me my entire life. I am not going to stand being bullied anymore! I want to ensure you can't bully or rape anyone again!" I was shouting but couldn't help it. I felt so alive. "My Demon, bring some friends!" I shouted. My body began to shiver uncontrollably as more shadows stepped out of my body. Each one took someone in the room and held them up against the walls.

Norris opened his eyes so wide I thought they would pop out of his head. I took a step towards him, and he tripped over his shoelaces. I looked at the shadow men holding someone and nodded to each one. “You get to watch what your buddies have to endure. They will be tortured until you tell me why. Why did you choose me? Why was it your life’s mission to hurt me?” I stood in front of Norris until I could see urine soaking his pants leg. “I’m waiting,” I said impatiently. He said nothing but kept trying to scoot away from me. “Do it,” I commanded the shadow men. Each one pulled out the eyes of the bully they were holding. I put each eyeball into my hands. All of them, including Norris, was sobbing loudly. I shoved an eyeball into Norris's mouth and held it closed until he had no choice but to swallow it. He was gagging under my hand. “Now, why me?” I asked once more. One of the bullies was screaming and begging Norris to tell me the truth. Norris ignored his friend and kept gagging as the eyeball slid down his throat. I kept feeding him the eyeballs of his buddies as he sobbed and choked them all down. He still didn't say a word. "You don't care about your buddies. I'm feeding you their dicks if you don't start talking!" I screamed.

Norris lost all the color on his face and began to shake visibly. "Your mom hired us. She paid us good money. The original plan was just to torment you to the point where you killed yourself. Then, when you didn't kill yourself, your mom gave us more money just to kill you. She was our biggest supplier for our parties. She just wanted to collect your death benefits from the state. She overdosed the day after we killed you!" Norris sobbed loudly. It made sense; my mother had thrown me to the wolves. I never stood a chance; she had doomed me from day one.

I screamed my rage until my throat

started to bleed. I nodded to the shadow demons one last time. They broke the necks of the bullies they were holding. Their bodies slumped onto the floor. The shadow men looked at me, awaiting my next command. “Rip their bodies to pieces.” I didn’t bother to see them nod. They were ripping the bodies like they were nothing more than paper. Blood was flying in every direction. “Norris, I loved you.” I sat down in front of him. He was sobbing harder than ever as he watched what had happened to his buddies. Someone’s brain matter hit him square in the face. It was time for Norris’s punishment.

I grabbed his arms one at a time and slowly snapped them like pretzels until bones were sticking out everywhere. Then I did the same to his legs. I ensured that at least six bones were sticking out in each limb.

There was nothing more than carnage that had been smeared every inch of the room. I saw a severed dick lying on the floor and picked it up. "I would have given you the world," I whispered to Norris as I forced the dick into his mouth. I broke his jaw so he couldn't spit it out, and it was stuck just below the uvula.

"You will survive quite a while. This is your food." I whispered to him. I sat down across the room from him and crossed my arms. "My Demon. You are all free to go." I roared. Each shadow man bowed to me and then disappeared. I didn't care if they were released to the world. This world was a cold place, and people needed to be punished. I hugged My Demon tightly as he left my body. "Thank you for everything." I looked at him deep into his red eyes. He smiled and bowed, then he too disappeared. I could feel my lungs slowing with my breath. It was great to sit here and watch Norris in pain. This time when I died, I would be in peace.

The End

Malina

I stopped reading and leaned over to the trash can. Immediately my lunch came back up in a hot rush. That was by far the worse story I had ever read. I felt so bad for the main character and I was happy she took care of the men who hurt her. I had never read anything so graphic and I felt like my body was sent into shock.

There was no more stories in the book but plenty of blank pages. Confused, I looked up from the book to see a woman standing there smiling at me. “I see you found my book,” she said in a voice that sounded like it was made from velvet. “What is this?” I asked as my fingers rubbed the letters on the cover once more. It sent a sensation through all my fingers with each touch.

"This is a book full of true stories. I go where there are troubled people who want revenge. I offer them a revenge if they write their story in my book." She smiled once more. Looking closer at her, I realized she was quite beautiful. She had long black hair that fell into waves down her back. She had the brightest green eyes I had ever seen that had been carefully done with a sophisticated makeup.

She had a slight scar by her right eye that looked like a crescent moon. Her lips were thin but done with a deep red lipstick to make them look fuller. She was dressed in a dark green, velvet dress that had dark red stitching. She was pale but looked magical.

"Tell me, do you want revenge?" She

asked as she walked closer to me. The air around her felt warm and I suddenly felt at ease. "I can't think of anyone who warrants that type of revenge." I said being as honest as I could be. She laughed quietly. "You must have someone who needs revenge. You found my book. No one finds my book unless there is someone who needs revenge."

She bent down to where she was eye level with me and grabbed my hands together. "This book is special, only the truly worthy find it." Her hands felt so warm, and I should have felt an uneasiness but I didn't. I thought back through my entire life and realized she was right. My home life wasn't the greatest, nor was my school life. I had been bullied and pushed around by everyone my entire life.

Before I could think of anything I

heard myself whisper, “Yes, I want revenge.” I was surprised at how easily the words flowed off my tongue. She smiled at me and tucked a piece of hair behind my ear. “You must write your story then,” she said as she handed me a fancy red ink pen. The tip of the ink pen was sharp and it cut my finger. Droplets of blood landed on the pen and the pen began to glow. Like my fingers had a mind of their own, I began to write my story. I had never written a story but I found the words easily. The pen dripped red ink onto the pages and with each word that I wrote, I could feel the book breathing once more.

The woman smiled and sat down in the chair in front of the desk. The room felt like warm, and inviting. I read the words that I had already written and was surprised to see that I wrote about being a baby. My biological dad was a young teenager with a cruel temper. He abused my mom and almost killed her several times.

Once she got pregnant with me, he changed for a few months. He wasn't exactly a charming guy but he spent months ignoring her completely. When I was about nine months old, my black hair turned almost white over night. My black eyes turned a bright blue color as well. My dad suddenly got religious. "This child is evil," he whispered to me while he held me in his arms. He tried to drop me down the stairs and was surprised that I had survived.

He then ran a boiling hot water bath and tried to drown me. My mom had showed up just in time for the water to touch my skin. She managed to stick her hands in the tub and pull me out to safety. I lay on the floor screaming and my body smoking from the hot water. My biological dad started to punch my mom until she was a broken mess on the floor. My mom never uttered a word and just kept trying to shield me from my biological dad's hands.

About a month later, my mom and my biological dad got into a fight. "This child must die, she is evil," my biological dad screamed at my mom. I had been napping, I remember that I was dreaming about water rushing over me. He picked me up and held me close to his chest. My biological dad picked up a sawed off shotgun from his desk and aimed at my face. My mom went pale and screamed the word no. My biological dad squeezed the trigger just as my mom lurched forward.

The sound of the gun being discharged made my ears rang for hours after that. The bullet had tore a huge hole in my biological dad's chest. Blood and pieces of flesh had dripped onto my arm. The air smelled of burnt flesh and gunpowder. Somehow, the gun missed me and killed my biological dad. "You see, you are so special," the woman said in a silky voice.

I nodded and continued to write. My mom and I spent five years moving from place to place after that. She worked hard but the people that watched me all turned out to be cruel. One daycare had never changed my diaper in the entire time I was there when my mom was working. I had a rash that went from my butt to my back that I had to get special ointment for. Another woman tied me to a highchair and forced me to sit up the entire time my mom was at work. We finally settled in the small town where I currently reside. She met my first step dad, Lawrence. Lawrence was a master at being cruel. He would smack me across the back and legs with a thick leather belt anytime I messed up.

There wasn't a time where I wasn't covered in welts or bruises. He would make a hot sauce with the hottest things he could find for me to eat spoonfuls of everytime he thought I was lying. Blisters from the heat broke out in my mouth, and on my tongue. My stomach would hurt for days afterwards.

He didn't work so my mom had to work long hours to make sure we kept a roof over our heads. When she was away, he took out his rage on me. He once spit on a plate saying I hadn't cleaned it properly. When I protested, he made me wash every dish in the house four times before I got dinner or could work on homework.

My mom had lost so much weight

because all she did was work. I hated my stepdad and I felt like it was time for him to pay dearly for how he treated me. I wrote his description in the book then scribbled out his legs. I scribbled out his eyes as well. The pen made a hole in the pages where his eyes used to be. On the next pages, I created every bully I had dealt with in school. I even created my best friend. Looking back, she was never a real friend to me.

She would see that I had lunch money and would come up with some story to take it from me. She didn't care if I didn't eat that day. I was breathing hard as I continued to my first boyfriend, Neil. Neil had started to date me because he made a bet with his buddies. The bet was who could take the virginity of the most ugliest girl in school. He had won the bet because he had told me he loved me.

At first, I had resisted but eventually I let it happen. It wasn't romantic like I thought it was going to be. It was painful and I had bruises everywhere. He had grabbed me hard and shoved me into the back seat of his car. It felt like agony and it lasted for an hour. After he shot his load all down my front, he got into the driver seat and began to drive. He dropped me off miles from my house on the side of the road.

The next day, he dumped me and I became quite the joke around school. The book was breathing harder and I felt a strange sensation pass through my body. The woman smiled and I dropped the pen on the table. "How do you feel?" She asked as she took the book from my shaking hands. "I feel alive," I gasped. It felt hard to breathe because I was so excited. "Thank you for continuing my story," she said as she quickly read my story. I thought maybe I was going to be sucked into the book for a brief moment.

"What will happen now?" I asked. "You can go home and see what happened." She said as she gently closed the book. She put the book back inside the book sitting on the desk. I shook my head. "I don't want to go back." I could feel tears welling up in my eyes. "Do you want to stay here with me?" She asked quietly.

She stood up and pulled me from the chair. She hugged me tightly and I could smell her perfume. It had a hint of cinnamon to it and it smelled so pretty. "Can I stay here with you?" I muttered. My eyes felt heavy. I couldn't keep my eyes open. "Oh yes! You may stay here and be part of my permanent collection. I will take good care of you." She said in a soothing voice.

I smiled and hugged her tighter. I could feel myself drifting off to sleep. I was in such a deep sleep I could no longer feel my body. When I woke up, I was in a nice and elegant room. It was filled with many shelves that had books to the ceiling. I was dressed in nice clothes and all my things had been moved into the room. I could smell the woman's perfume and heard her say, "You will live in my snowglobe and be safe. You will now be able to enjoy your life without worrying about getting hurt by others." Her voice sounded so melodic. I smiled. "Thank you," I said as I picked up a book. It was my favorite book and I curled back up in bed. I didn't care I was in a snowglobe and would never see the outside world again.

"If you want to see how your revenge went, you can turn on the tv. Their pain and anguish will play on a loop for all eternity." The woman said. Smiling, I turned on the t.v. to see life become cruel to the people I listed in the book. I fell back to sleep listening to their screams. The woman slipped out of the school and went home. No one paid any attention to her as she left. The cops and Malina's mother were running around trying to find Malina. She laughed quietly as they discovered the body of Malina laying in a hallway. The body was just a shell after all. The woman had taken Malina's soul and put it into the snowglobe like it was the easiest thing in the world. Malina was nothing more than a mangled heap on a dirty school floor.

The woman carefully put the snowglobe on the fire place mantel where so many others were. She smiled and patted the book with her hand. Malina's story was the best one so far. It was time to move on to the next school. In the dim light, each snowglobe twinkled with a happier soul inside.

The End

"And darkness and decay and the red death held illimitable dominion over all."
~Edgar Allan Poe~
****

Prologue

Growing up people always would tiptoe

around some people who had irrational fears. They couldn't help that they were terrified of certain things. But the world we live in today is too cruel for sympathy. Instead of understanding, people were ridiculed. I once did research on fears to pass the time and was surprised that there were some people who believed in past lives. However, a person who died in their past life would bring that fear into their current life. Died by bus, next life scared of buses. I like that idea better than just making fun of people who can't figure out what brought on this fear. So buckle up, these stories are from the most twisted depths of my mind. Not afraid of anything? This story will change that. It may not bring fear on but now you will always be looking over your shoulder, trusting people less, and making sure you take care of yourself. My name is Dr. Mortie Moore. I have compiled these stories together just to give you a taste of something that could really twist your world. I had my license revoked at the university thanks to a patient who had an irrational fear. She didn't like my theory that she had died in a previous life. She went to the board and complained I was a fraud. I am many things, but a fraud I am not.

I didn't medicate my patients, nor did I conduct experiments on them. I just gave them a different view on things. It wasn't my fault she couldn't handle it. I saved all the stories about the strange on a thumb drive and made a vow to myself that somehow I would make these stories reach the world. I got sick however by small negligence from my former partner, Grant. His lab was right by my office and never followed protocols. Grant cared more about the pretty girls walking down the hallways rather than the safety of anyone. Grant was working on experimental drugs and accidentally struck me with it when he tripped over his shoelaces. I won't make it to dawn. It is time I release these stories out to the world. Maybe then, people would believe me. Maybe I'll be famous like Edgar Allan Poe. He was famous after his death. Just like I hope to be.

I'll spend my last night on this Earth typing up this story as I cough blood into my handkerchief. My white handkerchief that is now horribly stained is the last remaining thing I have left from my mother. I killed her as I coughed up blood on her. My blood stopped her heart. I am highly contagious so I have barricaded myself inside my house. I am stuck in my house with no scotch, nothing to kill the pain, and no cigarettes. My wife left me a long time ago and my dog ran off. I am alone.

It hurts to take a deep breath and my fingers are shaking pretty badly. So here goes nothing.

This story is told to me by my patient Fara. She had started to come to me with nasty nightmares when she was 25 years old. She told me the story about how she got those nightmares. I told her she would be scared of clowns in her next life. She didn't handle that very well and opened up a vein using a piece of jagged glass. I am not going to change names, but I won't add any last names. Why should I? I'll be dead in twelve hours.

****

Coulrophobia, The fear of clowns

When I was a little girl about seven or eight I pleaded with my mom to throw me a birthday party. I begged her for months for clowns and balloons. Finally giving in, she planned a party I would never forget.

It started simple enough, all my friends from school and the neighborhood crowded into my backyard. We were all running around squirting each other with water guns, and playing robbers. I had about 20 kids there, it was a blast. The sun was beating down on us but we didn't care, it was summer.

My mom came out setting up a table with gifts, drinks and eventually brought out a cake she made late the night before when I was sleeping. It was a beautiful cake that must have taken hours. I remember looking down on it in awe. When no one was looking I ran my finger through the edge of frosting and stuck it in my mouth. Instantly my mouth started to water and for a few moments it was in my mouth I was in heaven.

One of the girls from down the block convinced her older brother to blow up a couple of hundred balloons for me. She came into the backyard clutching all the strings and barely on the ground. I squealed in delight and we ran around tying the balloons to everything we could. The plan was to release them after the party.

My mother hired a clown from the carnival that was passing through. Suddenly with a booming voice, he said, "You kids ready to have fun?" I admit I was startled and jumped at the sound of his voice. His voice didn't match the clown makeup he wore. It brought chills down my spine but not wanting to look like a wuss, I shrugged it off.

My mother went back into the house,

due to a phone call. I would learn later that two bad things happened on my birthday. My father died in a car accident and there was an escape from the mental asylum for the criminally insane. My mother sat sobbing at the kitchen table, forgetting the party and me.

The kids all wandered home, leaving me alone with the clown. Still, in character, the clown did his best to make me smile but I felt wrong. So wrong. “Come with me kid, I have a secret birthday surprise for you.” He boomed again, his blue eyes flashing with something I didn’t recognize.

I loved surprises, “Sure.” I said shrugging. I followed him out of the yard and into the woods behind the house. “A little farther.” the clown boomed smiling. Suddenly we stopped in the middle of the woods, by the creek. “Close your eyes and lie down.” The clown instructed. I remember laying down hoping the present was going to be the best ever.

Instead, the clown tied up my hands and feet. "Hey!" I shouted at him. He produced a small tape recorder from his clown suit and pushed play. "Hush, don't make a sound, or your mother will die." That was why his voice sounded funny, it wasn't even his voice at the party. I squirmed terrified of what the clown had in store for me.

He washed off the clown makeup in the creek. I wished he hadn't done so, his face was terrifying. He slowly peeled off the clown outfit. I realized that it had been bloody but he had hidden it well from us. He had a white jumpsuit on that read the words "Altru Asylum for the criminally insane. He had a long scar down through his eye to the middle of his cheek. He had sharp pointy teeth that were stained yellow. He put his dirty fingers to his lips and said, "Shhhhhh or I'll go kill your mother."

I tried to roll away but the guy caught me by my ankle. "Name is Burtie. You are my bargaining chip." He smiled showing off those nasty teeth. At the time, I didn't know what a bargaining chip meant. He grabbed me started to drag me through the forest. My legs and arms were getting scratched up from the rocks. I lost my favorite scrunchie from my wrist as I continued to be dragged like a sack of potatoes. He dragged me to an old farmhouse about three miles from my home. "I don't want you to get any funny ideas. You make one sound and I go back to that pretty momma of yours. I will slit her throat from ear to ear." He used the rest of the rope and tied me to a tree. I may have been young but was no idiot. As soon as he disappeared from my sight I began to slowly work my hands to get the knots untied. I could hear loud bangs from inside the farmhouse. I managed to my hands-free and was working on my feet. I had to hurry. I knew I couldn't outrun him. He was terrifyingly a huge man. Once untied, I climbed up to the top of the tree and quietly watched him walk to where I had been tied up.

He started to scream at the top of his lungs. Soon he was joined by another man in a terrifying clown costume. Another and another joined him. Each one was stripped out of their clown costumes. One man was wearing a cop uniform, and the others were wearing matching jumpsuits. There were four or five of them. I thought I was safe but could hear the branch crack from under me. I fell hard hitting my arm and head on the branches as I crashed down in the middle of them. One guy sneered at me while the others formed a tight circle around me.

"Stupid girl!" The man who tied me up in the first place spat at me. I wanted to get up and run but I couldn't breathe. I had gotten the air knocked out of me. I felt something sharp hit my stomach over and over again. It took me a few minutes to understand that they were stabbing me. "Guess we need a new bargaining chip." One of the men sneered. I wanted to die, to get away from the pain that was now in my gut. Unfortunately, I didn't die. At least not yet.

When the clown was done stabbing at

me, he reapplied his clown make-up and put back on his suit. My breath caught in my throat, scared to death of his newest make-up job. He picked me up and carried me further into the woods. After banging my head on a heavy gnarled tree a few times everything went black. All I could hear was the clown's evil laughter. I had never been more terrified in my life when I woke up in a dirty underground abandoned subway.

Once again, the clowns tried to make me laugh, and when I failed I paid a price for it. I had to learn to laugh at everything they did. He cut my mouth making me smile bigger like him. "One of these days you will be my clown," he whispered using his real voice this time. It was beyond scary. I knew then I would never see my mother again. I spent years with the clowns. They would bring me along to their crimes. I was the bargaining chip. It was like, let the men do what they want, rob what they want or they will kill me. No one ever saw their real faces. They were always terrifying clowns. This went on for years until I was 20.

I never knew what happened to my mother or even if she searched for me. My dad was her entire world and she had left me with a clown. One bank job the men did went wrong. As they were carrying bags of money, someone shot them all from behind. I was let go. I couldn't remember where my mother's house was. I couldn't remember my mother's face. Or even my name. I had been a shell of a person for so many years. I was badly scarred, burned, and bruised from the years of torture.

I went back to the subway. I had no other place to go. When I would close my eyes all I could see was the terrifying clowns grinning down at me. I wanted to make their laughter stop. I
wanted to remember my life before them.
****

*This next story is from Marci. She came to me briefly with a fear of mirrors. Before I could tell her anything she just disappeared. I never saw her again, but I bet in her next life, mirrors would be her

undoing.*
****

Catoptrophobia – The fear of mirrors. Being afraid of what you might see.

When my mother died suddenly, I was hospitalized for a few weeks. I couldn't calm down and ended up throwing myself into a panic I couldn't shake. It was one of the darker times in my life. I was really close to my mother, and one night when I was at work she got attacked. A man broke in destroying the house and mutilated my mother. The neighbors heard her screaming but did nothing to save her.

It took me many years to get over it, with every night a new nightmare, a feat I didn't think I could ever conquer. Eventually, I did and went off living my own life. I couldn't trust men enough to get serious with them so instead, I focused on my career. I was a therapist for a little while, but I couldn't keep my own personal demons from seeping

through to my patient's problems. Just before I decided it was probably time for me to quit, I saw another therapist about my problems. He didn't look like he was taking me seriously, so I left. Fuck him. I'll help myself. I was doing ok for the most part on my own.

That is, until a couple of weeks ago. Two weeks ago I took a hot shower after a long day of work. I wiped my bathroom mirror with my towel and began to brush my teeth. I looked at my reflection and screamed. The reflection looking back at me was not my own. It was the man who murdered my mother.

I backed away as quickly as I could slipping on the wet floor. I fell hard on my arm. Grey bone protruded through my natural pale flesh and blood pooled around it like an angry lover. "Fuck!" I screamed. I ran to the bedroom and quickly got dressed carefully not to touch the bone to my clothing.

I managed to drive myself to the hospital with one arm. I lied to the ER and

just told them I slipped in the shower. A couple of hours later my arm was in the cast and I drove home. I fell asleep grateful to put the night behind. I slept uneasily that night, nightmares from when my mother died resurfaced. I woke up with my arm throbbing and drenched in sweat.

I went to the bathroom and had a panic attack right on the floor by the toilet. The mirror was gleaming with images of my dead mother. She was burning in the mirror like she was stuck in hell. Her mouth opened in a silent scream. My mother was no saint by any means so hell is probably where she ended up, but it still pained me to gaze on her once beautiful face in pain.

"NO!" I screamed clasping my hand over my eyes. Fear kept me on the floor until a crack of thunder sounded. I screamed again then fled the bathroom as fast as I could. I banged my arm on the doorway and suddenly my eyes were filled with tears.

Another clap of thunder caused me to jump. I had to calm down so I sank to the floor by my bedroom. What was the matter with me? I hadn't had problems like this in so many years. I stood up and took a few deep breaths, forcing myself to calm. I made my way to the living room and sank on the couch.

The lights flickered from the storm and I could see lightning streak across the sky. I closed my eyes and when I opened them I realized I was staring at the mirror above my tv. The man that murdered my mother and this time was standing right behind me. I screamed and whirled around. but no one was there.

"Get a grip on yourself, Marci," I told myself hugging my knees close to my chest. "This isn't real," I muttered closing my eyes tight. Another clap of thunder. I opened my eyes and looked at the mirror again as if I lost all control. This time I could see myself hanging from the blind cord, my legs kicking. I grabbed the phone and ran to the kitchen. I shoved myself beside the fridge and called my best friend, Tommie.

"Tommie, could you please brave the storm and come over here? I need you, I'm scared!" I sobbed into the phone. "Of course Marci, I will come over but, what storm are you talking about? It's not storming." Another clap of thunder seemed to rattle the house. "Tommie, just get over here!" I screamed not really listening to anything he had to say. He lived three blocks over, of course, it was raining there. He must have not been paying attention.

It seemed like forever when Tommie showed up. He used his key to get in and pulled me out by the fridge. I told him what was going on and rain started to pelt the house hard. "See, it's storming!" I shouted and started to close the windows. "Marci, it's not raining," Tommie said, pulling me outside. He was right, it wasn't raining. "What the hell is going on?" I asked.

Tommie brought me back into the house

and dragged me to my bedroom. He laid me down and climbed in bed with me. Tommie and I had already slept together before, it wasn't what I needed at the moment but just gave in. Maybe getting my mind off of the weird things that were going on would be better. Tommie undressed me and started to pound me hard, harder than normal. To the point where I gasped in surprise and pain. "Tommie." I gasped hoping he would stop. Instead, he pounded harder and harder, knocking my head into the wall.

"Tommie!" I screamed but he didn't listen just kept ramming me harder than ever. Sweat started to roll down his face and he started to look like he was in another world altogether. I wasn't moaning in pleasure anymore, I was flat out screaming. Harder and harder my head made a hole in the wall. Finally, he came and when he pulled out, blood came out with his cock. He slumped face down on the pillow and I ran to the bedroom. He had done some damage because my inner thighs were stained with dark crimson. "You fucking bastard!" I screamed at him. The pain started to rack through me and the next thing I knew I was vomiting in the bathroom sink.

More pain caused me to grab a hold of the sink edges and glared at the mirror. I could see Tommie laying down in the bed where I left him, but I saw a shadow leave his body. I punched my mirror and walked into the bedroom. Tommie wasn't moving and I checked his pulse to find none. I heard laughter coming from the living room. I grabbed my gun and marched into the living room.

I destroyed the living room mirror and was face to face with the man that murdered my mother. I shot him until there were no more bullets in the gun. Blood sprayed me in a hot shower, but I didn't care. I brought the butt of the gun down on his face and kept hitting him until I felt his face bones crack.

I went back into the bedroom to destroy the mirror that hung on the back of my door and realized Tommie was no longer on the bed. I ran through the house forgetting the mirror and realized that Tommie was a crumpled heap in the middle of the living room. He had my house key in his hand and this time he was completely clothed. He must have just got into the house. I looked at the mirror again to see the scene change with Tommie laying on the bed then by the front door. In both images, he wasn't breathing.

"No, the mirror made me kill him." I sobbed and ran back to the bedroom. I touched the glass on the mirror wanting to smash it. As soon as I touched the mirror it pulled me in with my mother's burned hand. I became a part of hell watching the police come and carry Tommie away. Angrily I watched the news say it was from the same murderer that killed my mother. They blamed his murder on me. As well as my mother's murder. That wasn't right, it was the mirror! I pounded the inside of the mirror with my hands until they started to bleed. No one paid me any attention. I was trapped. My mother and I were trapped in a mirror of hell.

****

This story is from my patient Megan. She came to me a couple of times telling me her fears about being killed by her husband. I suggested she didn't need therapy but a good divorce lawyer and a woman's shelter. I always assumed she took my advice until I read in the paper that she had died. My guess is that her husband will kill her in any life she decides to live. Women like that never break free.

****

Taphophobia – The fear of being buried alive by mistake and waking up in a coffin underground.

I am afraid my husband is going to kill me. It started off as a regular fairy tale story. We met, fell in love, and got married. Now it's 8 years later, and the fairy tale has ended, replaced with a nightmare.

Jason started to drink heavily, plagued by a nightmare that kept him up at night.

I could hear him shrieking in his sleep then he would get up. It was the same every night. His temper got shorter and shorter until one night when I wasn't moving fast enough for him, he slugged me.

With a broken nose and a broken jaw, I managed to keep my distance from him from then on. I had to, whatever was plaguing him it was only getting worse. I came home from work one night only to find him standing in the middle of the kitchen smashing every dish we owned. Shattered glass flew everywhere, so I turned around and ran back to my car.

I spent the night in the car afraid he was going to come out and hurt me again. He never did apologize for hitting me in the first place, I didn't want to give him any more reasons to take his anger out on me. Late one night while he was drinking on the couch, I saw a dark shadow slid from the wall and go straight into his body. He jerked a couple of times, then hollered about how cold he was. I brought him a blanket silently and did my best to back away as fast as I could. His eyes had turned black they were once blue.

It would appear that no matter how hard I tried to avoid him, one day I failed. He went on a whiskey bender for the weekend and I was silently cleaning up the mess he made in the kitchen. He came up behind me grabbed my breasts hard. I pushed him away, I really didn't want to sleep with him. He smelled horrible and was wearing the same clothes for the entire weekend. I think it had been a couple of weeks since he showered.

"Bitch, time to fulfill your duties as a wife!" he slurred pushing me up against the wall. The next thing I knew he was kissing me hard, his slimy tongue entering my mouth. I did my best not to gag but pushed him away again. He angrily slurred something again this time picking me up and throwing me against the fridge.

"No, Jason don't!" I shouted not caring if it was going to anger him or not. He just laughed and ripped my shirt right off. I tried to run past him but he clotheslined me with his hairy, sweaty arm. I hit the tile floor hard and felt my skull crack as it made contact. The fall didn't knock me out and I did my best to fight Jason off. Suddenly I was naked and he had his fat arm against my throat.

I started to gasp for air then he started to slam his cock into me so hard that literally, it was slamming me on the floor over and over again. "STOP!" I screamed and pushed him off of me. I tried to scramble to my feet and he grabbed me by the feet and flipped me over. My face hit the floor and I could hear my teeth rattle in my head.

"Quit fighting me bitch. Just take it! Fucking boring cunt!" he screamed in rage. His cock started to ram me hard in the ass, shocked I screamed in pain. He had never done this before. I tried to crawl away but that made him pound me harder and harder. He grabbed me by the hair and lifted me off the ground. I was screaming and sobbing as loud as I could, hoping the neighbors would save me.

Finally, he was done, and I tried to run to the bathroom. He grabbed me by the waist and carried me to the bedroom. He had never done anything like that before. This was more than him being drunk. This was pure rage. I was going to have to get back at him for this. Suddenly, his thick smelly fingers were around my throat. I couldn't breathe, then everything went black.

I could hear him sobbing and screaming at me to not die. That he was sorry he hurt me, and he loved me. I did my best to stay in the darkness. Then there was nothing.

That is until I realized the fucker buried me alive. I woke up in a coffin. He must have thought he killed me, even had a funeral for me I bet. I knew better to scream because that would waste oxygen but I could feel the coffin closing in on me, a bad time for claustrophobia.

Another fear started to form a lump in my throat, what if I never could get out of this coffin? I wanted revenge, so that thought alone drove me forward. I was terrified, the coffin seemed to be getting smaller and smaller by the second. I ran my hand along with the nice silk inlay of the coffin and started to rip at it with my hands.

Once that was out of the way, I started to work on the coffin itself. I ended up breaking almost all my fingers. Small grey bones were sticking out jaggedly in my fingers. My nails bent back and ripped off, but I kept at it. Finally, I broke the side of the coffin and began to dig my way out. My lungs were burning, I needed air.

I was close to the top when I hit a rock. It was a big-sized rock and I couldn't dig around fast enough. I snapped one of my frail wrists on the rock and finally dug myself up to the top where I was able to gulp down some fresh air. I was terrified, I was going to end up buried alive again. I hid out in the woods by the cemetery.

I was hungry and killed a baby bird. I ate

it without tasting it, feathers and all. I only traveled at night back to my house because the fear of waking up in the coffin was so tremendous. Jason was still at the house, I must admit I was a little surprised. I figured he would have been hauled off to prison for "killing" me.

I snuck into the back door and found the newspaper. He had told cops that someone broke in and attacked me. I let out an angry hiss. That selfish bastard. I quietly snuck into the living room where he was tossing all my things into a goodwill box.

"Leave my things alone." I snapped at him. Surprised he fell backward on the couch. "You're dead." he sputtered. "Wrong again." I hissed at him. I lunged at him. I don't know what I was thinking, coming back from the dead makes one think they are invincible. I wasn't, he hit me in the forehead with my mother's cast iron pan he had in his hand.

I went down fast, and when I woke up I was tied up and lay beside my headstone.

Jason was digging my grave up. "I'm sorry honey, but you can't be alive. " He whispered to me. I growled at him, wanting to scream. I could taste burnt flesh in my mouth and to my horror, I realized he had cut out my own tongue. "You have to go back to the dead and stay there. My life is better without you around. I don't have to work, I get your benefits. I can get a hooker every night of the week." He kissed me then pushed me back into my coffin. He had reinforced it to where even tied up I couldn't break free.

I started to sob, I hated him. I wanted him to suffer. But that wasn't in the cards for me. Once again I was being buried alive. I fought with everything I had but this coffin was much stronger. The claustrophobic feeling returned and my lungs started to burn from my oxygen dwindling. My eyes hurt from the total darkness. Thirst hit me first, my lips cracked from being dry. My tongue stuck to the roof of my mouth. Then my stomach protested loudly. It had been a couple of days at least since I had eaten the bird. I tried to dig myself out, but I was too weak to do so. I broke my arm and decided it was time to accept my fate. I was going to die twice by my husband's hand and no one would ever know.

****

My last story in this book of fears is from Marge. She also had an abusive husband. Her fears were not of her own. As far as I could see, she was in a good mental state. She was another woman that just disappeared. I had a sneaking suspicion it was foul play.

****

Ergophobia The fear of work

Prologue

"Marge! Get me another beer!" Timothy screamed from the living room. Timothy was greeted with silence. "Marge! God damn it!" Timothy screamed heaving his heavy body up from the couch. He sauntered his way into the kitchen."Marge!" Timothy shouted at his wife. He surveyed the kitchen, it was a mess. Dirty dishes stacked to the ceiling and food that had dried on the floors. Marge's body lay slack in the corner, her once beautiful head slumped onto her chest. "Just because you are dead doesn't mean your ass can't get up and get me a beer!" Timothy angrily slurred and started to kick Marge. That was fun until his foot stuck in her side. "Oh gross Marge!" Timothy said vomiting on the floor. His foot came away from her body in a slimy sickening way. "Fucking disgusting," Timothy said once again vomiting. His nose was hit with the smell of decaying flesh. "I am going to need a new wife to wait on me," Timothy muttered to himself as he slowly passed out on the floor right into his vomit. By the time Timothy woke back up his was glued to the floor with his dried vomit and drool. His head hurt greatly and the mess of the house was making his stomach churn. Sighing heavily he began the task he disliked the most, cleaning and working on the house. "Fucking Marge had to die." He grumbled as he washed the dishes, cleaned the floor, and vacuumed the rest of the house. He had one more job to do, and that was the worst one. He put some Vicks vapor rub under his nose like he had seen on the tv and began to bag up Marge's soupy-like body. Finally, he got her bagged up and carefully hidden in an abandoned well on his property. He had to shampoo the floor where she was sitting for so long. By the time he finished, it was well past midnight. He took a shower and put on clean clothes, the first time in a week. Then made himself a sandwich. Time to go out and get another wife. Timothy had the perfect life in mind where he didn't have to work and his wife would wait on him hand and foot. Timothy was the epiphany of laziness and fully intended to continue on that path. He struck out at the bars horribly. Finally discouraged he went to a restaurant to get some food. He hated to cook, and the thought of dirtying up the dishes he cleaned the day before didn't appeal to him. He wanted spaghetti like the way Marge used to make for him, so he settled on a quiet

Italian restaurant.

There sitting at a table alone reading a book was the most beautiful woman he had ever laid eyes on. She was perfect with dark hair and green eyes that seemed to suck in his soul. She had full pouty lips and nice curves. He couldn't tell her age, but the sheer beauty of her made him ignore all that.

"Hi, I am Timothy," he said walking up to the table. She smiled and immediately the entire room seemed to brighten. "My name is Amy. Would you care to join me?" she answered putting her book away. Her voice was sweet almost like music. "Yes, I would love that," Timothy said sitting down. The night was filled with laughter and talking. They sat there for so long that the owner kicked them out to close. It was the beginning of something wonderful. Within a year they married. Once they were married, Timothy fell back into his old habits. He refused to work or lift a finger around the house. Little did he know that his new wife wasn't anything like Marge and wasn't going to stand for such behavior.

Chapter 1

"Amy, get me another beer will ya?" Timothy asked in a bored tone while he watched t.v. "No Timothy, get up and get yourself one. I have to go to work. You know that thing that pays the bills around here?" Amy said trying to hide her irritation. "Oh, what is that supposed to mean?" Timothy jumped off the couch snarling. "Nothing, Timothy. It's just that I am going to be late for work." Amy said quickly hoping to defuse the fight that was brewing. She kissed him quickly and practically ran out the door. "Fucking bitch telling me what I have to do, calling me lazy," Timothy shouted to the empty house, punching the front door. "I'll show her," he said to himself laughing. Timothy sat down and finished his show that was loudly playing on the t.v. He drank another beer. He sat there fuming and decided to trash the house. He pulled out every dish in the house smashing them with a fury that quickly exhausted him. It started to rain heavily, so he went outside walking around in it. It didn't calm him like he wanted it to, went back inside tracking mud everywhere.

He slammed back another beer hurling the empty bottle at the wall. He wanted to go for a drive but she had taken the only running car to work. "Fucking bitch stole my car!" Timothy yelled stomping inside. Timothy grabbed another beer muttering angrily under his breath. Soon, he passed out on the couch amidst the mess he made.

Chapter 2

Amy hated her menial job but did her best to keep it. She was sad most of the time, Timothy was not the man she married. She scooped up another order of fries sighing heavily. "Girl, just divorce him." Her best friend Jessie said coming up behind her. "You deserve better," Jessie said helping her with the fries. "I can't afford to," Amy said miserably. "You should make him disappear like my cousin Giana did with her husband. Just don't get caught as she did." Jessie laughed. Amy joined in laughing, but deep down inside a small idea was starting to form. Shaking her head, Amy said," I couldn't do that." Jessie nodded sympathetically to her and turned her attention to the fat customer standing at the counter, that was demanding half the menu. Amy pushed the thought that was forming in the back of her head, right now she had to focus on her shitty job. *Maybe tonight I can get Timothy to apply for some jobs.* Amy thought to herself. Her shift ended and she quickly changed her clothes to her other uniform. She had to get two jobs in order to keep the roof over her head.

Amy hated her second job even more than her first job although it wasn't as demeaning. She hated it because a monkey could scan groceries, it took no thought. And no matter what she had to be nice to the customers who hated the store as much as she did. They blamed her for all their problems so by the time she got home late at night she felt deflated.

Chapter 3

Amy sat in the car taking deep breaths, she was dreading going inside. With any luck, Timothy would be passed out. Sighing she made her way into the house. "What the fuck happened here?" Amy demanded waking up Timothy by accident. "I rearranged, bitch." Timothy stood up swaying. "Great, you are drunk again and trashed the house?" Amy said, putting her hand on her hip. Timothy growled and quickly grabbed her up by the neck, pushing her up against the wall. " You have some nerve complaining to me. I put the roof over your head. In case you forgot this is MY house." Timothy spat out angrily. "Your name may be on the deed but I am the one who pays the bills." Amy struggled to say. Timothy threw her across the room and grabbed another beer.

"Maybe I should be just like you and quit my job! Make you pay for everything! Then I can sit on my ass drinking myself into a stupor!!" Amy screamed, fed up with Timothy's behavior. Timothy growled again, tossing the half-empty beer on the floor. He closed the gap

between them and grabbed her by her hair. "You will do no such thing you ungrateful bitch." He slapped her hard making her teeth rattle hard. "You hit me!?" Amy screamed.

"You damn right I did," Timothy said laughing. He grabbed a dirty pan from the kitchen sink and hit Amy upside the head. Stars danced in front of Amy's eyes. "You fucker!" Amy said dazedly. She grabbed the lamp and yanked it out of the wall. "You stupid fucker!" Amy screamed again, wrapping the lamp cord tightly around Timothy's throat. Darkness swirled in front of Timothy and soon he slumped down unconscious.

Chapter 4

Amy watched him slump to the floor enjoying the thrill of giving in to her rage. She looked around in disgust at the nasty messy house. *"Maybe you should just make him disappear."* Jessie's words rang in her head. "Perfect fucking idea," Amy said to herself thinking of her next move.

She wasn't that strong of a woman so picking Timothy up was going to be a hard thing to manage. Amy decided to prop him on the rolling pins she had, one that was his and one that was her mother's. His fat belly rolled heavily as she scooted him to the back door. By the well that Timothy used as a trash can, there was a shed. Timothy wasn't going to roll out the back door, so Amy came up with another plan. She got the footstool that had wheels on it from beside the house. It was worn and as far as she knew, Timothy never used it. She pulled him up by the arms and laid his body over the stool. The added weight pushed the stool down and almost didn't want to roll. But after what seemed like an eternity she finally managed to get him to the shed.

She rolled Timothy on the workbench and tied him down. The shed was so organized, and clean, unlike the house. She stuffed a dirty rag into Timothy's mouth and went back into the house. She grabbed two beers from the fridge and an assortment of kitchen utensils.

Timothy was coming around in the shed when she made her way back to it. He was thrashing against the ropes on the table and screaming behind the dirty rag. Amy opened one of the beers and took a long thoughtful drink.

“What should I do to you?” Amy asked Timothy. Timothy eyed the beer in her hand. “Oh, you want some?” Amy said to Timothy, swinging the beer in front of his eyes. He tried to nod his head. “That is all that you care about, is your beer huh?” Amy took another swig off the beer. Timothy mumbled something.

Amy poured the beer on his face aiming for his eyes. “Timothy screamed as the liquid splashed in his eyes. Amy broke the bottle on the table and put a shard up to his throat. “I am so sick of your drinking, ordering me around, and being lazy. I am sick of coming home after my two jobs to have to wait on you hand and foot.” Amy said, scratching a thin line on his throat. She watched in fascination as his eyes widened in fear.

Amy looked around the shed taking in all the tools that were neatly hung up. “Oh, I think I am going to have some fun before I rid myself of you,” Amy said picking up a heavy wrench. She grabbed his hand that was curled into a fist. She uncurled his fingers and put them in the wrench mouth. Screaming he tried to jerk his fingers back closer to his body but Amy was already tightening up the wrench. She tightened the wrench until the fingers turned purple. Amy pulled out the dirty rag so Timothy could breathe. “Fucking bitch I am going to kill you.” He spat right in her face. Disgusted she wiped away the spit and twisted the wrench until the bones in his fingers began to protrude.

Chapter 5

Bones snapping is a rather loud sound, Amy was impressed. Timothy screamed and a spittle formed by his mouth. “Please stop. Please, I will be a better husband.” Timothy cried. “It’s a little late for that sweetie. You have been doing this for years now. You won't change." *Snap* Another bone snapped loudly as Amy continued to twist the wrench. "See now you have a reason not to work. You are going to need someone else's hand transplanted in order to work." Amy said, trying to sound brave. He started to sob even louder. Amy hated the sound of his cries. Digging around the kitchen utensils she had grabbed from the house, she found the very tool she was looking for. It was a salad tong that was made from hard plastic and had the shape of the fork on tips. She placed it by his adam's apple and looked Timothy dead in the eyes. "Always crying, always complaining and demanding." Amy started to slowly dig the salad tong in his throat. He screamed louder Amy dug in his throat deeper. It took some effort but she was able to dig out his Adam's apple. She lit a cigarette and placed the lighter on his throat to cauterize the wound. He was gurgling but wasn't screaming anymore. The shed started to stink of burnt flesh and Amy ran out of the shed as it hit her. It was

such an awful smell. She took a deep breath of the fresh chilly air. She had reached the point of no return, she had to go back into the shed and take care of him. "You can do this," Amy said to herself. "You have to do this, he will run to the cops if you let him live." She whispered to herself. She walked back into the shed to see Timothy trying to wiggle free. "Oh no, you don't!" Amy said tightening up the ropes. The rope was starting to dig deep into his pudgy flesh causing red welts to form. She grabbed a spoon and started to fish out his eyes. "There, now you can't see even if you do manage to get free." The eyes felt squishy in her hands that reminded her of fish eyes. She held them away from her body and threw them down the trash well. She shuddered at what she had just done, but only for a second when she remembered what all she put up with over the years. Determined, she walked back into the shed. "Are you hungry love?" Amy said joyfully. "I myself am starving. I worked a total of 12 hours today without any food." Timothy whimpered, shaking his

head from side to side. The hole in his throat jumped as he tried to speak. "I'll whip us up something real quick. Hang tight." Amy said laughing.

Chapter 6

It didn't take long to whip herself up a sandwich. She quickly ate thinking of her next move. She wanted to make him eat something gross. "What can I make him eat?" she wondered out loud. She went back out to the shed to check on him. Then an idea hit her. The trash well filled with nasty trash would be a perfect dinner for him. She grabbed some trash and crammed it into his throat. He started to thrash around and move his head around. That irritated Amy even more. She found a rusty saw and started to saw off his arms, one by one. He was choking on the trash and whimpering. Hot blood sprayed Amy in the face causing her to gag. Without warning, she threw up right in the empty eye sockets of Timothy.

" I just don't have the stomach to keep torturing you," Amy said, wiping her mouth. She took the wrench off his fingers and smacked him hard in the head. She kept hitting him until he was dead. Cracked skull pieces and blood sprayed her once more. It started to rain again, and Amy rushed out of the shed letting the rain wash away his blood. Finally, she was soaked through and shivering. She went into the house, changed her clothes and started to clean up the house. She bagged up all of his belongings and threw them in the trunk. She drove a few miles to the goodwill and dropped off his belongings by the drop-off door.

She went to the store and bought cleaning supplies. For the first time in many years, she felt free. She cleaned the entire house wiping away all existence of Timothy. It was almost 4 am and Amy was exhausted, but she had to get rid of Timothy. There was no way she was going to be lazy and leave him there until she got to sleep.

She ate the rest of the sandwich she made earlier and drank Timothy's last beer. She felt better and another idea hit her. To get rid of all the trash including Timothy she came up with a plan.

Chapter 7

It took her some time to clean out all the trash in the well. She found the body of Marge. She gazed at the swollen and waterlogged head with sadness. "Timothy probably killed you huh?" Amy said, wiping away a tear. From the pictures Timothy had, she was once a beautiful woman. He had told her that his wife Marge had died from cancer. Suddenly Amy got angry again. "What a lying son of a bitch!" She screamed letting Marge's head fall between her hands.

She stormed into the shed and untied Timothy. He was a little bit lighter minus his arms. She grabbed the arms and tied them together. She rolled his body off the table onto the stool and rolled him outside. The only thing she wasn't able to retrieve was his eyes. She bagged him up and threw him in with Marge's head. Then tied it tightly to where no air was able to escape. She threw all the trash in her trunk and once again drove a few miles to a landfill. Then drove back to deal with the last big garbage bag left in the yard.

The sun came up and Amy felt tired. It had been such a long night, she decided to get some rest. She slept for a couple of hours but not well. Nightmares plagued her causing her to wake up screaming. She showered and walked out into the yard. For the first time, she was able to look at the yard without looking at all the trash Timothy had thrown around for years. It was a nice pretty yard, Amy felt at peace. Until she looked at the shed and remembered what she had done.

She hauled the garbage bag into the shed. "Marge, give him hell, he is yours now," Amy whispered to the bag and shut the door to the shed. The great thing about where Amy lived was it was literally out of nowhere. She poured some lighter fluid over the bag and shed. She lit another cigarette and set the shed on fire.

Standing there smoking she watched the shed quickly engulfed in flames. The bodies in the bag started to whistle as the heat melted them together. Amy watched the shed completely burn to the ground and would feel at peace but the smell as the body turned to ash was turning her stomach. She went back inside and took a small nap. Marge was yelling at her in her dreams for binding her and Timothy together forever. Amy woke up and was happy to see a black square in the yard and it was raining.

A few days later on her next day off, she tiled where the shed used to be and planted a wonderful flower garden. She decided to paint the house and do some little repairs around it to make it look better. Between the two jobs, and the house repairs Amy stopped sleeping except for a couple of hours here and there. Every time she slept she saw Marge crying to set her free.

Chapter 8

Amy finished the house and the garden

was the best in the state. Amy wasn't able to relax and enjoy her hard work, she was plagued by ghosts. She decided it was time to set the ghosts free, she couldn't let Marge take over her sanity. Although being haunted by Marge allowed her to keep up appearances that Timothy was still alive.

Amy went to the library and found a nice quiet corner to do some research. She wasn't by any means a Christian but witchcraft and voodoo were not something in her wheelhouse. She found what she was looking for in the third book she opened up and made a couple of copies of the pages she needed. Then put the books back on the shelf and left the library. She went to the store and picked up the provisions the book had said she needed. Then drove home listening to lightning crackle across the sky.

Amy went to the middle of her garden and sat down on the dirt where Timothy's body would have been. She held a candle in her shaking hands and pictured Marge's head in her mind. "I set you free Marge, I am sorry," Amy whispered over and over again. The wind picked up and knocked the candle out of her hand. It landed on her pant leg quickly catching fire. "Ah!" Amy screamed and ran out of the garden, the fire moving closer up to her leg. She turned on the hose and sprayed her leg. That smell came again, that rotten burnt meat smell. "I'm so sorry Marge, I just wanted you to give him hell because of what he did to us, with his laziness." Amy sobbed as she tried to care for her blistered-up leg. Amy closed her eyes trying to not scream in pain as another bolt of lightning cracked loudly in the sky. Standing in front of her was Marge."AH!" Amy shrieked and fell backward. Marge stuck her rotted hand over Amy's eyes to let her see the last day she was alive. Screaming Amy tried to get away from the skeleton hand that had pieces of slimy flesh still clinging to it but it was too late. She was going to see this whether or not she wanted to.

Marge was cooking dinner for Timothy. It was their anniversary. She didn't mind the fact that he never worked, or even that he pushed her around. She loved Timothy with all her heart. It was his brother James that made her scared. James was Timothy's twin brother who was meaner in every way possible. He moved in once he lost his job. James would outdrink his brother Timothy until Timothy passed out. Then he would have his way with his brother's wife. Marge hated James. Even told Timothy what James was doing. She showed him the marks that James left on her. Timothy laughed a cruel laugh. "My brother is a saint. And if he wants a piece of my pie, you better give it to him!" Timothy shouted at her and slapped her. Marge couldn't believe what she heard. In fact both the brothers decided to be married to Marge at that point and shared her. Timothy's laziness got worse and so did his temper. James stopped working altogether and both would drink themselves into a rage. They hated working. The very thought of it would bring on massive panic attacks and more drinking. "The world owes me," Timothy complained to his brother. "You damn right it does." James would say every time egging him on.

Then on Marge and Timothy's anniversary, something happened. Timothy left the house to get some more booze for the night he and James had planned for Marge. James wanted Marge to do something she had never been willing to do and she hit him in the head with the cast iron skillet she was cooking with. Not only did the hot pan sizzle the man's face but cracked his skull open wide enough she could see his brains.

"Fuck!" Marge shouted. Marge put the pan through the kitchen wall and shoved Jame's body in the hole. She was trying to cover up the hole when Timothy walked in. He saw his brother's body shoved in the wall and flew at Marge with a rage that surprised her. "You bitch! I will make you spend eternity with my brother as his slave!"Timothy spat out and grabbed her by the throat. Timothy started to scream "Mounraire!" then plunged a kitchen knife deep into Marge's heart. He left her there for months decaying in the kitchen. But his brother, he took out of the hole. He cut his wrist and put his bleeding wrist over his brother's mouth. "Come back to life!" Timothy screamed.

James sat up with red eyes. But before the ceremony was completed James ran off.

Marge showed him living in the shed, his brother unaware. James was the one who organized it. Amy saw Timothy dump Marge's body into the well and began to fill it full of trash. James watched from the shed his eyes glowing red. James left the shed a month before she moved in.

"Oh, that means James is still alive!' Amy shouted understanding well why Marge had to be set free. Marge needed them both in death in order to be freed. "Where the fuck am I going to find James? Marge show me." Amy said, forgetting her blistered leg. The wind picked up and Marge was gone. "Marge! Marge!" Amy shouted running behind her garden. "Marge is dead." A man appeared from the woods from the edge of the property. His red eyes gleamed as he lit a cigarette. "James!" Amy gasped. "The one and the same." James bowed. He looked identical to Timothy except he had a nice scar where Marge had bashed his head in. "So you are the new wife huh? My brother has great taste." James said, offering her a cigarette. Amy took it and lit it. "Where have you been James?" Amy asked, trying to remain calm. "Oh around." He said smiling, showing off razor-like teeth. Out of the corner of her eye, she saw Marge point to the well. "I killed Timothy and put him in the well. " Amy lied. " Did ya now? He probably deserved it." Timothy said, taking another drag off the cigarette. "Do you want to see his body?" Amy asked not sure whether or not he would follow her there. "Sure," James said, keeping the smile on his face. Once by the well Amy pushed him in but didn't realize he had grabbed a hold of her blistered leg. Both James and Amy fell to the murky depths of the well, landing on Timothy's eyes. The fall caused Amy to break her neck at an unnatural angle. It was her neck bone that pierced the heart of James, killing him. Lightning cracked across the sky hitting the well causing it to collapse on itself. Burying them together for eternity. Marge laughed she was free and had tricked Timothy's new wife to take her place. She started to float away when she felt a hand on her shoulder. "Where do you think you are going, Marge? You and I are together forever." Timothy's ghost laughed as he kissed Marge hard. "Now that I am dead, I never have to worry about having to find a job. Just the thought of a job makes me shiver. This world was not designed for me to work in it." Timothy laughed. All four of them were now crowded in the well. Lightning struck the well and closed it up forever. They were all trapped with each other.

****

It's nearly dawn now, and it has become hard to breathe. Spots have started to swirl in front of my eyes. I think it's time I rest. Funny I should die by an accident. I don't believe in experiments. Maybe I will get lucky and in my next life have an answer as to why so many of my patients were afraid of the very things that killed them. But I am not.

The End

Table of Contents:
2022

Hell's door in the west
2022
Halloween
2022 Mama's story

"Words have no power to impress the mind without the exquisite horror of their reality."
~Edgar Allan Poe~

Prologue 2022

"Mama, tell me a story," My beautiful daughter said as she laid down beside me. I was tired and I knew I still needed to clean the house. Housework was one of those things I always hated to do but did them ever without complaining. My daughter is 14 years old, it won't be too long before she won't want to hang out with her mom. I smiled, hoping that the fatigue I was feeling deep in my bones didn't shine through in my eyes. "Sure love, what would you like to hear?" I pointed to the books on her

shelf that surrounded her entire bed. "That one!" She pointed and snuggled into her blankets a bit more. I rolled my eyes. "Our family history? You want a good night story about how we became cannibals in a modern world?" I looked at her curiously. "Yes, those are the best stories, the ones that ring with some sort of truth." She smiled. When she was younger, I always worried she would freak out once she realized that our family tree was nothing more than cannibals.

I didn't tell her for years, masking all the human flesh in a way she always thought was hamburger. That was how she lived up till about four years ago. She walked in on me butchering her father in the kitchen. I thought she would have sobbed or questioned me but instead, she grabbed a knife and began to help cut him up. She never asked why I had killed her father, but then again, she had hated him from such a young age. She had always called him a troll behind his back. Instead, of asking questions, she made sure she accompanied me to the trips where I got more people to eat. I showed her how to cook and prepare each meal so neither of us would get sick. One night, she found the book labeled I eat people by Allisha McAdoo in the attic. It was filled with short stories about how our family wasn't like others. Each person had written in it before their demise. They didn't always cook the meat right and many people in our family went crazy or got

so sick they died.

My daughter and I were the last of our family tree. For now. She closed her eyes and began to listen intently to the story she had now heard a thousand times.

"The first story is about your great-great-great-grandfather. Hell's door in the west," I read out loud. It was a shame what happened to him, but somehow he had managed to carry on his curse to the next family member. Some had said that once he turned into whatever he was, he became frisky with all the survivors he came across. I didn't know if any of that were true, but it felt nice to be next to my daughter. It didn't matter how our family tree grew.

Hell's Door in the West

Sheriff Clinton signed heavily as he read the newspaper filled with more bad news. The Debauchery Brothers were getting closer to his little town. It was only a matter of time before they showed up to rob his bank. Sheriff Clinton was not the sheriff but assumed the role because the town thought him as such. He had shown up years ago just as the old sheriff died. He had shot the sheriff by accident when he tried to blow the door off the safe. He found the combination written on his hand. He was a Debauchery Brother himself, except he went rogue. His brothers would be pissed seeing him posing as a sheriff. The entire family hated authority. He would have to do something about his brothers before the town found out his secret. To keep his secret and continue to rule the town he grew to love. He was going to have to kill his brothers, Eddie and Teddie. He rubbed his temples. He was not looking forward to seeing his brothers again. It had been almost seven years.

******

Claira was the most beautiful woman in Cedar Springs but also the meanest. She had a frozen heart and helped the sheriff keep people in line as she tended to the saloon. She was the type of woman who always had a gun on her. She had no problems making sure nothing bad ever went down in her saloon. Many men tried to claim her heart, but many failed the challenge. She wasn't ready to be tamed by anyone; besides, she would never say this, but she hated men. Not just men, Claira hated everyone. She was more in love with her guns. They had never spoken out loud about the night they spent together. Sheriff Clinton and Claira had spent the night together many years before, but in the morning, she had left. She left with just a small note that said, “If you tell a soul, I’ll kill you with a gun I love more than anything.” Sheriff Clinton had respected her wishes. He had seen her shoot someone for stepping on her shoe once. He was perfectly happy being a friend and was more than happy with her gun skills that kept everyone in line. “Howdy, Claira.” The sheriff said as he walked into the saloon. “Howdy, sheriff.” She replied, pouring him a tall glass of whiskey. He pushed the newspaper in her direction and gulped down the drink.

“They are getting closer to Cedar Springs. I need to find a way to stop them,” Clinton said, making sure his voice sounded desperate. Claira nodded, reading the paper with no emotion. She poured another drink, but this time Clinton waved it away. “I’m good, Claira.” She shrugged and slammed down the whiskey like it was water. He watched her for a moment with fascination. He would love to take her home for the night, but he knew she wouldn't come with him willingly. Sighing, he took off his cowboy hat and rubbed his temples. He had been rubbing his temples so much that it was starting to leave red marks.

“Why don't you wrangle up the most dangerous criminals out of jail and offer their freedom to kill the brothers or bring them to you,” Claira said simply as she gracefully wiped the bar down with a dirty rag. Sheriff Clinton was surprised at the idea. Why didn't he think of that? He thought. “Claira, I like the way you think.” He said, impressed. She managed a quick smile and went back to work. A plan started to form in his mind to rid the town of not only the most dangerous criminals but to get rid of his brothers for good with one hit. Getting rid of anyone who might make trouble for Sheriff Clinton down the road might be the best way.

He thanked Claira for the whiskey and put his hat back on. He strode out into the hot desert day, admiring the tumbleweed that swirled in the dusty wind. He would lure them to the abandoned mine just outside town, then blow it up. The mine was condemned for collapsing and killing 400 men. It would be the perfect place to get rid of his brothers once and for all. If his calculations were correct, his brothers would be entering the town by tomorrow. Sheriff Clinton planted the homemade bombs all over the mine until he couldn't get past anymore. He had just enough time to redirect the signs to the bank by the mine before he saw the dust cloud from their horses.

“Well, well, well, look who is here to greet us! It’s our missing brother Clinton. You must be out of your mind waiting for us after stealing our money from the safe.” Eddie sneered as he jumped off his horse. “Yea, taking all the money and breaking our guns," Teddie muttered. Teddie never said much, just muttered under his breath most of the time when he did decide to say something. Teddie was the more dangerous of the brothers. He was quiet but loved violence. Eddie was loud and could keep his own in a fight, but he chose to get revenge first before he resorted to violence.

Teddie got off his horse and peered deeply at Sheriff Clinton. "Look at this here, Eddie." He said a little bit louder than normal. "Our brother stole from us, killed our ma and pa, ran away to be a sheriff. Eddie's face darkened with disapproval and anger. Sheriff Clinton held up his hands as a peace offering. "I don't want trouble from you two. Things have happened since I ran with you guys. I'm offering you a case full of money just to leave this town alone. No one would even know you were here. You can go on to your next destination." Sheriff Clinton sighed heavily. He knew that his brothers would never go for that offer deep down inside. They had both known that they would kill him if they ever crossed paths again.

"What will it take for you just to pass through?" Sheriff Clinton said. Teddie smiled and shook his head. "I think we are going to take this little town." He muttered, smiling bigger. Eddie laughed loudly and went to draw his gun. Sheriff Clinton pushed himself back into the mine. He knew where he placed his bombs and could double out by a side entrance. He took off to the saloon. He was breathless when he arrived as he got off his horse and ran into the saloon. "Claira, it's time. They are in the mine. Go get the criminals and bring them to the mine." He said as he stole a glass of whiskey from a customer. He downed the whiskey, winced, and ran back onto his horse. He made it back to the mine in record time. Claira followed closely behind the carriage carrying about 90% of the jail. Sheriff Clinton snuck back into the mine using the side entrance. "Come out, little brother!" Eddie was shouting. "Quit being a coward!" They were deep into the mine, close to the last of the bombs. The criminals that were released into the mines were all carrying weapons. Sheriff Clinton sucked into his breath as he watched his brothers and criminals beginning to fight from his hiding place.

Both of his brothers were good fighters and were able to make a pile of criminals gasping for breath. Finally, it was time to set the bombs. He carefully made his way to the detonator and slowly raised the level. Right before he pressed the level down, he saw a glimpse of something bright purple. He smashed the level down on the box and was greeted with a hot searing wave from all the blasts. Sheriff Clinton was thrown back. He smashed up against the rocks that dug deep into his back. He hit his head hard enough to make him lose consciousness. He was woken up by screaming and growling. Sheriff Clinton sat up, rubbing his eyes with his dirty hand. Everything had a purple hue to it and looked distorted. He got up slowly to see the blast had torn through his shirt. He had multiple bruises and cuts all over. Standing up made him feel dizzy, and a jolt of pain coursed down his spine.

It was hard to see through all the rock dust and purple hues dancing all over the walls. Sheriff Clinton slowly made his way to where he saw his brothers last. He kept slipping on the sharp rocks. He had never felt so disorientated before. The air still felt hot as he walked as if he was still in the blast. He must have miscalculated the blast radius. When he originally set up the bombs, he had made sure he was far enough away, but something must have gone wrong. Rocks and debris were scattered everywhere. The screams died down, and the growling sound was almost a dull roar. When he got closer to where he last saw his brothers, he realized something was wrong. The rocks were hurting his eyes with the bright purple color, stained with blood. Blood was trickling down the rocks forming a small river at the base. Bodies were strung all over the place. No one was intact. Chunks of mangled flesh were hanging off rocks, and bone fragments stuck straight up like tacks. In the middle of the blood river stood Teddie and Eddie. They were covered in blood, but their eyes were glowing with a bright purple color.

"Come here, Clinton," Eddie said quietly. It was the volume of his voice that made Sheriff Clinton feel uneasy. Eddie had never used a quiet voice. Sheriff Clinton wanted to turn around and run, but his feet took him towards his brothers. Teddie growled and smiled. His smile seemed too big for his face. "Thanks for blowing up this mine. You chose the exact spot that led to a gate of Hell." Teddie's voice sounded distorted. Eddie and Teddie ripped off their shirts with a single try. They seemed taller, and their muscles were bulging. Sheriff Clinton took a step back. "Tsk, tsk, tsk, little brother. You aren't going anywhere." Eddie said, laughing. The laugh made a shiver go down Sheriff Clinton's spine.

Before he could blink an eye, Eddie and Teddie were on top of him. With one punch, Teddie sent him flying to the ground. Sharp rocks dug deeper into his back. He was pretty sure rocks were embedded into his spine. Eddie grabbed his throat and spat blood into his mouth. Sheriff Clinton started to gag as the rancid blood slid down his throat. It didn't taste like normal blood. It tasted like rot. It burned like it was made from acid. He could feel every bone snapping loudly as his body began to convulse on the ground. Sharp rocks created deep gashes all over his body. The rocks were slicing him like he was made from butter. Finally, he heard three growls and looked up to see a man that looked to be made from metal step out from the rubble. His eyes were glowing green and purple.

"Hello, son." The man said. His voice sounded as if razor blades were scraping across a chalkboard. Sheriff Clinton looked up as he continued to convulse. His vision was blurry still from the blast, and blood had started to drip into his eyes. He had cut his face on the sharp rocks as each bone painfully cracked at unnatural angles. "I was distraught with you when you killed Ma and me. You took the money we had so painstakingly saved up for her surgery. Your poor Ma was blind. You left your brothers without anything for survival. You are a despicable human being. You don't deserve the powers I gave your brothers. You deserve to be in pain for the rest of your life."The man said as he crouched down in front of Sheriff Clinton. Finally, he was able to see something that almost resembled his dad.

"Sheriff Clinton? You ok?" Claira's voice rang out from somewhere within the mine. "Go away! Don't come here!" Sheriff Clinton shouted. His brothers smirked and clasped each other on the forearm. Then, his brothers merged in a brilliant flash of red and purple. The only bad thing is how they looked exactly like Sheriff Clinton did. They took off towards Claira. "NOOOOO!" Sheriff

Clinton shouted. He never wanted to admit it out loud, but he had deep feelings for the only woman in town that no one could attain. His father laughed hard and hit him in the head. He could feel his skull cracking from the impact of his father's fist. He kept hitting him over and over again. Finally, sheriff Clinton's left side of his head was completely caved in. He knew he wasn't going to last much longer. "Here will be your punishment." His father said, looking deeply into Sheriff Clinton's eyes. His father forced his mouth open and stuck what looked like a maggot-covered rock down his throat. The rock felt like it was on fire, burning down as he swallowed it with no choice.

He could feel the maggots wriggling down his throat and into his stomach. Then he felt sharp pinches inside of his stomach. The maggots had grown sharp teeth and were eating him from the inside out. Sheriff Clinton screamed in agony. His father held up a mirror in front of his face so he could see the maggots eating underneath his face. Sheriff Clinton could feel the maggots into his sunken in the left side of his head. He had to warn Claira not to trust his brothers. Standing up, he realized he was no longer a man but a creature from hell. He ran out of the mine to warn Claira as his father laughed loudly. Once he got out into the sunlight, his skin caught fire. Claira screamed and lifted her rifle. My brothers, who were now me, also raised a rifle. "No! It's me, Claira!" Sheriff Clinton tried to scream. All that came out was a horrifying growl. Claira started shooting, hitting Sheriff Clinton in the chest. His brothers began shooting, battering his body with bullets.

Sheriff Clinton didn't die even though they must have pumped forty bullets into him. He lunged at his brothers but only managed to bite them on the arm. Their blood tasted amazing, and Sheriff Clinton forgot about trying to warn Claira for a minute. Instead, he lunged at her and took a big bite out of her neck. Her blood was the most amazing thing he had ever tried. He was biting her neck in a frenzy and didn't realize when her head had been severed. Claira's head rolled down towards the town. His brothers shot him in the knee cap, dropping him and slowing him down for a few minutes. It was enough for his brothers to climb on their house and ride into town. Sheriff Clinton had no doubt they would rally up the rest of the town to stop him. He would go back into the mines until night time then make his move. He moved back into the mine and saw that his skin blackened from being on fire. The blackened skin became like heavy-duty armor. He could see his heart beating with a reddish glow. He found himself in a nice hiding place where he could rest and wait for his brothers to return. He no longer cared about anything else.

He just wanted a meal. He would be remembered as a legendary monster, while his brothers would be forgotten over time. As the years went on, Sheriff Clinton devoured everything and anything that came into the mines. He never did see his father again. The glowing purple rocks became buried deep in the decay.

The town that he loved became a ghost town. Today it's a marker for tourists.

2022

I checked to see if my daughter was asleep, but found her smiling. "Keep reading, mama," she whispered. I tried to stifle a yawn and took a deep breath. She would probably stay awake until I finished the entire book. I looked in the kitchen at all the dishes and blood. Letting all those dishes and blood stay like they were was going to be a pain in the ass task to clean. Blood once it congeals is one of the hardest things to get rid of. It usually took about a 12-hour process. My house never looked like any sort of crime ever happened, no one in town knew we were cannibals. We had disguised ourselves

well, and I had enough information to make sure no blood was ever found in any way. The hair we always donated to cancer patients. My sister, worked miracles with people's hair, to the point no one would have ever guessed that their new wig could have come from someone they used to know. She died last year from eating someone who had caught a bad virus. Fingernails, toenails, and teeth were always put into a biodegradable planter and then planted at the bottom of the local lake. The lake was the only body of water for miles and had the prettiest plants grow from all the planters we had planted over the years.

"Next story is about your great-aunt. It's called Halloween." I moved a piece of hair off of my daughter's face and began to read once more.

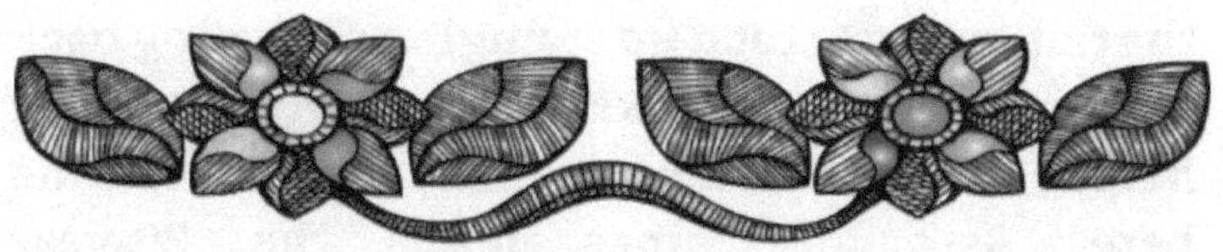

Halloween

I grew up never afraid of anything or anyone. For some reason, nothing scared me even when I dipped into the darker side of everything. I saw many things I couldn't explain and still can't to this day. Still feared nothing. One night I went to

the park to think. I couldn't sleep like every other night since I was 7. Hunters park was so beautiful at 2 am. No one ever played at the park and left it abandoned for no real reason. Slowly I started to swing, gazing down at the ground. My nightshirt clung to my body and my feet dangled as I picked up speed. Suddenly I heard a noise in front of me that startled me and caused me to whip my head up. There standing directly in front of me were two kids in my college class. "No one really knows the true story about Aimee Milner. There were two men hanging beside her lifeless body on this very swing." The taller one said to the other. I waved my hand in front of them but they acted like they didn't see me. The shorter one grabbed the chains of the swing and ran his finger right over my hand. It sent a chill down my body. "That's a sad fucked up story." He whispered to the taller one. I stood up swinging the swing back and it crashed into his knee caps. "Let's get out of here! I can't believe you talked me into coming here. Especially since it's the 20-year anniversary of Aimee Milner's death!" The smaller one grabbed the taller one's arm and both took off running. I stood there watching them run. I had no idea what kind of prank they were pulling. I didn't die. I was really going to let them have it at school on Monday. I walked home with my long hair sticking to the back of my neck. Ugh, I hated the heat why was it always so hot? I couldn't remember when was the last time it got cold or even snowed. It was almost like I was stuck in hell. I got home and switched on the lights. My sister screamed as she jumped off the couch. Curious I looked at her, I didn't remember her sleeping at my place. "I'm sorry I didn't do anything to save you, Aimee. It was 20 years ago when these carnies kidnapped you when I was busy making out with my boyfriend. 20 years ago when they found your body. I'm so sorry. Please stop haunting me!" She broke down sobbing holding the necklace I wore every day close to her heart. Suddenly it all came crashing back to me. I was in hell. I had died from those two carnies who had hurt me. I tricked them into hanging themselves and as a result, this was my hell. I wanted to comfort my sister but instead turned off the light and went back to the park. I felt bad for my sister, I didn't mean to haunt her. On most nights I couldn't remember that I had actually died. Once the carnies had hung themselves a demon popped out of the ground underneath the tree. He looked like a normal person except had red glowing eyes. "Tsk, tsk, tsk, Aimee Milner. Now you must face the consequences. You made my two top men hang themselves. They kept Hell alive with the souls they would collect." He said in a weird voice. The voice didn't match his face at all. It was too deep and sounded off.

I couldn't remember if I spoke to him, but I knew that I had kicked him in the balls. He had grabbed my arm and cut me in a weird design with a knife that was bigger than his hand. I didn't feel it much. It was like a searing pain that lasted only for a few seconds. The cut took my memory of the fact that I had died. I went to school every single day. I always thought it was weird I had all math classes. Math was the one subject I always hated and did poorly in every year. It would seem that every Halloween I would get my memory back for a short time. Did I hear those kids right? I had been dead for twenty years. What was I supposed to do? Just roam the Earth doing math all day? Surely, that wasn't the whole reason why that demon marked me. Why was I the one punished, when those carnies hurt me? I felt rage boil up inside of me. That was complete and utter bullshit! I was going to go to that spot where the carnies died and give that demon a piece of my mind.

It was a long walk and the heat was making sweat pour down my entire body. The heat made me angrier. Once I got to the tree in which both carnies died, I started to yell as loud as I could. "Hey! Demon! Get your ass out here now!" The hot wind picked up around me as the ground seeped with red. He once again appeared under the tree this time smoking a cigarette. "Why am I being punished? Those guys of yours hurt me! They killed me! I only made them hang themselves after I was dead. How come I have to endure this shit? Where are the two guys?" I was angrily shouting and panting because I had run out of breath. "You are getting punished for tricking my top men into hanging themselves. That's the ultimate sin for a demon. Their souls vanquished like a squished grape. You possessed their bodies until they were hanging themselves. I am still not sure why a simple dead human with nothing special about her was able to control both men to the point of their undoing. I had to spend the last 20 years finding out why you were able to do such things. Why aren't you in Hell, and free to roam around like a lost puppy."

He tossed the cigarette aside and laughed as the leaves caught fire. "Why can't I leave?" I asked afraid to hear the answer. "Because it turns out, you are special. You have a very special lineage. Turns out you are the daughter of the devil himself. You are the result of the devil having a one-night stand with someone he thought was a human. Your mother was a siren, luring him in. Your blood would have made you royalty. You can't move on, nor can you be cast to Hell. How about you come work for me?" He said as pulled out a flask from his jacket pocket. He took a long swing of something that smelled like whiskey. "Why would I work for you?" I asked pulling my long wet hair into a ponytail. I was getting beyond pissed off. "You just said, I can't leave and can't be dragged to Hell. What's the point of working for you? I don't remember my own name more than half of the time."

I turned around to leave when he appeared in front of me. He grabbed the scar on my arm until it started to pulsate with pain. "I own you. I won't make you collect souls, but you will have to pay." He started to really hurt my arm so I let out a yelp. He put his mouth over the top of mine and kissed me. His breath smelled like something had rotted away. I pulled away and spat in disgust. "What the fuck is wrong with you?" I hit him hard enough to make him fall back. "What I did was give you your punishment. You will be alive now, a brand new life. However, no human food will sustain you in any way. You have to eat people. That's right, you heard right. You are now a human, not a spirit. You won't look like you used to, that girl died a long time ago. You will be nameless, and you will be a cannibal. I'll let you die, once you have eaten enough people to pay for taking away my two best men."

I couldn't hold back the vomit anymore. The smell of his breath was making my stomach churn. I started to vomit harder than I ever had in my entire life. I was panting and out of breath when he patted me on the back. "Have fun!" He laughed, then he vanished back into the ground. I had thrown up all over my nightshirt. It wasn't normal vomit, it was thick and clumpy. It looked like the blood that had been congealed for many years. Clumsily, I stood up trying to get the strength to walk. Did he really mean, I was alive once more? What did I look like now? I had no place to go, so I broke into the motel by the highway. They never locked their doors and most of the doors no longer had keys. I showered and then looked at myself in the cracked mirror. I had long jet-black hair with red streaks that looked like blood in my hair. My eyes were no longer blue but the darkest shade of green I had ever seen in my life. I was no longer tanned, but so pale I could see my veins. My lips were a dark blood-red color. I had long fingernails that looked like black talons. The first thing I wanted to do was trim them, I always hated long nails. I found a fingernail clipper on the table beside the bed. I sanitized them as best as I could with some hand sanitizer I found in the bathroom. It looked fairly new and was still sealed in its package. I tried to clip my fingernails but I couldn't even make a dent. They were rock solid.

I was not digging my new look at all. There were a couple of outfits that people had left in the tiny, dirty closet. At least I wouldn't be naked when I went outside. The clothes smelled but at least they seemed to fit okay. I checked under the mattress and was happy to find some money under there. At least I will be able to get some decent clothes. I put the money in my pocket after I counted it. There was a little over 5k that had been stuffed inside the mattress. Lucky me. Taking it would probably get someone killed, but at this point I needed it to survive.

I was happy I was no longer having to take math classes, but I had died without finishing high school. I was only 16 when I died. I had no skills in order to survive. I walked to the store and bought a few new outfits, some toiletries, and a burner phone. I went back to the hotel in a different but cleaner room. I barricaded myself in the room so no one could enter. I first tried to cut my long hair but found that nothing could cut it. Frustrated, I decided to embrace the new look. I spent a couple of hours trying out different makeup styles until I found one that suited my new look best. I missed my old body and my old life. I waited until the sun came up and hid in the bushes at my sister's house. I followed her around everywhere she went. Eventually, I was sitting across from her at her job. "I need a job," I said simply. My sister rubbed her eyes, she looked tired. "Ok, what's your name?" She asked as she was filling out a form. Fuck! I had forgotten to pick out a new name. I shifted uncomfortably in my seat. "My name?" I started to look around to see if anyone was watching me.

I felt like I couldn't breathe. "You ok?" My sister asked me as she poured me a glass of water. I held the cup with shaking hands. Time had not been my sister's friend. She had worry wrinkles all over her face. Her hair was long when we were kids, but it was cut short and looked messy. “Uh-” I couldn’t get the words to form out of my mouth. “Hey, come with me.” my sister said gently. She brought me to a bigger, more secluded office and closed all the blinds. “My name is Tina, and if you are in danger, or escaping from something bad, I can help you. If you don’t want to use your name, you are more than welcome to choose another name. Are you in a dangerous situation?” She asked while pouring me a glass of water. Her eyes were so piercing I couldn’t look at her in the eyes. I had terribly missed my sister but seeing her alive just broke my heart. “I- uh,” I still couldn’t say anything. I looked around the office and could see my sister’s face in everything in the office. Not only did she help people find jobs, but she helped kidnapped victims and families who lost their kids. She lived in our old house, our parents had died when we were both young. She had raised me and kept us from going to foster care. I could tell she still blamed herself for what happened to me. She was a force to reckoned with, somehow my disappearance and death made her a woman made of steel. “Are you in a dangerous situation?” She asked again.

“No,” I whispered. I tried to smooth out my hair and sit up straight. “I need a job ma’am. I don’t have much schooling. I am shy and not very strong. I’ll work hard,” I managed to whisper.

She looked at me and gave me the look like she didn't believe me. She was furiously typing away and her brow deepened. "Honestly, I'm not lying Tina." I crossed my heart in the shape of an X with my finger. She gasped slightly. Fuck! I had forgotten I was no longer my old self. I had no name. "I'm sorry, did I do something wrong?" I asked hating the fact that my voice was quivering.

"No, it's ok. My sister used to do that all the time to show me how sincere she was. She died over 20 years ago. I miss her." She quickly wiped away a tear. I wanted to hug her but I knew I had to be someone else for right now. My stomach was growling loudly. I hugged myself tightly hoping my sister didn't hear it. "My name is Amber," I whispered. My stomach was growling so much it was starting to become super painful. "I can set you up with a night shift as a cleaning woman for the hotel. They can give you a free room if you need it. It's not the scary one that never locks. It's the nice one they built by the new highway." She gave me the address and some paperwork to fill out. I quickly wrote out what I could, lying about everything. I thanked her and then hurried out of the office.

I ran all the way back to the motel. My stomach was convulsing against itself. I grabbed all my stuff and began the slow walk to the motel I would be working at. It was over nine miles. I wasn't going to turn to eating people. I couldn't do it. Let him come for me, I whispered as my eyes narrowed. I hugged my jacket closer to my body and snaked my arm around my stomach. The job was easy and I kept eating hamburgers. It didn't help with the hunger pains. It didn't make my stomach hurt less. The other employees wrote me off as a meth head going through withdrawals. I didn't talk to anyone and kept my head down. The stomach growling got worse, and people were starting to talk.

Months later, while I sleeping the demon woke me up rather rudely. "Why aren't you eating people?" He sat down smoking a cigarette. "Put out that nasty shit." I snapped at him. My stomach growled loudly. I was exhausted. I had been working so many hours because I couldn't stand the sound my stomach was making. "I don't answer to you. Now get the hell out of my room. I have to get at least two hours of sleep before my next shift!" He stood up and put his cigarette out on top of the scar he created. I didn't bother to flinch. I was used to the scar throbbing constantly. I pushed him out of my room and locked the door. I flopped back down on the bed only for him to grab my leg and throw me onto the floor. "You will consume people. You hear me?" He spit as he yelled in my face. "Or what? Are you going to drag me to hell? Punish me?" I laughed. "You going to give me a spanking because you are a big mean scary demon?" I said in a mockingly sweet voice. I almost couldn't hear myself over the growling of my stomach. He screamed and opened the floor of the motel room. The hot searing heat blasted me in the face. Sure enough, he was dragging me to Hell. I smiled as the hot rocks embedded into my legs. The demon was strong I was starting to think he was going to rip off my arms. Slivers of my flesh kept getting caught on the rocks.

"Why are you being like that? Get up and fucking walk!" I could barely hear him over the roar of flames that surrounded me. "Fuck you, you want me here, drag me bitch." I screamed. I didn't care if that pissed him off. Judging how he tightened his jaw and started to stomp faster, I could see his anger building up. In Hell, there was no way I could ignore my stomach pains. Then an idea hit me. I would just eat him and everyone else that was part of the carnival. I remembered every carnie's face from when they kidnapped me. After so many years of wandering around, my memory of that night came rushing back to me. Tina was as she had said making out with her boyfriend in her room. She didn't hear me sneaking out to go to the carnival. I had planned on coming back before her boyfriend left so she wouldn't have noticed me gone.

The guy in the ticket booth smiled at me as I tried to peek inside the metal fence they put around the carnival. He smiled and whispered in my ear that I could go in and just tell no one I didn't have a ticket. I remember him saying something on the phone as I passed through the gates. All the carnie's let me have free prizes and free food. I got to play all the games and was having so much fun until they lured me into a room that held a single cage. Somehow, I tripped over something on the floor and landed face-first in the cage. They locked the cage door and refused to let me out. I couldn't tell you how long I was in the cage. They all took turns whipping me with horse whips and breaking bones. My eyes had matted shut from the crying and blood so I was never able to defend myself. They had played really creepy music on the speakers loudly 24/7 until I thought my eardrums were going to burst from the sheer noise of it all. They sealed the cage up entirely once I stopped crying out. I was no longer fun to them. I just lay in the corner of the cage, letting them do whatever they wanted from me. I had no strength to fight back, and my bones never healed. If anything looked like they had started to heal, the carnies would break it all over again. They threw the sealed-up cage into the local lake, right by the school playground.

Water had rushed in from the bottom of the cage and still, I lay there. There was no point in trying to fight to save my life. There was no way I was going to be able to break free from that cage.

They found my body in the cage almost a year later as it was washed up by the swings at school. I had found myself wandering by the carnival shortly after I died and found it was easy to jump into the two carnie's bodies. It was so easy to hang them.

I continued to let the demon drag me until he stopped in a big room. The room looked exactly as the carnival did all those years ago. Even played the same music. He probably thought I would sink to my knees and start sobbing once I recognized the place. Instead, I stood up slowly and picked out the smaller rocks that had embedded themselves into my joints. I clapped my hands loudly and started to laugh. "Thank you for bringing me here!" I shouted. Everyone stopped what they were doing and looked at me with curiosity. All I could hear was the roar of the fire and my stomach growling. I didn't bother to elaborate on why I was thanking them, I sprang into action. I was so hungry so I was able to bite through demons' throats with two bites. Soon, there was nothing but a pile of bodies strung all over the floor.

Once everyone had died, I sat happily on the floor crunching loudly on the bones. I could see black smoke lingering around so I started to stab at them with the bones that I hadn't eaten. The smoke made a weird puncture sound like a balloon had a small leak in it. I took as many deep breaths as I could in order to inhale all the smoke I could. "Thanks, guys for such a great meal. I was so fucking hungry." I laughed as I continued to eat. Looking around, I felt at home. The heat wasn't so bad. I could stay right here and never have to worry about my stomach ever hurting again. I didn't have to eat any people, I got to see my sister one last time and I got revenge on the fuckers who were hurting people. I could feel the smoke bubbling around inside of me so I laid down on the wet, squishy mess I had made on the floor. Closing my eyes, I could hear the soul's scream, which brought a smile to my face.

The End

2022 Mama's Story

My daughter's eyes fluttered for a brief second as she began to lightly snore. I looked at her, then looked at the kitchen once more. "One more story. This one is ours." I whispered. I began to write in the book as I read each word out loud. The kitchen could wait just another hour. I would make sure I spent the rest of the night cleaning. I was proud of my daughter for not causing a big scene once she found out we were cannibals. She deserved to know how we came about as well.

It all started in 2008 in a lab a few hundred miles from our home. I was taken to a hospital because I had fallen and hurt my back. My mother back then was all cloak and dagger when it came to leaving the house. I thought she was just paranoid. She hated people and our front door had 12 locks on it. I couldn't stand up properly and my mom had said a piece of my spine was poking through. My mom left me in the hospital not by her choice though. The doctor recognized her and turned her into the authorities. My mom had been hiding from the police for years after she started to eat human flesh. Hiding in plain sight until she had to take me to the hospital.

She never got the chance to come back for me. She was shot down after she attacked a cop. I was being wheeled into surgery for my back when I heard the gunshots. I knew that day, I was going to have to do anything to survive. Once the surgery was complete, I was in the hospital for months. I made friends with a male nurse on nightshift by name of Kyle. "Once I'm released here, I'll be put into foster care," I confessed to him one night. Kyle never said a word to me but nodded as he understood. He put his finger to his lips and shushed me. He smiled and it seemed like the world got brighter. He started to inject me with something he created. Not only did it help me heal faster, but it meant I could eat flesh without getting sick. True to my word, when I got out, I was put into foster care.

At first, my foster family was abusive to me. I was kept in a closet for months and given just enough food to survive. I got sick and almost died. They took me to the same hospital my mother was killed in front of. I stayed a week that time in the hospital. Kyle looked at me and shook his head sadly. "I injected you with something that was supposed to protect you." Kyle had whispered. He injected me again to heal me quickly. He slipped me a hamburger and let me eat in the darkened room. It was the best hamburger I had ever tasted. In the morning time, my foster parents came with the news that the state granted them complete guardianship of me until I was 18.

Kyle came in right as they told me the news. He shooed them away saying I needed to stay in the hospital for a couple more days. "If you go back, they will continue to hurt you. That burger you ate was made from human flesh. I killed a nurse that was trying to have sex with coma patients. That is how you will gain enough strength to make it to the end safely." Kyle had said once my foster parents were out of the room. I smiled and finally understood. I was a powerful beast and they weren't going to hurt me any longer.

It took a few months after I went back to the

foster home before they started their abuse once more. They wanted to make sure that the police weren't looking to take away their guardianship. I was worth a lot of money a month. This time I was ready for them to go back to their ways. I was far more confident than most teens. I had to play my cards right. I was still afraid of crossing that moral line. I let them hit me and hide me back into that closet for a year.

I finally couldn't take it anymore. I remembered thinking to myself in the dark, that my mom wouldn't want me to live like that. I had to stop feeling sorry for myself. I waited for my foster dad to drag me out of the closet. Like most nights, he was drunk and was unsteady on his feet. He pulled me out of the closet by my long, matted hair.

He was too drunk to see what he was doing, and tripped over his own feet. I pushed him down the stairs. His body bounced down the stairs as if it was made from rubber. His neck made a weird cracking sound as his body went still. My foster mother was passed out drunk on the floor beside the door. I didn't have any foster siblings at that moment. The house was silent except for the occasional snore coming from my foster mom.

I slowly and quietly made my way down the steps. I didn't know the first thing about eating human flesh. I did know that I needed my foster mother to join my foster dad in death. I couldn't have her waking up in the middle of me trying to figure out why I was trying to eat someone. I wasn't sure I was going to be able to kill her but somehow, I dug down deep inside of myself. I grabbed my foster mother's favorite cast iron skillet, she cooked everything in. She never washed it, but that didn't matter to me. They only fed me bread anyway thankfully. I thought about all the times my foster mother hit me, or put her cigarettes out on my skin.

I had bottled up so much rage for so long, that once I hit her in the head with the cast iron skillet, I couldn't stop. Chunks of disgusting dried on food came flying off the pan and landed on my foster mother's dead body. Blood splattered all over me. I didn't know how to cook, my mother never got the chance to show me before she was killed. I decided to eat them both raw. Human flesh when it's not cooked is so stringy, it took a while to chew. I was beyond hungry I was able to consume both bodies within hours. I had never eaten so much before and fell into a deep sleep next to the bodies.

A neighbor must have peeked inside the door the next morning and reported to the police that we were all dead. I didn't feel them lifting me up into the body bag, I had slept for almost 20 hours straight. When I woke up I on a tray inside a cold freezer. Feeling around in the dark, I was able to find a pressure release button that made the door swing open with a hiss. Thankfully, there was no one in the room. I ran down the street covering my body with the sheet they had put on me while I was laying on the tray. I ran until the bottoms of my feet were bloody.

I stole some clothes off of a scarecrow and kept walking. I walked out of town and eventually I figured out how to steal a car. Learning to drive was easier than I thought it was going to be. After scraping the car a few times on trees and guard rails, I figured it out. When it ran out of gas, I stole car after car. I made it all the way to Maine, in scarecrow clothes. Once in Maine, I hopped on the first ferry that came in the morning and took it to a little island.

The island was filled with cannibals. At first they wanted to eat me, but after a few failed attempts I finally was able to tell them I was a cannibal too. They cooked me a meal after slaughtering a man in front of me. It was the best meal I had ever tasted. When I cleaned my bowl and asked for seconds, I was accepted in the tribe. I lived there for 14 years. Then your father and his crew crashed their boat on the island. We ate many of the crew but I had fallen in love with your father. Instead of eating him, I begged the people to let me and him escape. They wouldn't let us leave the island instead they built us a home on a neighboring island. This house was built with

several others that had been for other people in the past.

Your father decided to cheat on me with one of the woman that had been in a house four doors down. I killed him in the kitchen. Not only did I make him into meals for us, but I went to the original island and fed everyone there. After I told them what I had done, we are both accepted over there once more. We are royalty. I have decided to marry the king of the island. It's better to stay on the island then trying to survive out in the world where people like to hurt anyone who is different. When you grow up, you should write your story in this book as well. We may not live forever, but words will.

I stopped writing and massaged my hand. I was excited for my wedding. It was time to get the kitchen cleaned back up. I was making my own wedding cake and needed the meat in the freezer. I signed my name to the back of the book and quietly put it on her shelf. I smiled and kissed her on the forehead gently, then went to clean the kitchen.

The End

LIFE *after* YOU

MAGDALENE MAVEENA

Copyright © Magdalene Maveena 2023
All Rights Reserved.

ISBN 979-8-89067-785-3

This book has been published with all efforts taken to make the material error-free after the consent of the author. However, the author and the publisher do not assume and hereby disclaim any liability to any party for any loss, damage, or disruption caused by errors or omissions, whether such errors or omissions result from negligence, accident, or any other cause.

While every effort has been made to avoid any mistake or omission, this publication is being sold on the condition and understanding that neither the author nor the publishers or printers would be liable in any manner to any person by reason of any mistake or omission in this publication or for any action taken or omitted to be taken or advice rendered or accepted on the basis of this work. For any defect in printing or binding the publishers will be liable only to replace the defective copy by another copy of this work then available.

For every one of you who thought you weren't worth being loved or worth anything, this one's for you.

Lots of love,

M

"Love is patient and kind; love does not envy or boast; it is not arrogant or rude. It does not insist on its own way; it is not irritable or resentful; it does not rejoice at wrongdoing, but rejoices with the truth. Love bears all things, believes all things, hopes all things, endures all things.

Love never ends."

Playlist

They Don't Know About Us by One Direction

Living Proof by Camila Cabello

Strong by One Direction

I miss you, I'm sorry by Gracie Abrams

Someone To You by BANNERS

Gorgeous by Taylor Swift

Risk It All by The Vamps

It'll be Okay by Shawn Mendes

More Than This by One Direction

You Took My Heart Away by Michael Learns To Rock

Fallin' All In You by Shawn Mendes

Sign of the Times by Harry Styles

Little Things by One Direction

No Tears Left To Cry by Ariana Grande

Imagination by Shawn Mendes

Begin Again by Taylor Swift

It Is What It Is by James Miller

Falling Like The Stars by James Arthur

Flightless Bird, American Mouth by Iron & Wine

Chapter One

They Don't Know About Us by One Direction

I think I've read an ample amount of romance novels to figure out or half-plot whatever happens in a book by just the first few chapters of a book. Mostly. I also tend, well, *used to,* believe in love. I used to believe I was capable of loving someone or for someone to love me. Did that happen?

Sure.

Maybe.

Sort of.

The answer is no. I did. But I don't think *they* did.

Like all romance novels, every relationship is different compared to so many right? Maybe mine was one of the *different*, way different ones compared to the rest. It's different because how can something or rather, *someone* who meant everything to you at some point completely shatter you into pieces? It's human to like, love, hurt and eventually hate.

"Hey Isabelle, can I talk to you for a second?" I turn around to see Steven coming down the stairs towards me.

"Oh hey, sure. What do you want to talk about?" I smile, trying to contain the excitement that just took over at the sound of his voice. Gosh why am I so...naive? More like sensitively naive.

"It's more like what I have to say to you.." he says slowly, trapping me with his eye contact.

"Okay. I'm all ears." I smile even though my heartbeat just increased its pace.

"Have you realised it's been only like a month since we started dating?" He asks with that dreamy smile of his. I nod and then notice a crowd of students gathering just a couple of stairs above from where we're standing.

"Steven.." I feel my hands shaking while my heart keeps beating faster by the second.

"I know, but wait. I've been dying to say this to you." He says gently. He looks down at the mere distance between our hands. I smile sadly. I shake my head at him, feeling the tears pool my eyes. He sighs. "I love you, Isabelle. I don't want to keep it in anymore.."

"You love me?" I whisper, completely taken aback. That's an understatement by the way.

"I do. I know we can't be like an actual couple, we can't but-"

"I love you too." I say, cutting him off mid sentence. I'm staring into his eyes, his face trying to grasp his expression of what might be running in his mind. And then he smiles.

I look away from him because I'm not sure I have the strength to keep staring at him when I know I'm capable of letting my emotions take over, forgetting our surroundings and acting as if it's just us alone in the area. I didn't want to take a chance so I waved goodbye and ran away towards the closest ladies room I could find.

In class I was so distracted by what he had said not a long time ago, it kept on ringing in my head over and over again. After what seemed like forever the last bell rang and all of the students rushed out of the doors where as I took my own cool time packing my bag and leaving to meet him at our spot which is on the ground floor staircase which thankfully is the only place we could be ourselves around each other.

I get slightly nervous when I realise I'm only steps away from him. He is smiling which only makes me smile even more.

"Hey," I smile when we're only a foot away from each other.

"How was your day?"

"The usual," I start to say but break into a smile.

"Better than usual I hope." He catches on and takes a seat on one of the stairs so we're eye level. Did I mention he's like a foot taller than me?

"Mh-hm. It had a little to do with someone," he smiles at that.

"Now, I'm jealous. What'd he say to get you so happy?" He has this smug smile covering his face, I can't help but want to close the distance between us.

Silence fell over us for a bit, but it was a comfortable silence. Until he breaks the silence like he always does.

"You remember what I said back at the stairs earlier today?"

"I do. I feel the same way, Steven. I have, for a while now. I just didn't know how to go about it." I find myself saying it openly.

"Come here," he gestures towards him, and I gladly close the distance between us.

"Why are things so unfair?" I whisper against his chest.

"I know. Life is like that I guess." He says above my face.

"I wish we could do this everyday. I miss you so much!"

"I'm right here, Isabelle. I'm right here," He rubs my back soothingly and I hum.

"I love you," I say softly, slowly looking up to face him.

"I love you." He looks down at me with a smile.

"How long do we have?" I suddenly asked, standing up.

"All the time in the world," he grins. "A few more minutes, really." He says after glancing at his watch. I frown. "Isabelle, I'll see you in a couple of hours, okay?" He stands up, walking closer to me.

"Hmm. I'll miss you all evening through the night." I sigh.

"I have something for you. Read it when you get home." He says and pulls out a yellow paper out of his pocket and hands it to me.

"I will. Bye now." I say with a smile, hoping it would hide my sadness within.

"Bye." He says just when I feel my hand brush through his face, goosebumps suddenly rise on my skin. I just touched his face!

When I get home, the house is empty, which means my parents have gone to work. I do a happy dance and quickly hop in the shower, eat and take the note he gave me today.

Dear Isabelle,

I know what I'm about to say now is going to make you sad. I didn't want to say anything earlier because I didn't want to ruin our day. We just told each other we love each other. That's something that doesn't happen everyday. I just couldn't ruin it for you. I'm sorry.

I won't be coming to school for a couple of weeks. Remember the mid-terms we had last semester? Well, now I've got the actual exams coming soon. School has given us study leave so I'll be home for the rest of the month, till exams finally end.

I'll see you soon, very soon okay? I'm sorry but wait for me. Two months. Just two months, I'll see you soon.

– Steven

Just like all first love romances, I felt like I had mine the first two months after getting to know him. Steven. The first ever boyfriend I had. The first *ever* time I felt my adrenaline running high and also the *most* damaging experience I've ever gone through in my entire life.

The day he said he loves me was the most beautiful thing ever, and also the most hurtful memory to remember. Everything about that beautiful memory made me smile so much but also cry equally as much.

I was sure everybody in school knew about us. I was called by so many disciplinary committee teachers admonishing me to stop seeing him. So many students in my grade made fun of me about it and even though I was happy, or I thought I was, I cried so much everyday at night when everybody was asleep.

Six months. For six months, I dated the school's best student. I should've won an award for it honestly. But like they all say, 'all good things come to an end'. This love story, or whatever it was, came to an end in just a snap of a finger. It was so fast that I hadn't even realised how just months could completely change everything. But it wasn't a '*good thing*'. We didn't call off things because of school rules. We broke up, or at least I did, because while we were still dating, I saw him with someone else. They were happy. Of course they were happy, they were *together*.

Love is a funny thing sometimes. You can love somebody so much that you'd be willing to go through hell for them only to know that it was all a game to them. Still, you love them because your mind keeps flashing all those moments when it was just you and them. Moments you couldn't stop smiling because of the guy who said he cared about you. Moments you giggled so much, your mouth hurt because of the guy who said he loved you. Moments you cried so much because you loved the guy you thought loved you.

Breakups are hard, yes. Moving on is *harder*.

It's harder because you have to constantly keep stopping your mind from going places you were once able to. You're constantly on the move and that is exhausting! Twenty-four seven, you've got to be on the watch-out, because almost everything, even the littlest things would remind you of that person and that doesn't hurt. That *kills*. It kills because you're constantly reminded about someone who you thought loved you when no one did.

The day I cried myself to sleep, the day I decided it was time to move on, the day I wanted nothing more to do with him or to even to be in the same room as him, the day I never wanted to love again, the day I became someone I never was, was probably the hardest I've had to go through. And the best part was, nothing helped because like I said, when things weren't that well at home, school would be a distraction but in this case, it was the opposite. School made things so much worse than it already *was*.

Like I said earlier, it's human to like, love, hurt and eventually hate. It's just emotions until the said emotions happen to rearrange everything about you into a complete stranger.

And yes, I was officially alone again.

It was like drowning in this never ending sea with waves that keep crashing and almost choking you and you're in a position where you could either get too much water into your system and get choked or just keep letting the waves keep pushing and tossing you in the sea ruthlessly.

* * * * *

Few Months Later

"Remember you're a nobody!" My father yells in my face and kicks my mid thigh making me shut my eyes automatically letting the pain sink in. It feels like my muscle under my skin just broke open.

When I open my eyes, my vision blurs as I let out a deep breath, more like a reluctant sob.

"George! Do you realise what you did?!" My mum rushes to my side, looking horrified. My dad remains silent until I speak.

"I'm sorry, daddy," I say, sobs leaving my mouth as I say the words for probably the millionth time since I grew up. I turn around to walk out of the room only to realise I have to limp. I hold my thigh in one hand and limp my way to the door and to my room which is on the other end of the house. Tears keep trailing my way as I walk around the house.

"I'm going to school. I'll see you in the evening," I say, not bothered to know if they heard me. I just leave my house and limp all the way to the bus station. I texted my mum on the way, saying I left for school in case she got worried where I went and waited for a few minutes until the bus finally arrived.

"Um, hey. Do you mind if I sit here?" I ask the girl seated in the second row with her bag occupying the space next to her.

"Sure," she says without looking at me and places her bag on her lap and looks at the window. I say a quiet 'thank you' and sit down and absentmindedly place my bag on my thigh making me grimace so I set the bag down and keep my eyes closed the whole ride to school because I don't want to cry on the bus. I don't want the girl next to me to say, 'why are you crying' or 'are you okay?' Because, I'm not and I haven't been since I can remember.

"Have a nice day." I smile at the bus driver while getting down with difficulty of course but manage to deny the pain until I'm standing on the ground. I take slow but also fast steps to ignore the pain, entering school and the familiar environment.

I make my way with just a book to the secluded corridor just like every other day.

"Good morning," I instinctively gasp at the unexpected voice.

I thought I was the only one to occupy this corridor especially at 6:30 AM at school because the whole point was it was the only time of the day, I could actually appreciate my surroundings and the peace that comes from being solitary.

"Uh, good morning sir," I turned around to see Mr. Reynolds, the principal. Have I gotten myself in detention or something for being extra early to school just to read in the corridors?

"Sorry if I scared you, I didn't expect to see any students this early." He states as a matter of fact.

"Uh yeah, I come here every morning." I say, mentally slapping myself for blurting that out. Great. Now, he's really going to give me a detention slip.

"Oh I see. You live far away?" He asks. I smile but shake my head no. "Oh. Okay, well have a good day, miss." He smiles.

"Please call me Isabelle," I smile politely, he returns it with a nod and then walks away, leaving me by myself. I guess he forgot to hand me a detention slip. I laugh to myself quietly.

"Phew…" I sigh and grab my paperback for the time being because I've been so devoted to this book called 'Regretting You' by Colleen Hoover that got me hooked from chapter 1.

I mean, how could you put down a book with a logline that says,

'How do you pick up the pieces without the glue holding everything together?'

I love that reading helps me forget my environment or the everyday events that happen in my life. It helps me move on just a little bit every time something bad happens. And especially when you find books you completely dive into the minute you read the first page because that's how much you know you would relate to the book.

"Shoot!" I dump the book in my bag and start running down the stairs to my first class but end up falling on the floor because I just aggravated the pain in my thigh. How clever of me. I wince as I get up but limp all the way down two stairways and reach my class.

"Quickly, Heathers. Sit somewhere," my English professor, Mr. Williams says in his usual insouciant voice I've gotten used to in the past couple of years. "What's with the leg?" He asks, halfway as I walk to one of the seats in the last row.

"Uh, I got a muscle pull." I lie shakily, hoping he buys it. Like always.

"Really." I sigh but slowly nod my head, settling myself in my seat. "Right. Whatever. Let's start." He says and gives us the usual lecture on how we should start practising past papers for the exams that are a year from now I think and then starts off with the actual lesson in the syllabus. Grammar check tests. Great.

He sends each one of us a one paper test and that's what we do for the rest of the period while he types away who knows what on his laptop. Probably semester-end exams.

My school life is very uneventful to say the least. I never enjoy going to school to be honest, I just go to study obviously, but also to be away from 'home'. It doesn't really help as much as I thought it would but do I have a choice? Unfortunately, no.

"Isabelle. How's your day going?" I look up to see Mr. Reynolds again. I nervously smile and put the book down. I guess he finally remembered about giving me a detention slip.

"It's been good," I say softly. "Am I going to have to stay for detention after school?" I blurt out.

"Detention? Why would you think that?" He asks, looking confused.

"Because.. I don't know.." *because it's the second time today I see you and I can't help thinking I'm in trouble because you saw me in the corridor, reading, early in the morning, when no one was around.* "Do you think coming to school too early is bad?" I ask him bluntly. He almost laughs. Almost.

"No." He smiles. I sigh, relieved. "How are your classes going so far?" He asks.

"It's good." I nod my head. I'm grateful he doesn't ask any further questions about school because I haven't rehearsed conversations in so long, I barely know how to keep up with people talking about anything.

"What are you reading?" He eyes my book in hand.

"A book," I stated timidly. He chuckles before saying,

"I know. What's the book you're reading called?" He smiles and probably thinks I'm childish.

"Oh uh. It's called, 'Regretting You' by um, Colleen Hoover." I stutter.

"Interesting. How are you liking it so far?" He asks, seeming interested which makes me smile involuntarily.

"I really like the book. It's only been a couple of chapters though," I reply with another smile.

"Nice. Well, I hope you enjoy the rest of the book. Have a good day, Isabelle." He smiles and then walks away towards the office.

Why am I still smiling? Maybe because I don't do it much and every time I feel my lips tugging upwards, it feels unreal and strange and just *different*.

Chapter Two

Living Proof by Camila Cabello

Five Years Later

A lot of teenagers generally love school. But did I? Not one bit. I had never liked school since I can remember, maybe because all I can remember about my 'school life' is about all the picking on, bullying and the constant harassment. But with all that, it only helped me keep my mind busy when things didn't go too well in my caustic life.

I never *liked* living or even the idea of *living* for many different reasons thanks to my childhood memories–I mean that in a good way by the way. I felt like I didn't deserve to live or to even breathe with whatever that was going on all those years. I hated that it was easy to pity my own self. I hated living with pity. And I wanted all of what was going on to end. *With me.*

But, I was wrong.

So wrong.

* * * * *

THUD. THUD. THUD.

I mentally groan as I see three of my cardboard boxes scattered around the hallway.

"You guys toppled down a little too early!" I say to the boxes mindlessly as I begin picking the contents of the boxes that fell out and start tossing them back into the box.

"Who toppled down too early?" I gasp at the new voice but turn around to see a young girl with blonde curls hanging down her head beautifully standing by the doorway of the room opposite to mine.

"Oh hello. My boxes just toppled while I was trying to get them in my room." I explain to the girl looking at me and the toppled boxes.

"Can I help you?" She asks sweetly, holding both her hands together.

"Thank you," I smile at her, which makes her small face lighten up as I gesture for her to help me with the first box. "Where is your mummy and daddy?" I thought of making conversation with the young girl with pretty hair.

"Home." She answers, not looking up from her 'workplace'. I smile and continue picking up some of my clothes that fell out of the second box.

"There you are. *Addy*. Addy, what have I told you about strangers and messing with other people's stuff?" The only things I register for the past fifteen seconds are: British, deep, smell of cologne, probably a dad. I'm not sure about the 'dad' part though.

"But *Jerebear*, she is a *pretty* stranger. You didn't say not to talk to pretty strangers. Also, we need help on the third box." I don't know how old this girl is, probably five or six.

Either way, she sure knows her way around with words which is really cute because that's the kind of energy I'd kill to have. I don't even know why I am comparing myself to a child.

"Sorry..I didn't mean to call her to help me. She offered and I found that sweet so I allowed her. I'm sorry though." I stand up with a box full of my clothes and plan to turn around to set the box in my room but my legs have seemed to have forgotten how to walk.

I'm not sure about the guy being a father now because *ohmagosh!* Not to be too dramatic but I was definitely not expecting to see a drop dead gorgeous model. He appears to be in his twenties. He definitely isn't a dad.

"I see. You just moved in?" I didn't expect him to stop and lean against his door frame, let alone talk to me, but he is and that made me a little embarrassed because I smiled. *He just talked. To me.*

"Yeah," My voice sounds as if I've been running on a treadmill for hours. "Sorry again," I mumble and proceed to take the boxes to my room because I don't like the way my body is behaving right now.

When I get back, the tall super hot brown haired guy isn't leaning against his door frame but is squatting down in front of the third box picking up my *lingerie* and tossing them in the box. *Oh no.*

"Uh, I can get it, thanks," I stumble forward towards him and grab the last black panties from his hand and dump it in the box and stand up and head to my room. I'm definitely *not* embarrassed right now.

"Your welcome!" I hear him say, just when I place the box in my room. I smile to myself before walking out of my apartment.

"Sorry. Thank you." I say to him, he smirks and nods his head. I have half the heart to walk back inside and close my door because of this guy because I definitely want to skip getting settled in but just hear him talk.

"What's your name?" He smirks. Okay, I think that's my new favourite thing.

"Isabelle,"

"Isabelle.." he says my name like it's important to remember.

"And yours?" I am in no way ending this conversation without knowing the guy's name.

"Jeremiah," he smirks. I have no doubt that my cheeks have turned red for probably the tenth time now since I laid my eyes on him.

"Where's Addy? I mean, Adeline, sorry. That's her name right?" I ask him, seeing that she isn't in the hallway or near him.

"Inside," he nods, gesturing towards his apartment.

"Oh." I mumble not knowing what to say now. It's like I have forgotten to make conversation with somebody.

"See you around, neighbour." He smirks, dismissing the conversation.

I don't know how long I've been staring until my face snaps out of its trance when he closes the door behind him.

"Jesus, Isabelle.." I scold myself before walking in my own apartment and start putting things in their new places.

* * * * *

"Hey mummy," I answer the phone quickly as the call comes in.

"Hey Issa! Have you settled in yet?" She chirps. I smile at her voice, imagining her excited face as she talks. My mum is a talker and I love that about her.

"Somewhat. You should come see it." I take a seat on one of the stools of the small island in the kitchen.

"I'd love to! Have you seen the campus yet? I'm regretting letting you buy an apartment instead of getting a dorm room.." There she goes again. I sigh before trying my best to stay calm.

"*Mummy.* I don't want to talk about this again. Please. I'm perfectly happy on my own." I try my best to sound firm but not too harsh. She knows why I preferred having an apartment instead of a dorm room. She knows I wanted to be a little let loose this year. I didn't want to put much effort into making new friends on campus and all that stuff that comes with 'being a college student' subject.

"Fine, fine. Just saying. You would've befriended someone by now if you were in a dorm room. Don't you want to make friends there? Not all principals are young and nice, Isabelle." She says and I fight the urge to roll my eyes. I mentally groan but then smile because I know she is right.

"Mummy..." I purposely drag the word, silently pleading with her not to dig the past.

"What? It's true. You have to get out there and not just be by yourself all the time at some point you know? And Issa, you know *you*. We all know you'd get excited when someone talks to you and you'll consider them your friend fast." She says as a matter of factly. I hate that about myself though. "Stop secluding yourself, you've done that enough. Go out there. Enjoy college life!" She says enthusiastically and I know she's trying to encourage me but as much as I hate to disappoint her, it just won't happen. I'm not the same person I was years ago.

"Okay. I need time though. I will try to mingle though." I assure her anyway.

"That's my baby. You'll do just fine, okay? You're smart and mature, you know when to draw the line and you know what to do when. Just believe in yourself." I hum, while tracing circles on the counter.

If that were that easy.

Chapter Three

Strong by One Direction

You know when you don't feel loved in your family, you try to find other ways to be loved. I used to do that. A lot. That explains the many 'relationships' I had. If I could even call them that, because I had thought they loved me or that they're my source of happiness. Let me rephrase that. I had thought they were my *only* source of happiness.

I was wrong to even think my happiness or anything good depends on the people I befriend or my family. Growing up to be this weird, social but also asocial, I realised I get very close to people, very fast and end up expecting them to sort of be the same way I am to me.

When I realised how wrong and weird that was, I stopped getting involved in a lot of things. I wanted to give up on relationships with people or anything that has 'talking' to do with.

But being my weird self, I still did pursue friendships that exposed me to things I didn't even know existed. It's something like how you get to know things a little too early for your age because you're still a *kid*.

I gave up on love. It didn't exist to me. To me it was complete crap and disgusting at one point really. I felt like being born was a huge mistake. I hated that I was such a bad influence on my sister. I hated that I never fit in any crowd. I hated myself because I knew my parents worried about me like I was a burden. Maybe I was, so I wanted to end my life. I was alone and young and was nothing but a piece of nothing so what harm was there in me wanting to end my life right?

Again, I was *so* wrong.

* * * * *

It's been about two weeks since I started going to classes and so far I think it's been good. I've successfully made sure I spend every free minute that I have in a corner or the library or some place where no one is around.

"No, okay? It's just books and besides I need them. They're my pals." I'm walking on the stairs since the lift was delayed, one step at a time holding ten books in a stack with me, while speaking to my mum on the phone. Very wise, I know.

"Hold up, so you're telling me you just wasted a whole lot of money on books?" And here we go again.

"Mummy, *c'mon*! How many times do I have to tell you? They help alright? Besides, I love reading. I thought mothers know their ki-ahhhh, no-no-no-no-ahh!" I tumble down the stairs along with a few books in my hands, screaming my lungs out until I stop, but end up knocking some guy down which thankfully stops the tumbling.

"Goodness, are you alright?" The guy I practically tumbled over asks, from the floor. I don't answer him immediately because I'm in total shock. "Wait, it's you.

You-you're the one," I hear him say, making me look up at his face which also makes me realise I'm literally on top of the guy. And then it hits me.

"You-you're, Addy's um..someone.." I manage to say, still on top of him. "Oh I'm sorry, I'm sorry.." I crawl to the floor to the railing of the stairs, trying to help myself get up.

"Uh, are you alright?" He asks me again. I can't stand up for some reason. It's like my legs have forgotten to walk *again*. I'm not sure if it's because of the tumbling about twenty steps down or the fact that I'm meeting this super hot guy I avoided since the day I moved in.

"N-no I think, I think *gosh*.." I wince when I try to stand up.

"It looks like you've sprained your ankle." He states the obvious. I just nod, helplessly.

"I guess and I can't walk…and I'm sorry-so sorry I landed on you..it's just my mum…oh no, my phone!" I try to walk to my phone on the floor forgetting I've just sprained my ankle and end up whimpering, falling right on the floor again. I am such an idiot.

"You should've just asked me to get your phone," he says, retrieving it and bending down beside me, handing me the device. I take it and wipe under my eyes and take a deep breath because I'd rather not cry in front of Mr. Hottie here. What's his name again? Jeremiah wasn't it?

"S-sorry I-" I wince again as pain shoots through my ankle, making me clench my fists and squeeze my eyes shut.

"Do you have to go to a hospital or something?" He asks slowly. I shake my head no. That's the last thing on my mind right now.

"N-no, I'll be fine," I'm on the verge of crying. I hate that my ankle hurts and I feel like crying. Gosh, I feel like such a baby.

"Clearly you're not. I'm gonna carry you up. You can barely walk.." he says and before I could protest he carries me in his arms within seconds. What on earth have I gotten myself into?

"Thank you..it's Jeremiah right?" I hesitantly ask him, not fully making eye contact with him because his face is inches closer to mine.

"You remember, Isabelle." I feel him smiling as I nod my head slowly.

"Oh wait, my books!" I suddenly remember midway up the first flight of stairs.

"I'll come down and get them after I get you to your room." He says. Why is he being such a gentleman? He chuckles. Good lord, *please* no. "Do you always say what's on your mind out loud?" I want to shrink into a ball and hide right now. This is the most embarrassing thing I've ever done in my entire life.

"No...you weren't supposed to hear that.." I groan slightly, avoiding eye contact with him.

"It's fine. Happens sometimes," he smiles genuinely. I laugh at myself, clinging onto his shoulders. "So, are you from here?" He makes conversation as he carries me up the stairwell.

"No." I'm not sure if I can tell him the story of moving into a new country I've never been to.

"So you moved for higher studies?" He guesses. What, is he a teacher or something to figure that out so fast?

"Yup. What about you? You must've not moved obviously cause' clearly you're British but what do you do?" I ramble a little. When I make eye contact with him he has that smirk on his face. I roll my eyes to hide the weird tingly feeling in my gut.

"Right. I go to Cardiff." He states. Wait what?

"You're joking right?" I ask with disbelief.

"Why would I be joking?" He asks, clearly confused. I clear my throat before I form my next sentence.

"I don't know. You're going to Cardiff?" I say more than ask, letting the new information sink in. He's been going there? How did I not notice him?

"Yes, Isabelle, I do. What's wrong with that?" He chuckles, looking at me expectantly probably waiting for me to uncover my thoughts.

"I go there too! But, I'm just wondering why I haven't seen you in any of my classes so it-just..yeah," I say, he smiles.

"You're a freshman and what are your classes?" He inquires and I have no choice because I literally can't dodge the question being in the position I'm in with him.

"Um, I actually finished freshman year. I'm kind of on holiday for a bit but I have these exams coming up in like a month, but to answer your question I did English, Maths, IT, Business, Accounting and Economics and Society and Culture which I thought was Psychology but it wasn't, that was pretty disappointing because I was looking forward to studying that and it wasn't what the student counsellor said it was. I'm glad it is over now though." I ramble, forgetting that he is technically a stranger. Good lord, Isabelle, ever heard of keeping your mouth shut?

"Wow, that's a lot. Did you atleast enjoy the other classes?" He gazes, which obviously makes it even more challenging to answer him. Is he really that oblivious to the effects he has on women? Or is it just me?

"Um, not really but it wasn't so bad I guess," I shrug. "Do you mind if I rest my chin on your shoulder? It's kind of hard to keep looking up at you when you talk, it hurts my neck." I admit shyly. He chuckles. "I'm sorry, you're just so tall!" I laugh on his shoulder, hiding my embarrassment.

"Sure." I smile as if I've won an award and slowly, hesitantly wrap my arms around him and rest my chin on his shoulder making sure our chests aren't touching too much. "Better?" He asks and I nod my head yes.

"What are you studying?" I take the opportunity to ask him.

"Eh, I'd love to answer but guess we've reached your home sweet home." He smiles playfully.

"Oh-oh…that's not fair but alright. Thank you by the way..I apologise if I was heavy.." I say awkwardly. Now just thinking about it I feel embarrassed. What if I was heavy?

"No problem, Isabelle. You weren't heavy." He says, amused.

"Now you're just saying that." I conclude. "Um how are we..can you very slowly put me down?" I ask, not sure if I could walk.

"I thought I could lay you down on your couch or bed or something," he offers, making me look straight up at him.

"Are you sure? I mean, you walked me up so many stairs. I can manage." I say, planning to hop to my couch.

"Yes, it's no problem," he says, making my heart sink. That's not even supposed to happen. It's too early for that to happen. But it does.

"Thank you," I smile, grateful to him. He smiles and gestures towards the door. I reach for my jean pocket and pull out the keys and then unlock the door to my flat. I'm thankful I've been on a cleaning spree because the place is neat as a pin.

"Where do you want me to put you?" He asks as we walk into my flat.

"The kitchen? It's just the left from here," I say so I can give him something to drink.

"Sure," he turns the corner, slowly taking in the place as he walks by the small living room and then entering the kitchen that is spotless.

"Hold on." I say and he stops right in front of the fridge, giving me the opportunity to open it and grab two iced coffee cans and then close it. "Okay, we can sit at the counter." I smile and he does just that. He carefully lands me on one of the barstools. And then looks around the kitchen.

"Nice decorations," he points out. I smile, thanking him. I'm not a major fan of decking the house but I do have an interest in interior designing.

"Have a seat," I gesture towards the bar stool next to me and hand him the can of iced coffee.

"Thank you, but I can't stay. I have some errands to run. You get some rest and take care of your ankle. See you around Isabelle," he says. I nod reluctantly.

"At least take the coffee. I'll be happy." I tell him. He smiles and takes it from my hand. I ignore his hand brushing through my skin and force a smile. "Thank you again." I say. He nods and turns around to walk towards the door but then stops.

"Your books. I'll get them but is it alright if I keep them in my flat for tonight? I'll hand them tomorrow to you during the day." He says, turning halfway around.

"Oh sure, yeah. Thanks again. I almost forgot about them." I say, as relief washes over me. He nods one more time before turning around exiting the kitchen and a few seconds later I hear the front door close quietly.

I spend the next thirty minutes squealing every two minutes just by reminding myself of the feeling of being in his arms and talking to him and replaying his words, the voice in my head. I almost knock down the coffee I was sipping by hitting the counter a few times every time I feel a shiver run through my body.

How many times can you tell yourself to stop liking the guy you just met?

This is probably going to take me a while now because plan A which was to avoid him clearly is a forgotten story now that we met and had a whole conversation while being carried which oddly isn't still hitting me that that should have been weird. Before I know it, I'm already opening my notes app on my phone, typing out everything that just happened a while ago since I couldn't walk to my bedroom to grab my journal with my injured foot.

Minutes later, I called my mum to explain the sudden disappearance after the call and the fall. I carefully leave out most of the details because obviously she'll flip if she knows some stranger. Well, an *almost*-stranger carried me so many floors up to my apartment.

After we exchange 'I love yous', I hop off the stool to make some instant noodles for myself and then hop fifteen steps to my room for the night.

I turn off the lights after making sure I lock the front door and freshen up in the bathroom before getting ready for bed, which is basically me getting comfortable with a book to read to put me to sleep.

I apply some ointment of my grandma's on my ankle before getting under the covers and then let Elizabeth Bennet and Mr. Darcy lull me to sleep for the rest of the night.

Chapter Four

I miss you, I'm sorry by Gracie Abrams

I don't think there's a perfect definition to explain the love you have for someone you chose to let go. It depends on the person and the situation, maybe. Or maybe it's just that you had no other choice but to put an end to the never ending cycle with that person who once was your everything.

It's insane sometimes when you remember the most trivial things about that person even after so many years of not being in contact. Like their birthday, their favourite music or even better, their favourite colour! It's like no matter what you do or how much you try to forget all those years, it's as if all those things are permanently inked in your brain.

Maybe some things aren't meant to be forgotten. Even when you know you'll see or hear from the person again, you still can't find it in you to forget them because even though they're not a part of your 'now' in life, they were once part of it.

In spite of all that, you *still* love that person even after all those years.

It's May now. My ankle is better. It's been more than two weeks and it healed after a week's time after mostly bedresting. I joined online classes and have been submitting assignments online.

I haven't heard or seen Jeremiah lately. In a way I've been a bit relieved I haven't had to have unexpected meetings because, being brutally honest, there have been days he's occupied my mind which have resulted in my poor journal to have regular sheets of paper vomit.

Happy birthday! I hope you have a good day and year :)

After contemplating sending the message the whole night, I hit 'send' and put my phone on silent mode and grab a book to keep my mind off of the 'waiting' if he ever responds, which is probably unlikely.

I don't even know why I'm texting this guy when we haven't spoken in years. Maybe that's what happens when you spend hours reading your childhood journals of a guy you once loved so much, it hurts.

The next morning I don't bother looking at the notifications on my phone for the day, I just do whatever I can to prevent myself from grabbing my phone and opening Instagram. It works for most of the day until I notice my phone ringing. I grab my phone to see my sister calling.

"What's up Merebelle?" My sister is a year younger to me and yes, my parents wanted us to have similar names or something common that was in both names like they planned not to have another child after us which still disappoints me to this day.

"You haven't spoken all day. Wanted to see if things were okay." She says simply.

"Oh. Sorry. Just didn't want to use the phone much." I say which isn't the entire truth but it isn't a lie either. It's not like she would tell on me to my parents, my sister has passed that age where she would annoyingly give an update on everything I do but now she is more like my best friend. She doesn't share a lot like I do but I'm starting to understand why she doesn't.

"Trying to have self-control I see," she jokes, I laugh. That's a word for it.

"Something like that. How are things?" I hate asking her that because she always responds with either 'good' or 'okay' and doesn't go any further but now, I just wanted the focus to be away from me because I'm scared I'll admit I actually texted *him* after all these years for his birthday when I didn't the past few years. She might wonder 'why now?' Jeez, I've been wondering that since last night but I can't seem to come up with anything as to why I would do something after so long.

"I think I have a crush on someone," she admits and I feel my lips turning into a wide grin. I stay quiet even though inside I'm screaming 'OH MY GOSH!'

"Yeah? Is it alright if I ask who?" I make sure I don't sound too pushy because she telling me this is a big step itself and I don't want to go back to square one.

"You know him. He was in your class. I think you used to like him, I'm not sure..." she trails off while my heart begins to increase its pace. I used to like the guy who now she has a crush on?

"Okay. I'm gonna guess who. Hmm," I think back to the last year of highschool. The last grade I was in school. There weren't many students; only seven girls and five boys and as much as I remember I don't remember liking anyone that year. "Are you referring to Shawn?" I ask her with anticipation.

"Yeah." She admits and I almost laugh but clamp my mouth shut and make my way to the kitchen to drown a glass of water to prevent myself from laughing.

"I never liked him enough to date him but I did like him as a friend. He's changed though. I mean, I know he's still nice but he isn't quite like he used to be. He's changed don't you think?" I say and then wonder what she saw in him to like him. The guy is nice, don't get me wrong but the last thing I remember of him was standing me up at a class when I was assigned to assist him on a paper for one whole period. When I found him in the science classroom with his friends, I questioned him but he just stayed silent which gave me the idea he wasn't going to turn up so I left. Talk about the end of something of a friendship. Besides, it always felt like such a burden being just friends with him seeing that school wasn't exactly mature to see it that way.

"Yeah, but he talked to me the other day. I still feel like he's the same. He just puts up an act or whatever when there's people around." She says, seeming convinced about knowing him more than I do.

"Okay then. Have you guys talked? Does he know you like him?" I ask and then instantly regret it when I feel like that was a question she might not be ready to answer.

"We don't really talk a lot…and no. I don't want him to know until I feel like whatever we're feeling is mutual." She tells me, quite boldly for someone who said, '*relationships suck and I think I have enough assurance after seeing how your only relationship took a toll on you. So, no thank you.*' I laugh remembering the day she said it the first time I asked if she had any crushes on anybody in school. "What's funny about that?" Oh no. She thinks I laughed at what she said.

"No, sorry, I didn't mean to laugh at what you said. I just remembered something you said about relationships and that made me laugh." I say hoping she isn't mad at me.

"Oh yeah. I'm not sure if we'd even date. It's just a crush and he doesn't even know I like him and I doubt he likes me or feels a fraction of what I feel for him." She says and I get the feeling that it's my turn to give 'relationship advice'.

"Right. I honestly have no advice on relationships to give. I had a bad example, well, the only example which obviously isn't the best to share so no. I hope you find the right guy." I say, hoping she'll understand and not feel too pressured about it. I just don't want her to go through what I went through. "No one deserves to be feel the way I felt when I got dumped by my ex boyfriend." I say hoping it made sense to her because I've never given her advice especially when it comes to relationships.

"Alright. I have to go now. I'll text you if something happens?" I smile. She didn't mean to say that but she did and that makes me feel good about not giving up on our relationship because it *is* improving.

"Of course. Love you Merebelle." I say. She says 'love you too' quietly and then we hang up.

Right when the call ends I get a notification that makes my heart almost stop.

Thank you! I hope you're doing alright too.

Is it possible for the heart to suddenly just keep banging on your chest just by a text message received from someone you haven't spoken to in ages?

I heart the text and exit the app and pull up my music app and play the recent playlist while I put away some of my clothes into the closet and then complete some homework but then find myself getting distracted with the lyrics of some of the songs.

It's never a good thing to listen to music especially when you realise you may or may not be crushing on your neighbour who happens to be living right opposite your apartment.

What can I say, I'm in deep, deep, deep trouble.

Chapter Five

Someone To You by BANNERS

wake up sleepyhead 7:00 AM alarm rings.

It's one of those days when you snooze your alarm for five minutes but then you end up sleeping thirty minutes more. Which in my case is the time I spent getting ready to leave the apartment and drive the fifteen minute ride to work by seven-forty-five. I have to be at work by eight!

"Oh-my-gosh. This can't be happening!" I throw the covers and sprint to the bathroom and shower while brushing my teeth under the chill water.

Fifteen minutes later, I'm throwing on a beige tulle sleeved blouse and buttoning my blue jeans and grabbing my backpack that thankfully I didn't unpack last night and run out of the door only to freak out at Jeremiah standing by his door buttoning his shirt.

"Guess I'm not the only one who overslept," I say under my breath, Jeremiah smiles.

"Can I ask you a favour if it's no bother? I need a ride." He says without waiting for me to respond which makes me chuckle.

"Sure yeah. I'll get even late to work, guess that's alright since I'm already late." I mumble knowing he can hear me but motion for him to follow me nonetheless.

"Sorry but I only asked because it's on the way to Cardiff so you wouldn't get late." He says with a smirk as we enter the lift.

"Yeah except for the fact that I'm not going to school today. I work on Tuesdays." I say with a smile and then wait as the lift takes us down to the basement. I unlock my car and we both get in.

"You work? Where?" He asks, clearly surprised. I may be young but thanks to finishing school early, I'm already working by the age of eighteen. I'm only working so I could pay rent every month and have the liberty to be independent or act like it at least. My parents help with university fees, while I pay for everything else, since I disagreed with getting a dorm room, but it still works out perfectly, plus, I'm lucky I found the perfect job fifteen minutes away from my apartment and Cardiff was thankfully on the same road. So yes, it really worked out perfectly.

"Why, so you could stalk me?" I ask with a smirk. He laughs.

"It's a left from here," he says but he didn't have to because I was about to turn left anyway.

"Jeremiah, can I ask you something?" I ask him, while having my focus on the rearview mirror and the road.

"I guess," he shrugs casually, looking at the road.

"How old are you?" I ask him, slightly glancing at him. We've known each other for about a month and half now but I haven't been able to learn basic information about him.

"Old enough to be working," he winks, which makes my eyes go a little wide. "You can stop here by the way. I can walk." He says and unstraps his belt but I'm already driving towards the parking lot and finding a place to park. I turn off the car once I'm parked and grab my things and step out of the car and wait for Jeremiah.

"This isn't what I think it is right?" I say when Jeremiah gets out and we walk towards the sliding doors.

"Depends on *whatever* you're thinking," he says like he has no idea. Hasn't he realised it yet?

"Jeremiah, why are you in this building?" I ask him. *Because he works here of course.*

"I work here Isabelle." He smiles but then it falters as he eyes me and then eyes my backpack and then at me again. He looks as if he's finally putting two and two together. "What in the world?" He mutters. I smile.

Why oh why is the guy I potentially may have an annoying crush on working and studying in both the same places I work and study too?

This is definitely not *fate!*

"How have I not seen you around? Today isn't your first day right?" I ask as we walk to the lift.

"I don't come here everyday. I prefer working from home." He says after I press the button for the tenth floor. He presses for the thirteenth floor. Whoa, isn't that floor for the highest employees of the company? He's young and is already a millionaire? Why does that sound like a book plot?

"That's probably why I haven't seen you at the office." I just say and stare at my reflection during the journey to my floor. I cannot believe this is happening. Just thinking about how many times we might or might not see each other almost everyday terrifies me because since the day my stupid, stupid, stupid self spoke to him, I've wanted to avoid him. But now it just feels like that crappy word I don't even want to use right now. *Fate*.

"Didn't know you were into publishing." He makes small talk. I mentally sigh.

"I could say the same." I smile sweetly. "So you work while studying too huh?" I give up being silent since I've got more floors to go.

"Yup. I've been here for a year now." He says with a smirk like he knows that was a piece of information to me. I shake my head. "Which days do you work?" He asks, facing me full on.

I hesitate a little before answering, "Tuesdays, Wednesdays and Thursdays."

"I'm impressed." He smiles, I smile back. I want to ask 'why?' but I stopped myself.

"This is me. I'll see you around then," I say when I exit the lift. Jeremiah nods and waves and then the doors close.

As I'm walking to my office, the chairman of the company so generously offered, I can't stop thinking how blind I've been or it's probably because I rarely leave my office especially when I have manuscripts to read and edit. I get soaked a lot. I hate that I'm more curious about Jeremiah now though.

To: isabelleheathers@cp.org
From: jamesbrown@cp.org

Subject: Greetings.

Good morning Isabelle,

Thanks for the word on yesterday's script. As always, your work is commendable. Good work.

I've dropped off two files I'd like you to have a look at today. Don't worry about finishing manuscripts today. Have a look at the files and maybe we can chat about it on Thursday.

Best regards,

James

I open the first file and rummage slowly through the sheets of paper and come to a conclusion that it's about a book to be published. Okay. I open the second file and see that it looks like a list of things to do for the month.

I sigh in content and email Mr. Brown back before getting to work for the day.

* * * * *

“Don’t scream, it’s just me,” I hear as someone taps my shoulder making me swallow my gasp.

“Jeremiah,” I breathe in relief. “You already scared me.” I smile. He does too. I think I smile too much when he’s around. It’s crazy and weird because for a girl like me, I tend to cover up smiles whenever possible and especially in front of someone I *fancy*. Great, now I use British words.

“Are you getting lunch?” He asks me, motioning towards the almost empty shelves of food.

“Yeah. I missed breakfast so I’m kind of hungry today.” I say and look at the almost empty lunch room.

“Burger King’s close by. We can get lunch there.” He suggests. I think about it. I never leave the building even during lunch break.

“Is that even okay? Leaving the building, I mean.” I ask him.

“Yes. You haven’t eaten out for lunch before?” He asks as we walk outside towards my car.

“No. I thought we weren’t allowed. We can walk right?”

“Yeah. So, how was work?” He asks on our way to Burger King.

"Good. Hey, why didn't you tell me you work at a publishing company?" I ask him since that's been bugging me today ever since the lift.

"Oh yeah. I don't usually go around telling my neighbours I work here," he says, looking serious, making me stop in my tracks before he bursts out laughing.

"Urgh!" I groan and walk faster. He catches up to me though.

"James is one of my dad's friends. So I've known him and he offered me a job here when I used to work at SAGE. He offered more so I came here. Plus the guy doesn't really care if I'm at the office or not. He just wants the work done and I work better at home anyway." He explains and I process the information.

"You're lucky." I say and he shrugs. "And I'm guessing you're older to me?" I ask more than say.

"Maybe," he grins. My gut says he's probably twenty. Maybe twenty one.

We sit at a small booth and order burgers and chips and he gets coke while I get iced coffee.

"So you're a coffee addict?" He asks matter of factly. I nod. "And you read way too much," he points out. I nod again wondering where he's going with the conversation. "And you sleep late," he says, making me look at him suspiciously.

"Care to elaborate on the last one?" I barely ask.

"My assumption is, you come late after work or school and you clean up your place for hours and then probably take a long shower and then maybe have dinner. Make coffee for the night and read all night with music on." He says and I have to bring my palms to my lips to hide my smile. I can't believe he's right.

"Wow. Is that what you do every night? Eavesdrop whatever I do?" I tease but also ask him. He just smiles. Okay, I don't know what to think about that.

"Don't be too surprised Isabelle. You must know that the wall of your room is the same wall of my room." He says with a stoic expression. What?

"How do you even know that?" I ask, dumbfounded

"Our rooms are the last ones in the hallway and they're opposite each other which means the corner of your apartment and mine are connected. It's the same wall that separates our rooms. How come you never thought about that? I thought you figured that out too." He says looking surprised.

"I just didn't." I say, a little embarrassed.

The food arrives which stops me from asking Jeremiah more about 'eavesdropping' me through his room because now since he brought it up, I'm more than curious.

"Do you mind if I join you when you go home? I thought I could pick my car up from the garage, but they told me to come the day after tomorrow." He asks.

"Sure." I smile, while wiping the corner of my mouth with a napkin.

"I'll take you to dinner then," he says and then gets the bill and pays for our meal before I could stop him. We leave Burger King and start heading towards CP.

"First off you shouldn't have paid for everything. And second, are you sure? Because we just had lunch together. I don't want to bore you." I laugh.

"I don't think you would." I catch him smiling sheepishly as we walk towards the building we both work in.

"See you in the evening then, last-minute-dinner-date" I joke. He laughs. I smile and then head towards the lift. *Last-minute-dinner-date? Really man?*

* * * * *

"Ah, Isabelle, I was just about to come to your office." Mr. Brown says just as he lets me into his office.

"No problem, Mr. Brown. Can I have a word with you? It's about the book report." I tell him as he gestures for me to take a seat.

"Please, go ahead," he closes his laptop and crosses his hands as he awaits for me to speak.

"I think it's a good book and it deserves an audience. I feel like it has an amazing ring to the title 'Everyone Deserves Love'. The plot is amazing. It's entertaining, heartwarming, educational and I feel like it has a moral that can impact people in not just one or two ways but so many. Basically, there's a lot to learn from the book. It's a book you will definitely enjoy and also learn a lot too." I say, mostly avoiding eye contact. When I finally look at his face, he appears to be thinking about what I said. I guess he is.

"I agree with you, Isabelle. Can I have a look at whatever you looked into today?" He asks and I nod eagerly as I hand him the file that consists of all the work I did for the day regarding this book. "Wow. Good work Isabelle. I will have a word with the committee and will get back to you on this. I'm sure they'll agree with what your thoughts are on this book." He says and I can't help but grin.

"Thank you Mr. Brown." I say as I stand up.

"Have a good evening Isabelle." He says and I thank him before leaving his office and heading to mine to pack up to leave for the day.

It's 6:15 when I take a seat at the lobby to wait for Jeremiah to come down but I don't see him. I figured maybe he's at a meeting or something so I grab a book from my backpack to occupy myself.

* * * * *

"Isabelle," I feel someone shaking me. I almost want to groan and push that hand away but my eyes stop me miraculously. I immediately sit up and wipe the little drool on my chin with the back of my hand and wipe it on my jeans, embarrassed.

"Sorry," I don't look up at him. I just rummage through my backpack for my perfume bottle. When I see it, I sigh, relieved.

"Sorry for keeping you waiting for so long. I see you occupied yourself though," he hands me my copy of 'Book Lovers' I was reading before falling asleep on the c-shaped sofa.

"Thanks," I mutter and stand up. "I'll be right back." I tell him and rush to where the restrooms are.

I look at my reflection in the huge rectangular sized mirror and cringe. I look sleepy. I wash my face and dry it and spray perfume in all the needed places and tie my hair up in a ponytail and exit the restroom.

"Everything alright?" Jeremiah asks as I make my way outside towards my car in the parking lot.

"Yeah. So where are we going?" I ask him as we get in and leave the building in my car.

"Have you tried Italian food?" He asks, pulling out his Iphone. I have the sudden feeling to turn on the radio but I don't. I don't think I want to reveal the kinds of songs I listen to everyday.

"No. I've tasted lasagne. Just that though," I say and glance at his phone to see him browsing through restaurants.

"You're not mad at all that I got late?" He asks suddenly. I wonder why he just brought that up now.

"No," I just say and shift my attention back to the road.

"You seemed a little off. I'm sorry I kept you waiting-"

"You said that already and it's okay. I'm not mad." I interrupt him when I stop at a red light. He smiles, shaking his head a little, "what?" I smile.

"Nothing. You just- nevermind. Are we good?" His eyes cut to mine.

"Yeah," I laugh a little as I look at his face. Instantly my eyes scan his face at the details. It's like whenever he faces me full-on, I can't seem to stop myself from staring and I hate it. I hate that I can't look away.

"The lights changed to green. You have to drive." He points to the green light for a split second and then his eyes are back on my face. I almost forgot how to drive forward. But I do somehow.

The next few minutes, Jeremiah directs me to some restaurant he keeps saying is so good and that I have to try their food. He says it a lot that I have to swat his arm to remind him I heard him all those times before.

When we reach the place, Jeremiah leads us to a small but not too small kind of place that is all lit up with lanterns around that gives the place nice lighting for pictures. It's a bar. I see the small stage in the front end of the place and the drum set, guitars and a keyboard and mic stands.

Why was he talking about Italian food if he wanted to take us to a bar?

"Good evening people!" The girl, probably the lead singer, says into the mic. I like her. From her clothes to the vibe she is currently giving me. Only because I wish I had the guts and the opportunity to be like her. I could never go up on a stage and sing my heart out in front of a crowd.

"I thought you said 'restaurant'" I finally say, air quoting his words. He smiles. Cheeky.

"This is a restaurant. And," he smiles again. I sigh but nod and look at the stage again.

"A bar too, I get it." I interrupt him rather childishly without looking at him. He laughs and then we find two seats by the bar. He orders something I couldn't really hear, thanks to the loud blaring music in the place paired with the chit-chatter from the people around us.

"So, how'd you start working at CP?" He starts up a conversation and I'm forced to face him in the bar stool that is literally inches away from his.

"A friend's friend's contact." I state. He raises his eyebrow as if to say 'really?' or to elaborate but I just nod. What's the point of explaining anyway when I'm already working there?

"James is happy with you," Jeremiah says, smiling. I smile and nod. "Do you mind if I ask where you're from?"

"Do I even have a choice?" I smile. He laughs. "I'm from San Diego. Moved here because it's been my dream to live here. I didn't really like my country to be honest. I never saw myself having a life there like here. So I moved and here we are." I say, trying my best to keep it precise and not give away too much.

"I see," he taps his knee as he nods. "Are you happy here?" He asks just as the waitress lands two plates of what looks and smells like lasagna in front of us.

"You should know I'm not a big eater. I'm sure this is a large potion. Can we get a small potion? I'm not sure I can eat all this," I quickly say, feeling a little embarrassed and nervous.

"It's actually a small potion. And it's alright if you can't eat everything." Jeremiah pats my shoulder. He shouldn't have done that.

"It's a waste of money. Someone else can eat this." I almost snapped at him.

"Fine. We'll pack it then." He says. When I look over at him, he's smiling. What is with him and smiling?

"Thanks. For ordering this," I wave around the plate with a smile. He smiles back as he nods.

"You didn't answer my question." He brings up. I lift up my index finger motioning him to wait as I swallow.

"I am happy." I finally say. *Lie.* "What about you? Have you figured out what you want to do after college? And why, publishing, if I may ask?" I ask curiously.

"Not really. Maybe become a writer? I'm not sure though. Publishing? I've always just found something I can do there. It's a possible job I could do." He says and I ponder over his words.

"So you're an English major." I say. I had already guessed that earlier today. He nods. "I wanted to be an English major too." I say as I twirl my fork around my food and take another bite.

"What made you change your mind? To study Psychology I mean? That's what you want to do right?" I don't look at him as he talks to me, but I do listen to him. He makes me want to answer his questions when in general I'd be a little irritated if someone else did the same.

"I don't really know. Maybe the fact that the world needs someone to care for them?" My subconscious answers for me. He stares at me now. And I mean really stares at me like I would disappear any second. "I want to make a difference in the world. Even if it's just a tiny one. I want to do something to help. I want to understand people better without judging them. I want to reach out to people hurting. I want them to know that the world is a better place with them in it..." *And that maybe they need to know that they are worth it. That no one is ever considered less important or otherwise. We're all equally important and unique and amazing in our own ways. Except me though.*

Jeremiah just stays silent. Smiles. Shakes his head to himself. Smiles again. And again. Or maybe he's still smiling...

Chapter Six

Gorgeous by Taylor Swift

How long does it take to not think of a guy you really like?

It's just been sixty seconds since I said goodnight to Jeremiah after walking up to our apartments but I have this weird attachment to him now that I find myself wanting to go see him again. Which I know is a little overboard.

My heart is swelling just thinking about the time we had, basically spending the whole day with him; starting it with him and ending it with him. It's like we're both parts of a magnet. He's the blue side and I'm the red. And we attract.

"You can't be crazy over someone so fast. You don't even know him! For all you know, he may be some serial killer living next door apparently. Oh my gosh I just spent time with a maybe-" a knock stops me from pacing around the living room, my focus snatched by the door knocking.

"Hey," I grip the door just as I open it to reveal no one but Jeremiah.

"Hi. Did you leave something in my car or-"

"Are you doing anything?" He asks after his laugh cuts me off. I look backwards at my living room before answering him.

"No. Why'd you ask?"

"Would you like to have some company?" He asks, smiling and I think I notice his dimples showing.

"S-sure" I mumble unbelievably. Did I just agree to hang out with someone who can be a serial killer or worse?

"Really?" He asks, hopeful, like he didn't expect me to just agree.

"Yeah. I'll just grab my phone. Meet you in five minutes?" He nods and disappears in his apartment while I grab my phone from my bed and switch off the lights except in the living room and grab the keys.

"If you're wondering, we're going to the rooftop." He informs me as we make our way to the lift. *Perfect place for a murder.* I mentally roll my eyes at the thought but follow him and stand in one corner of the lift while he stands in the other.

The journey up fifteen floors was spent mostly silent with just our breathing and the 'dings' the lift makes when we reach the rooftop.

"Wow,"

"Yeah," Jeremiah agrees as I take in the surroundings of the highest place in the building. The last time I went up a rooftop or a balcony was months ago. Balconies were my comfort places when I couldn't visit libraries.

"It's beautiful." I whisper as I look down at the city, gripping the metal railing made to prevent people from falling.

As it's a reunion between me and the view from up here, I take the next several minutes in silence just staring at the night sky and feeling the cool breeze hit my skin on and off. I never realised how much I've missed the feeling of being high up on a building when it's night, the peace it brings and how I used to just be myself for a few hours and then wear the invincible mask when I leave the place.

"I've missed this." I say, not particularly to anyone.

"Me too," he replies. When I look at him, I smile because he does. I want to ask what he meant, but I face the sky again. "I come here up alot." He says, making me look towards him again.

"I used to also…" I say not meeting his eyes. "Earlier tonight, at the bar.."

"I asked if you were happy," he basically finishes my sentence. Am I that apparent or is he a vampire or something to read minds that fast? Plus he didn't ask.

"You did." I smile.

"You said you were," he repeated what I said. But he looks at me like he wants more than that. "But why do I feel like that's not true?" Now the question is, what would he do if I told him?

"I wouldn't say I was 'happy'. I'm just okay." I sigh, not wanting to look at him so I go on. "I moved here because I needed time away from where I was from. I needed a fresh start. I wasn't exactly doing that well back home. I was a mess and just not great back home. I was lost." I say, chipping off the black nail polish from my nails.

"Did that help?" He asks in the most gentle voice I've heard in a person.

"Yeah. Just a little lonely," I laugh a little but it comes out strained. He gives me a gentle smile, like he understands me.

"You're not alone, you know. Whatever that happened there..maybe it was for the best?" He says, standing closer to me leaving just a few inches away between us. "Sometimes bad things happen but that doesn't mean you're a bad person. Maybe the mess moulded you into a better person and maybe, that's because you'd be able to be an example to so many around you." I watch his face as he speaks, even when he finishes, I'm not able to tear my eyes off of him.

"You're the- you're the first person to ever say that to me." I have to look away from him to breathe away my tears when he turns to face me already crying.

Who does that? Says you're not a bad person when most of your life, you've been nothing but just a bad person?

"Maybe because it needs to be said." He says just above a whisper.

I don't know what comes over me but I hug him, absorbing all his warmth and his incredible scent from his skin and clothes both. The fabric of his shirt, soft against my skin, his warmth transcending to my body like a blanket.

"Remember how Lily and Ryle met on a balcony?" He suddenly breaks the silence making me pull back in shock. "why are you looking at me like that, Isabelle? Is there something on my face?" He touches his face while looking at me with adorable gorgeous green eyes, a smile on his lips with his cute dimples making an entrance.

"No, it's just...how do you know that?!" My hands are clasped on my cheeks in surprise. I've never met someone who has read my favourite book! And the fact that he connected the book to this very moment.

"What was your favourite part?" He asks and I smile before looking at the starts first. I never thought I'd get to experience a moment like this. A moment I've dreamed of having so many times.

"I wish I could have a bottle of wine right now.." I say ad bite my tongue to suppress my laughter.

"A bottle of WHAT now?" Jeremiah's eyes widen and I burst out laughing at the sight of him like I've never before.

"You should've seen your face!" I'm cracking up so much, my stomach hurts and I almost hit lose balance but he was quick to catch me, making me lean on his hard chest. I smile though, ignoring the fluttery feelings. I guess this is what romance books mean when they say 'butterflies' because there's definitely lots of them flying around.

"You should laugh more often, Isabelle. Looks good on you." Jeremiah says, more like whispers over my head with his warm arms wrapped around me in an embrace and I sigh in content.

Chapter Seven

"Come in!" I call from my office, not shifting my eyes from my laptop. I hear the door open, I stand and do a double take when I see Jeremiah closing the door behind him. "Jeremiah, hey," I send him a smile as he walks to me.

"Hey, Isabelle. Busy?" He asks, smiling. I shake my head no when in reality I am. I have exams this week starting in two days and also have work in between to attend to. "James told me to give you a hand on the manuscripts you're working on," He smiles while my mouth forms an 'o' shape. Feeling relieved would be an understatement.

"Oh my gosh, he did?" I ask in disbelief.

"Yeah." Jeremiah smiles and walks toward the stack of files on my desk and opens the first one. "Tell you what, you go ahead and call it a day, I'll finish this up, okay?" He looks up at me from the file. I stare at him, unbelievably. Am I dreaming?

"I-I.. you would do that?" I almost whisper, fidgeting with my fingers.

"Of course." He smiles kindly. Without another word, I start packing my things and thank Jeremiah before leaving my office and the building and heading home to study.

I don't know what it is with Jeremiah, I don't understand how someone could go from being a very nice neighbour to a strange therapist and now to just a life saver in a matter of just days!

* * * * *

"There you are. How was studying?" I gasp at the voice but relax almost instantly when I see Jeremiah. "It's just me, sorry," He apologises and slowly walks toward me.

"Good. Thank you again for um, earlier today.." I trail off as he gets closer to me. "How was your day?" I finally ask after debating in my head. He smiles before saying,

"It was..good," he says with that same smile. "You do a lot of work for a day." He says, getting my attention.

"Oh. Is that a good thing?" I ask. Something about his tone makes me want to watch him doing my work now.

"Yes. Definitely yes." He says and then he looks at the stars just as I move my gaze to the sky.

"Do you see that? Isn't that… a butterfly?" I almost squeal as I connect the dots, well, the stars that make up into a butterfly. Something close to it at least.

"Oh yeah, that's the first time I'm seeing a butterfly in the stars." We are still gazing at it and then I realise I'm leaning on his shoulder. "So when are exams finishing?" He asks after a few minutes of silence.

"Two weeks."

"Okay. You have plans? After exams I mean." He clarifies.

"Um, not really…" I mumble.

"Okay. Well…" he starts but then stops. I look up at him silently asking him to continue. "Would you like to hang out with me? We could do some things together..like-"

"Like what?" I smile, interrupting him on purpose. He smiles, amused probably.

"What do you have in mind?" he asks thoughtfully.

"Uhhh," I chuckle before racking my brain for ideas. "Maybe I'll think about it after exams." I finally say when nothing interesting pops in my head.

"Sure." He says, looking pleased. He brushes his curls backwards and then shakes his head as he looks slightly up, towards the sky maybe. "Would you like me to walk you to your apartment?" He asks, gesturing towards the small door.

"Uh, sure. Thanks." I smile and then follow him downstairs. "How is Adeline doing?" I find myself asking as we enter the lift.

"She's good. Started school. New class." I nod along as he talks. I just realised that his voice is something I can listen to over and over again without getting tired. "Why didn't you call her Addy?" He adds silently. I didn't even know he'd notice it.

"Because I haven't earned the right I guess?" He chuckles and then looks away. "What? Do you think I've earned the right then?" I ask him curiously.

"Maybe..." he shrugs. "She likes you, you know." He informs me when we reach our floor.

"She does?" I can't help but ask. He nods.

"Good night, Isabelle." He says when I say,

"Thank you for finding me. On the rooftop." I laugh at my own words. Jeremiah stands in place, his movements halting.

"Of course," he smiles. It's not like his usual charming smiles though. This one's different. He smiled with *care.*

Chapter Eight

'Risk It All' by The Vamps

I would be lying to myself if I said I haven't thought about hanging out with Jeremiah a handful of times during the past two weeks. To be frank, Jeremiah has been on my mind almost everyday since I met him, which was like three months ago now, or a little more but still, *why* is the problem? I meet guys, maybe not everyday but I do meet people, why not one of them but him?

I smile knowing what I've thought through last night to do today with him for our hangout. I put up a checklist of things I've always wanted to do but never got the chance or better, had anybody to do them with.

My alarm for extracting the gel from the aloe leaves I just had kept to soak for the last twenty minutes rings snapping me out from my thoughts. Once I pour all the gooey stuff in a bottle I get ready to start my routine for my hair. I may sound a little too self conscious but really, aloe vera does wonders on hair.

I spend almost two hours in the shower thinking about all the ways a conversation could go between me and Jeremiah about the hangout and then spend fifteen minutes talking myself out of hanging out with him while dressing up and doing my makeup for the day before hearing the door knocking.

I'm about to open the door to possibly Jeremiah, when I suddenly think, 'what if he just pranked me? What if getting me all ready and hyped up was a joke to him?'. I open the door anyway.

"Heyy," He smiles his signature smile.

"I made a checklist." I blurted out. He smiles.

"Getting right to it, I see." I laugh, agreeing but also disagreeing with him.

"If you think some of the things there seem silly, you could just cut them off..." I trail off as I hand him the book I wrote the checklist in.

"I don't think that will be necessary." He says, skimming through the list and then starts reading them out loud. "Number one. Go book shopping." He looks up at me with a raised brow. "Why, if I may ask Isabelle? Don't you already have so many?" He says in a more daddy-tone. I laugh when I realise what I'm thinking.

"There's no answer to that. I have to go book shopping. With you." I say. He smiles like he's pleased with my answer and reads the next.

"Plan a beach trip. That's wonderful actually." I nod as he smiles. For the next couple of seconds he reads the entire list,

- *Visit the biggest library in the country.*
- *Visit an orphanage.*
- *Volunteer at an elder's home.*
- *Maybe fly to France (if possible).*
- *Read a book in a day. (maybe with someone).*
- *Try surfing.*
- *Learn a new language. French maybe?*
- *Plan a picnic on a boat.*
- *Watch the sunrise or sunset.*
- *Write a song, poem, whatever that feels like something you feel at that moment.*
- *Love somebody.*

Jeremiah is still holding the book. He holds it for a whole minute. Then another. Then smiles. Snaps a picture of the page. Then runs his fingers along the page, I don't know which sentence or what but he does. And finally closes it after a solid five minutes.

"What should we do first?" I ask him just as he says,

"That's an excellent checklist."

"I do love a good checklist." I smile. He laughs and hands me the book.

"Maybe we can start with book shopping." He suggests and I agree.

"Good choice. Do we go now or?" I ask him, hesitance clear in my slightly shaky voice.

"Sure. If that's what you want," he says. I mumble an 'okay' and scurry to my bedroom and grab whatever necessities I'd need for an outing and leave my apartment with Jeremiah. He suggested we use his car remembering the night where I drove him around to work and to the bar slash restaurant. So that's what we did.

You know how usually the first thing you do when you get in your car or even your parent's for that matter, you turn on the radio right? Jeremiah didn't. And yes, that bugged me until after a whole ten minutes, I mustered up the courage to ask him.

"You don't listen to music?" I can't help but ask.

"I do." He says, glancing at me for a second. Two seconds. And then back at the front.

"What about listening to music in the car?" The words just tumble out of my mouth.

"You should've asked me if that's what you wanted. Was that why you were silent for so long?" He smirks and turns on the radio, making me smile in both victory and embarrassment.

I hate being read so easily.

"Thanks." I mumble when an unfamiliar melody plays.

"For reading you or turning on the radio?" He teases, looking straight at me through the rearview mirror. I look away as soon as he makes eye contact. He chuckles while I focus on the window for the next couple of minutes.

When we reached the bookstore, I got out of the car first, before he could walk over to open the door for me.

It's not that I don't like that he does that, I just don't want someone I care for to treat me extra caring. It makes me feel guilty for some reason. Or maybe I don't deserve his care. I don't know why but for some reason the littlest things affect me when they shouldn't.

"Where do we start?" I ask him, excited as we walk towards the entrance and into the bookstore.

"You tell me," he says. I scan the place for a few minutes, eyeing all the bookshelves and the genre labels labelled on the walls of each section that separates each genre from the others.

"There." I pointed towards where the stationery was. He looks at me and then where I pointed before I start walking towards the big shelves with notebooks, journals, pens, pencils, etc…

After a good fifteen minutes of checking out the different kinds and sizes of books on the racks, I pick two books, one big and the other one small. A couple of pens, highlighters and a box of tubes of paint, a canvas board, one big and a smaller one. I pay for all the items and then make my way towards the 'fiction books' corner. Jeremiah follows silently.

"You're being awfully silent," I say, smiling his way, not meaning to point that out but just tell him.

"Sorry. It's interesting to see you 'book shopping'," he says. Not smiling or with any humour.

"Are you being serious?"

"I am," he says, truthfully. "Why?" He asks. I just shake my head and look at the highest shelf, hurting my neck.

"This reminds me of the part when the Beast shows Belle the library in his castle." I find myself saying as I scan all the books.

"Yeah. Do you want a ladder or something? Looking up like that can hurt your neck." He says. I look around but see no ladder or anyone in sight to help.

"No one is around. It's fine. Just for a few minutes-ahh! Wha-Jeremiah!" I scream-laugh as Jeremiah carries me up. I grip one of the higher shelves to hold me still because Jeremiah is carrying me from the back, his hands wrapped around my thighs.

"Your wel-"

"Don't you dare say your welcome!" I whisper-yell. He laughs. I laugh too. This is ridiculous. I get that I am short and all, but he shouldn't have to carry me. This is the second time!

"Hey, aren't you getting a book or not?" He asks, making me look down at him, a smirk plastered across his pretty face.

"I am, I am. Just getting used to my new position," I say and then manage to grab two books from the highest shelf and one from the shelf below. "Okay. I think I got what I wanted." I say, still holding the shelf for dear life.

"Let go. I won't drop you, Isabelle. Let go." He says gently. I nod and very slowly let go of the shelf and take the books, holding it to my chest as he slowly, carefully lands me on my feet.

"You know you don't have to always do that." I say as nicely as possible but already know that can hurt him. He only was helping. I know he was only helping. But knowing myself, how everything he does affects me on a different level, it's best to nip in the bud then and there.

I don't tell Jeremiah I want to go home after exiting the bookstore. I didn't have to, surprisingly. And when I go to ask him why he's behaving like I didn't hurt him, I feel like my mouth is duct taped for some reason which leads me to believe maybe I just should be silent. But I can't stand being silent when I know I hurt him. But here he is acting hurtless.

"Jeremiah-"

"I know, Isabelle." He says before I can even form an apology or explain anything. I don't keep silent though.

"Know what?" I boldly ask him, not ready for what he might say or do next.

"I just know," he says like he means it. My tongue has the words 'I'm still sorry' ready to be said but I don't. Instead, I silently nod and shift my focus to the window.

"What if we go to the beach the day after tomorrow since Monday and Tuesday are holidays next week?" I don't even know how I managed to come up with something to say after such an awkward fifteen minutes but thank God that I did. Jeremiah seems to relax too, the awkward silence earlier slipping away and soon out of the car into thin air.

"You mean 'we' as in the two of us? Together?" He asks and 98 percent of my eyes want to roll my eyes at him, but I ignore the urge to.

"Jeremiah, answer the question please." I fake-plead and he laughs muttering 'sure, sure' just as I say, "I said what I said."

Chapter Nine

It'll Be Okay by Shawn Mendes

A normal person would describe a good day or a good feeling with the word 'happiness'. At least most of them do. The word 'happy' hasn't been in my vocabulary since, wait-I-don't-even-know-when. I never thought I'd have to remember the word until now. I'm going to go with joy.

Joy. That's exactly what I feel right now.

"Want to go for a swim?" Jeremiah asks for the third time in a row. I laugh.

"But I'm winning here. I don't want to stop yet." I smile teasingly and drop a wild card. "Changing the colour to blue," I giggle. Jeremiah groans. This is probably the fifth time I'm changing the colour in the last fifteen minutes.

"Again?" He whines. I was expecting it.

"Told you I'd win." I playfully wink. "Do you want to keep playing or?"

"Or. I want to see you winning." He smirks and I try to suppress a smile.

"Game's on Remy!" I cheer. Jeremiah laughs.

"Look at you giving me a nickname," Jeremiah smirks, and then drops a four-plus card.

"Whoa. Was that a thank you?" I huff, taking four cards and then arranging it in an order on my hand.

"Do you have any two's?" He asks casually, arranging his cards in his hands.

"You can't ask that." I quickly said, He laughs, shaking his head.

The game goes on with us managing to drain our cards, competition increasing with every card that we drop. When I have only two cards in my hand and his three, I smile.

"UNO!" I almost yelled. Jeremiah smirks.

"Finally!" He groans and then throws his cards in a pile and then sprints to the beach. I laugh, a little surprised by his actions but nonetheless run behind him to keep up.

"*Oh Isabelle!*" Jeremiah yells just a second before pouncing on the water, soaking me too because I was right behind him.

"Thanks for the heads up!" I say, wiping the salt water from my face.

"You were going to get soaked anyway," Jeremiah shrugs as he walks deeper into the water, the water already up to his chest. I follow but don't go that deep.

"I love this… It's beautiful isn't it?" I say when trying to get myself to float on the water.

"Indeed it is." Jeremiah says, moving his hands in waves under the water. I wonder if he purposely got himself wet with his shirt on because of me. And my possible distractions.

"I don't know what it is with beaches and me. It's like it does something to me." I mumble, playing with the water.

"You know what they say about beaches. It's the best therapy." He smiles and in less than two seconds he dives down, disappearing for a couple of seconds. I laugh when I think maybe he wants to go coral collecting or whatever but I was proved wrong when a minute later I get pulled under water.

* * * * *

I hear him laugh and then just like that the next few minutes of the band singing about three songs that actually were pretty good. And I mean, good that gets yourself involuntarily swinging your hips and moving your body like you've never before.

"So this is the Isabelle with an e?" I hear Jeremiah saying with an amused grin covering his pink lips that look like he's coated them with lipstick.

"You're talking to her," I wink and then point my thumb backwards towards the beach. He looks at what I'm pointing at and then at me.

The next minute, we grab our phones from the table and walk with our shoes dangling in our hands by the side of the sea, leaving two pairs of feet along the sand.

"This is breathtakingly peaceful.." I find myself saying. It still feels like I'm living a dream. Moments I spent with Jeremiah. I don't want anything to ruin it, I'm scared *I* might ruin it and I wish that doesn't happen because this has been the happiest I've ever been in such a long time.

"Sing something." I hate that his gentle-toned request makes me want to obey him. I shake my head with a shy smile. "Please," I think I even sigh a couple of times but he waits, he just waits with a smile. A gentle one.

"I don't-"

"Stop, I know you do." He says.

"Right here?" I ask looking around the beach. Nobody is around, it's just us but still I'm nervous as if I'm in front of a crowd of people.

"It's just me, Isabelle." He assures me.

"Okay, but keep walking. Don't stop." I say and rack my brain for a song.

"Okay. Let's walk."

"I've been listening to this song like on and on and it's all in my head.. I don't think it's a song that'll suit the environment or the mood today.. It's different but I think.. I think it's a beautiful song." I say with a nervous breath. I can't even believe I'm considering singing to him. If this was a month ago, I wouldn't even be considering doing it but here I am, about to sing. To him, when I barely sing to myself anymore.

"Okay," he gives me an encouraging smile.

"Okay." I breathe before humming the song out loud and then start singing the words. "It's called 'It'll Be Okay' by Shawn Mendes." I say before breathing in and exhaling.

"Are we gonna make it?
Is this gonna hurt?
Oh, we can try to sedate it
But that never works
Yeah

I start to imagine a world where we don't collide
It's making me sick, but we'll heal and the sun will rise.

If you tell me you're leaving, I'll make it easy
It'll be okay.
If we can't stop the bleeding
We don't have to fix it, we don't have to stay.

I will love you either way
Ooh-ooh, it'll be oh, be okay
Ooh-ooh.."

All I can think about right now is what a fool I've made out of myself. Apart from how the silence is so loud and killing me as every second passes with him being silent. He probably is coming up with a 'nice' compliment to say for my horri-

"That was-"

"Horrible, I know." I mumble, knowing he heard me. I'm still walking, wanting nothing more than to hide in my room but he stops walking. I turn towards him.

"It was beautiful," he says from where he is standing, a foot away from me.

"The song, yeah." I agree. He chuckles but not because it was funny.

"Isabelle, why?" I look at him, more than confused. First he says the song is beautiful and then he chuckles and now he's asking me why? Why what? As if he read my thoughts he answers, "why wouldn't you take a compliment when it's for you? I didn't mean the song, I meant you. Your voice is *beautiful*."

It's unbelievable how many times my mind keeps echoing those words over and over again for several seconds, minutes even until it sinks.

I can't even find my voice to say 'thank you' or anything. Words keep piling up and right at the tip of my tongue but nothing comes out. I know for sure I'd write a whole page once we go back to our rooms about this very moment. I already see myself doing it.

"So, um what do you like doing?" I thought I'd ask.

"I'm not sure what interests me would interest you." he smiles.

"I disagree. How could someone as amazing as you be boring? C'mon, fill me up on something about your life." I prompt. He chuckles at that.

"Well," he starts, us both walking by the side of the waves of the beach just when the sun starts to set. What a perfect combination. "I like figuring people out. People fascinate me. *You* fascinate me." He says, taking me completely by surprise. "It's weird, I know. I probably sound creepy to you now.."

"It's not creepy, but it's definitely different." I say and stop walking just to see the sunset. "Look at how beautiful this is," I find myself saying.

"Yeah," Jeremiah says, but something about the way he said it made me want to look at him. And I did. Only to find him looking back at me. I smile because that's all I could do.

"I like figuring you out, Isabelle." He then says.

"There's not a lot of interesting things you'd find then." I say, looking back to the sunset.

"Hey, look at me. you'd be surprised about the stuff I've come to know about you. You're one of the most interesting people I've met, Isabelle." He says and I want to believe him but there's a lot of things people say and I'm not saying he is 'people', but it's better this way.

"You're crazy, you know?" I smile.

"I'm a lot of things." He shrugs. "Hey, you dance right?" He suddenly asks.

"No, why?" I laugh.

"Yeah, you do." He says instead and pulls me behind him towards a small crowd playing some cool music. No way. No freaking way.

"Jeremiah, I really don't-"

"Stop lying. I know you do. and I know all of the types of songs you like dancing to." He says and grabs both my arms and *dances*. With me.

Chapter Ten

Is surfing in the night, specifically past midnight a good idea to surf?

Google says ***'The biggest danger of night surfing is of course low visibility. Lesser the light, more prone you are to get hurt or to get disoriented when a wave hits. This means that you should be well prepared when you are surfing at night.'***

I don't see a big fat 'no' in there so I guess I just have to be prepared if something happens.

"You stole it?!" I almost shriek when Jeremiah tells me he 'just took' a board that no one was using which was lying on the sand.

"Calm down. No one was there, besides, I saw a different guy having the same so if the owner thinks somebody stole it, hopefully he goes there first so that gives us time to-"

"To put the board where it was and pretend nothing happened with that board." I finish his sentence and he smirks. I sigh.

"What are you waiting for? Get in there." Jeremiah nudges my arm playfully.

“Have you done this before?” I ask him, removing my slippers and setting it next to the quilt we were laying on and start spraying body spray that literally says ‘Ridiculous Idea’ all over my body hoping whatever fish I come across would smell that more than my blood.

“What, spray perfume all over my body?” He teases. I roll my eyes. “I have surfed a couple of times. Haven’t done it in a while though.” He admits. My subconscious screams ‘All The More Reason To Sit This One Out’. I ignore her.

“Great. Let’s just hope I come back in one piece.” I attempt to joke while I make my way towards the ocean. It looks calm tonight. “So how do I start?”

“Try sitting in the middle of the board and try to paddle yourself around, get used to the waves,” he says and when we go deep enough. By deep enough, I mean, standing on my tiptoes to keep my nose out to breathe while Jeremiah calmly stands, the water only reaching his mid stomach. Tall people!

“Okay,” I say and lift myself up and swing my leg on the other side of the board.

“Now paddle for now.” He instructs, I nod. I lie on the board because I’ve seen people doing that in the movies and move my hands in free-style. It works. This feels like training freestyle in swimming back in fourth or fifth grade. I used to swim back in school. It was the only sport I was actually good at apparently. I kind of liked it. I loved the water and being in it, minus when it’s boiling. It sort of felt like home to me in some weird way.

"You sure you haven't done this before?" Jeremiah asks when I paddle myself the eighth lap.

"Yeah, why?"

"You seem pretty good at it." He beckons.

"Thank you. I think it's the movies I've watched growing up." I say and continue the paddling for about ten more minutes and then take a break.

The next hour goes by with me trying to swim with the board towards a wave to see if I could handle it without falling off the board. Very safe, I know.

I fail a couple of times and even scare Jeremiah but when he sees that I can manage and swim back to the shallow side of the ocean, he calms down a bit. I don't know if he noticed but I'm actually having a great time, even with the water going in my nose and failing to stand on the board without being knocked down by the waves.

After Jeremiah says it's late enough and that it's time for bed, I oblige and help to gather the quilt and stuff and walk to our rooms. I bid him good night first, feeling the exhaustion kick in from the day and all the energy I had to use earlier.

I only go to bed when it's fifteen minutes to three in the morning once I've noted down the day's events in my journal. Call me cliché, but I'll be blissfully re-reading all of these good memories five or ten or more years from now and maybe even reliving those moments or just enjoying reading them, picturing them in my mind, cherishing them…

Chapter Eleven

More Than This by One Direction

It's been a month. If only there was a word to describe the said month, since we, as in, Jeremiah and I, tried checking out all of the boxes on my bucket list. I knew I wouldn't be able to check them all out, of course but we did the ones I really, really wanted to do.

But, there were some things. Things that kept bubbling inside me or was it just my head? The point is, even though the past month has been amazing, at the same time, I've wanted to run away. A lot. I feel maybe it's something to do with a guy. To be specific, the same guy who is graciously nice, amazingly beautiful, ridiculously funny, smart and a lot of things combined who also happens to be living right opposite of my apartment.

What's even funny is my journal running out of pages because of the past month and this week spending all my free time on scribbling the past days' happenings as if my life depends on it.

The past few days have been an ongoing cycle of me avoiding Jeremiah on some days and then some days where I let him in. I hate it. I hate myself for letting him in sometimes. I hate that my dumb self is still naive. I thought after all those years of calamity and countless tears being shed on a daily basis, the amount of times I kept telling myself 'there's just no one for you Isabelle. No one. Just live.' I didn't mean in any way to be selfish, quite the opposite actually, but I wanted to limit myself with my surroundings, the people around me.

I wanted to put a stop to relationships.

I didn't want to go through the pain of not being loved back or to be made a fool or to be taken advantage over and over again. I didn't want to feel lifeless just because phases in life, or rather the people that come along are just sometimes hard.

Training yourself to do the opposite of what your true character is is hopeless. No matter how you try to just be closed off when in nature you're not. No matter how much you push yourself to be an introvert when you're not. No matter how much you try to be that someone who is not you… it won't work. Like a cycle, you force yourself in a bubble that's not yours to be in.

"I had a feeling you might be here." I gasp for a second but then calm down when I recognise the voice. *Jeremiah.*

He's leaning against a bookshelf with a smile and an unreadable expression on his face. I cover my face with the book I'm reading wanting to be away from him right now. I'm embarrassed. I'm embarrassed he must have noticed my sudden disappearance the last couple of days.

"What's up Bells?" *Bells*. I can feel him squat down and sit next to me on the mat. He takes the book from my hands and sets it on his lap.

"Aren't you supposed to be at work or something?" I ask, finding every way possible to distract him from the real problem here. That is, me.

"Stop doing that. You know why I'm here. You'd know I'd show up anyway." He says softly, making me want to cry right then and there, but I don't.

"I wouldn't know…" the words were out of my mouth before I could even process them.

"Yes, you would, Isabelle," he immediately adds. I think I smile. "Do you want to tell me what's bothering you?"

"No, no. It's happening again. I'm not going to fall for it…" I don't even know what I'm saying but all I know is I'm crying when I stand up and run out of the library without looking back.

I have to wait for the lights to change from green to red to cross the road, making me quickly wipe my eyes, smudging my mascara in the process. I cuss at myself for not thinking.

"Isabelle," I feel my breath hitch in my throat. This is not how the story goes. It's always me running out crying or breaking down in the situation with nobody following me behind. But this is different and unexpected.

"What, what are you doing?" I ask, completely taken aback.

"What do you mean? I just don't want you crying alone and if that's to do with me... I'm sorry. Please tell me.."

"No Jeremiah, stop." I cut him off.

"Then tell me. Tell me what's wrong. I can help. I want to be there for you Isabelle." With every word that leaves his mouth, my tears only increase.

"I'm scared. I'm scared everything will change if I talk..." I tell him honestly for once without beating around the bush.

"Is that what it is then?" He asks completely different from all the scenarios I imagined this kind of conversation would be with him.

"Jeremiah, you don't know what you're talking about. I'm not like other people...other girls... you wouldn't want to even look at me if I tell you things from my past." I breathe out and start walking along the street.

What surprises me is hearing footsteps behind me. *His* footsteps.

"Jeremiah-" he cuts me off by engulfing me in a much needed embrace, shutting me up completely.

"You don't have to always stay strong and push your feelings away. It's okay to break sometimes. We're all human, we need somebody. You're not alone in this. I'm here, Bells."

Chapter Twelve

You Took My Heart Away by Michael Learns To Rock

Flashback

"Okay? Your brother-in-law touched me and that's nothing to you?" I don't know how I'm talking because right now it feels like with every word that leaves my mouth, my throat bleeds even more.

"Yeah because I know he didn't touch you like that! He loves you. He's your uncle, Isabelle!" he shouts, making me back away against the chair.

"Oh yeah, my uncle who made me sit on his lap and touch me and kiss me in all the wrong places!?" I fire back, tears prickling in the corners of my eyes.

For a moment he looks… shocked? Shocked, taking in the information I just spat and opened his mouth but closed it again.

"You're lying!" He scolds after several seconds. It takes a second for his words to process and when it does I feel something incredibly painful. I feel stabbed. I feel my heart quench and maybe even bleeding.

"You don't believe me but you believe him? Wow. Just, wow. I'm *your daughter and you choose to believe him over what I just*

told you which is the truth daddy." I cry but I don't think that's really possible at this point because my whole body feels like it's crashing down.

"I know what I'm doing! I know better than you so watch your stupid mouth!"

"I can see that because you don't give – that I was touched by your sick brother-in-law!" I have to whisper, louder than I normally would. He hears me.

"I'm gonna call him and ask." I laughed because what else can I do at this point? I can't cry so might as well laugh. Even though that too kills.

"Of course you will." I say and run upstairs to the balcony, finding the sharpest object I could find.

End of flashback

Seconds pass. Then a minute. Then another.

I know I'm on the verge of crying. He looks like he wants out of this place, his living room, his apartment, I don't know because I'm only trying to read his face with a clouded vision thanks to the tears filling up my eyes, blinding me.

"Are you.. Are you okay?" His voice is just above a whisper as if whatever I've just spilled out to him has absorbed everything in him.

And that was all it took for all the burning tears to make their entrance.

I buried my face in one of the cushions to drain out the noise from my sudden sobbing but what surprises me is what he does just a second later.

"Jeremiah-" he embraced me for the second time today and it's not just for a second. It's different. He doesn't just stop there. He *holds* me.

"Shh. I can't just sit here and watch you break down. Use me as the cushion," he says ever so gently making me slightly laugh through my tears and then bury my face in his shirt while he holds me.

* * * * *

It's been over two hours now since I was able to let all of those suppressed tears for so long all out at once. And surprisingly, all I've been able to think about is how I have someone right now when I've spent so many year's nights crying all by myself into my pillow thinking I would never be able to experience *this*.

"Thank you." I finally said after finding my voice.

"Of course. I'm sorry I can't change anything that happened to you but I'm here for you now. I know that may sound crazy to you but I'm serious." He says running his fingers in my hair naturally.

"I know. Thank you."

"Enough of that. Let's watch something. You're a sucker for romance aren't you?" He muses and I laugh.

"Something like that." I mumble, hiding my smile.

"Yeah, yeah. Tell you what, the bathroom's a left from here, my room. You go and freshen up while I get the popcorn ready and coffee." He says and before I could say a thing he disappears in his kitchen.

I walk to the bathroom on the left which leads to his bedroom and stare at myself in the mirror.

I look around the room and notice how *him-like* his room is. The shade of marshy green on the walls. The bed is a dull grey and blue. Some of his stuff is being laid out on the table. His dresser with some framed photos and some of his colognes and lotions and things like that stacked in rows. He even has a floor to ceiling mini bookshelf that is fully fitted with books. That's where I go.

I contemplate in my head about checking out his books but the temptation takes over and I end up grabbing a copy of 'Wuthering Heights' from the shelf and inspect it.

My eyes catch the here and there texts that's been highlighted. *Annotated.* I have half the mind to go ask him if he annotates too because that's something I love doing but I stay and run my fingers along the lines of a verse.

> *"Be with me always - take any form - drive me mad! Only do not leave me in this abyss, where I cannot find you! Oh, God! It is unutterable! I can not live without my life! I can not live without my soul!"*
>
> *"I have to remind myself to breathe-almost to remind my heart to beat!"*
>
> *"..he's more myself than I am. Whatever our souls are made of, his and mine are the same."*

Just as I process the words of the last highlighted text, I feel the door open and Jeremiah walking in, startling me.

"Of course you're here. I forgot to warn you." He smiles, standing in the middle of the room with his hands on his hips.

"You had a huge bookshelf filled with books and you never told me?!" I walk towards him, still with the open copy of 'Wuthering Heights'. He notices. "And you annotate?" I couldn't help but ask.

"I used to wonder why you had your books so differently and then I started seeing why." I can't believe he actually started annotating because of me.

"Wow. I'm impressed." I say and continue flipping slowly through the pages.

"Your popcorn's going to get cold. Plus I've got Pride and Prejudice ready on the TV." He says and leaves the room fast, getting me to speed-walk to catch up to him.

"You did not." I mutter, walking behind him towards the living room and true to his word, the TV screen is lit up with the Pride and Prejudice menu. "Oh my gosh, I can't believe this." Why is this dream oddly familiar?

"Say you'll stay for the movie?" He asks from the kitchen.

"I'd love to. Thank you so much..." I couldn't help but hug him, catching him off guard.

* * * * *

I don't know how Jeremiah just knew the exact atmosphere I would need right now, like how he made so much coffee and had Pride and Prejudice ready on the TV. How did he even remember my favourite movie? The fact that he does remember the littlest facts like this somehow makes me feel so squeasy because literally no one does that.

"What are you thinking?" Jeremiah speaks, getting me out of the cloud of thoughts my mind ran into.

"Nothing. Just tired I guess." I half-lie. I am tired. It's been a long day and he somehow got me to lay all my emotions out in the open and that was a lot.

"Alright. I'll walk you to your flat." he says, standing up immediately and then reaching out for my hand.

"You don't have to walk me. You've already done enough today.." I say, taking his hand but not standing up yet. "I'll help clean." I say and then start picking up the plates and the cups from the floor.

"Isabelle, you don't have to. I can clean this up," he says, now standing in front of me.

"This is the least I can do. Please let me." I almost beg and move past him towards the kitchen and load the dishwasher and start scrubbing the dishes.

"You're something else," I hear him say. I choose not to look at him because I can feel him staring and him staring is making me nervous even though I'm just washing dishes. My heart's already starting to race and this is precisely the reason I choose to do things to avoid him even though I hate doing it.

No matter how much you try to avoid something, or in this case *someone*, they just keep showing up almost everywhere and everyday and as much as it pains you to get yourself together every time you have to face them, you can't help but smile at the thought of them.

"Good night Jeremiah." I make a bold move and kiss his cheek, in a way to say 'thank you' and immediately leave his apartment.

Chapter Thirteen

Fallin' All In You by Shawn Mendes

It's been a couple of days since the 'breakdown'. Ever since that day, I've been feeling my feelings towards Jeremiah growing day by day. I'm not proud of it but to be honest it's been impossible to *not* think about him or all those tender moments with him.

Maybe psychologically, I'm feeling all of this is because he's just there. Maybe it wouldn't last long like all those relationships. Maybe it's just another terrible, terrible phase where I'm making the same mistake yet again.

I still can't help but think otherwise.

I rush to the door when I hear the pounding of probably Jeremiah. There's nobody else I know of from the building who'd knock, or rather pound on my door at six in the evening.

"Adeline?" I almost gasp, more than surprised.

"Hello, Isabelle," she says sweetly as I bend down to match her height.

"Hello angel," I hug her in greeting and then look up to see Jeremiah by his door smiling. I smile back. "No school today?" I shift my focus on the cute little girl in front of me.

"Nah. I took a day off," she giggles. I laugh and then tickle her sides making her giggle even louder.

"I wonder who's idea it was to take a day off." I say, eyeing Jeremiah with a smirk as I carry Adeline and rest her on my hip.

"Doesn't matter now. Since we all are here, can we go to the park and then maybe get ice cream?" She chirps, clasping both her hands and making that puppy dog face towards Jeremiah. I laugh at both of them.

"Alright. But only if you make sure you make up for missing today's school work." Jeremiah says in that daddy-voice. Adeline pouts then groans but eventually agrees.

The next few minutes go by us getting ourselves ready for the short trip to the park. Ironically, if a stranger looked at us, they would've assumed we were a cute family seeing Jeremiah driving, me in the passenger seat with Adeline seated comfortably on my lap chatting away the whole drive there.

Adeline dances her way entering the park with me and Jeremiah following close behind her laughing at her high-spirited charisma.

"Oh my gosh! Oh my gosh! Oh my gosh!" Adeline squeals, squeezing her small hands in fists as she hops to us. "They're throwing water!" She says, her voice filled with excitement, tugging Jeremiah's shirt, getting his attention. I look over to where she is pointing at and see that it is towards the water play-place. The area that sprays water all over with a bunch of equipment.

"That's cool. We can't go today though, we didn't bring a change." Jeremiah says making me want to swat his arm but then remind myself they're family. I'm just an outsider here.

"Hmph! Plea-"

"No Addy. We can go next time, okay?" Jeremiah says, not stern, not lenient either. Adeline pouts but then spots a couple of kids playing on the swings.

I feel my phone vibrate in my jean pocket. When I look at the notification, I gasp.

Candidate results June 2021

But that's all I do.

I don't open the page or bother seeing the rest of the notification but instead turn off my phone and put it back in my pocket like nothing happened.

I buy myself and Jeremiah a packet of chips and sit next to him on the bench he is seated on watching Adeline play.

"Hey, you." He sends me a friendly smile. I return it and hand him the packet. He smiles again.

"Hey. Looks like she has made new friends already." I say, motioning towards the little girl mingling with four other kids looking her age.

"Hmm," he hums, popping chips in his mouth. "How's your day going so far? Besides the time being here," he adds with a smile.

"It's been okay. Was a bit boring but mostly I had a lot on my mind to think about.. I guess it was an ok-day." I smile.

"Did any of that thinking have anything to do with the guy next door?" He smirks playfully. I swatted his arm and then burst out laughing.

"Stop flattering yourself." I mutter with a slight smile, only partly looking at him.

"Oh, I'm not actually," he smiles, teasingly.

"Sure, sure." I reply sarcastically with a laugh. "How was your day?" I changed the topic.

"Same old. I have to go shopping-"

"For your apartment?" I perked up just as the word 'shopping' left his mouth. He nods, smiling. "Finally!" I exclaim, probably sounding a little too excited. Couldn't help it though. The guy's apartment is so plain. It literally looks like he just moved in.

"Well, would you like to join me?" He asks, making me quiet down a bit. "I could use some ideas from an interior designer..." I didn't expect him to just go out and ask me that. Plus I don't know why I feel awkward now because we've spent time out before. But I find myself smiling at the thought of spending time together.

"Okay. When will you go?" I ask him. He smiles, probably surprised I agreed so fast.

"Um, I'm thinking maybe this Friday? That way we could work on them during the weekend." It's like he's planned all of that out already. I don't even know why I'm smiling so much. The thought of doing things together with him does sound appealing and the fact that it does so much is annoying.

Thankfully, Jeremiah moves on to talking about his family which I found nice of him to do seeing that I've been wanting to get to know him more. More than I've ever wanted to get to know anyone else.

When it gets to my turn to talk about my family, I tell him the basics. Then talk about Merebelle and our progressing relationship. Talking about my sister gets him to talk about his which gets the conversation to escalate onto a deeper, longer conversation to the point where we only stop talking to check on Adeline.

"You ever had time to do a little sightseeing here in London?" He fully turns towards me as he asks me this.

"No, but I've always wanted to. Just didn't get the opportunity to, I guess." I reply, while playing with the soft grass on the ground.

"When's your next day off?" He asks, making me smile, even though I'm not directly looking at him.

"You are not asking me out, Jeremiah." I say immediately. I'm smiling even though I hate that I blurted that out. Jeremiah's face contours a bit but he still is smiling which is now making me wonder why.

"What's so wrong with that Isabelle?" He smiles, and I groan into my hands at his use of my name in that sentence. I hate that he is smiling but I also love it because it's so beautiful.

"It's wrong because..because I don't.." I sigh at a loss of words. "You just can't." I whisper, hoping he would understand.

"Fine, I'll drop this conversation for now only because Adeline is walking towards us." He says and true to his word, a second later, Adeline is in front of us. I laugh at him, he smiles but shoots me a look as if to say, 'I'm not going easy on you'.

"Alright, can we go now? I'm hungry." She says, more like announces.

"Oh. Why? Did something happen back there?" Jeremiah asks the same question I wanted to ask.

"No, just hungry. Can we have burgers and chips now? I'm kind of hungry," she asks sweetly, rubbing her small belly to prove her point.

"You said that twice in the same sentence, silly." Jeremiah scoops her up in his arms and leads the way to his car.

The drive was short, just five minutes since there was a Burger King closeby, just a couple of metres away from the park. Once the three of us found a booth and ordered, I excuse myself when my phone rings.

Merebelle

Just when I was about to swipe 'answer' the call got cut making me furrow my eyebrows in confusion.

I called again but the line said 'line busy'. I called two more times, getting the same response making me worry a bit.

Merebelle never *just* calls like that. For a second I think maybe this is a prank but that is so unlike her.

I sigh, noting down a mental reminder to call again when I get to my apartment later and walk towards the booth where Jeremiah and Adeline are seated.

"Everything okay?" Jeremiah asks, softly so Adeline couldn't hear. I just smile and nod my head.

"What did I miss?" I asked Adeline, who currently is busy colouring with four crayons on a printed paper. The ones they give the kids.

"Nothing really. Just that mum called and said I have an explanation to do and grandma wants me to spend the weekend there and Bailey told me the homework on the phone a second ago." Adeline says, not moving her eyes from the paper. I laugh silently at her. She's a funny girl.

The food arrives five minutes later and Adeline ends up laughing at a waiter, forgetting she has food in her mouth, staining the waiter's uniform. She gasps, clasping her hand over her mouth with wide eyes but then bursts out laughing again, saying 'sorry!' about ten times in a row.

Later that evening we watched 'Lion King' since Adeline kept asking. After the movie, Jeremiah got a call, his sister who apparently got stuck in work so she needed Jeremiah to drop Adeline. I left shortly after saying goodbye to her and hung out in my room ever since doing nothing but staring at the ceiling.

I've ignored the notification from earlier all day and now it's all I can think about.

"Screw it." I mutter and get my phone from the living room and *finally* open the notification, gripping the phone in both my hands not knowing what to expect.

English - A

Economics - B

Accounting - C

Mathematics - D

Business Studies - B

Computer Science - C

Instinctively, I screenshot the page and then just stare at it for what feels like forever.

I guess this is what 'disbelief' feels like.

I don't even have the time to process that I *passed* the exams when my phone starts ringing, my dad's name flashing on it.

The best part is, with all the excitement in me that evoked me to tell my dad about the results, thanking God for the perfect timing, the conversation never really had even the slightest gap for me to say *anything*.

Chapter Fourteen

Sign Of The Times by Harry Styles

I've never wanted to visit home with feelings like *this*. It was all planned, I visit my family for all the holidays after every semester or when the course ends. Never while doing the course, not even a long weekend. And I planned out, pictured how I'd spend my holidays with my family in my dreams often, waiting for the first semester to end to fly out to my family, my home.

When my dad called, he didn't waste time telling me all the details. He didn't have to, I already knew right after he said, "*we need you home for a couple of days. We're struggling here Isabelle.*"

I did nothing to waste another minute but started packing my dad's green duffel bag I brought here with me and booked the next flight to San Diego.

Once I get all the flight details, I lock up wishing Jeremiah were around to tell him everything that happened the past few minutes. But, he wasn't there. He was still out. I don't even know why I felt like telling Jeremiah. I wanted to so badly. I wanted to just talk to him so bad. Even if it was just goodbye for I don't know how long.

My mind is debating leaving a note for him or to call him and let him know but it feels selfish for some reason so I push the thought to the back of my mind and carry the duffel bag and my backpack towards the lift.

Five minutes later, I walk out of the apartment building scanning the road for the cab I called and spot it but then I spot another car too.

I spotted *his* car.

He makes eye contact. And I don't glance away.

"Isabelle? Where are you going this late at night?" He approaches me and I want to move but it feels like my feet are glued to the ground.

"I.." I inhale, trying to find enough oxygen but I feel the air thickening. "I-have-to-go.." I exhale, just as my tears make an entrance and this time I rush towards the cab, ignoring his calls after me.

"Isabelle, wait!" Was the last I heard before his voice disappeared as the car kept driving even farther away, making me block my mouth, as I *sob.*

To say the least, I'm terrified. That's actually an understatement.

I don't know how I'm going to have to act there or answer any of the awaiting questions from mummy about my sudden visit. I don't know how long *this* phase is going to go. I'm clueless as to what caused *it* to happen and I don't even want to find out because it's probably the same never ending cycle. It always is.

"Have you left?" My dad says just as I answer his call.

"Yeah. I'll be there in a couple of hours, daddy." I answer. "Hang in there okay? It'll pass soon." I try to sound encouraging. When it comes to times like this, I have no idea how to comfort my dad or even my sister since they both are basically the same person.

"Yeah. See you soon darling," he says before he hangs up. I feel like crying, daddy's voice ringing in my ears still. But I hold those tears. I can't cry again. Not now. Not even when I've reached there.

After paying the cab driver, I thanked him and then made my way to the entrance of the airport through the small groups of people. It feels like actually saying goodbye when I just got here only months ago. I shake my head forcing back the tears and get checked in and safely make it to the plane.

I hate that tears keep forming the more time goes while being seated on the plane ready to depart. I hate that I feel selfish right now. I hate that my emotions are all over the place. I hate how everytime this happens my mind knows only how to flash all the past horrible memories.

The night my mum refused her medicine and literally threatened to kill my dad with broken glass right in front of me and then I ended up being locked up with my sister when my dad could be in real trouble or worse which was the most horrifying thing I have ever had to go through.

The day my dad had to pick me up from choir practice at school to leave for mummy's doctor's appointment because she was refusing to leave without us. The whole ride there was just so disturbing and literally hurtful to be in.

The day mummy left home without any of us knowing but thankfully daddy finding her at a train station a few kilometres away. And then the whole drive to the christmas party...

The week being left at my grandma's place until my mum was being discharged from the hospital.

Just when my first tear falls, *Sign of the Times* starts playing, making me laugh bitterly at the coincidence. The plane takes off minutes later while I still cry alone facing the window overlooking the dark city lights.

* * * * *

Seeing my dad at the airport exit made me feel all emotional again but thanks to the whole crying session I had on the plane hours ago I was able to keep the tears out of the way. We hugged longer than we'd usually do without words being exchanged.

The drive home was quiet mostly other than the here and there conversations about my classes and all until I started feeling drowsy.

"Oh. What on earth are you doing here Isabelle?" My mum says, her voice an octave higher than her usual voice, much deeper, scarier.

"Uh, hello, mummy," I literally had to pause in between each word as she stared at me up and down as if she's scanning my flaws. Out of habit, I asked her, "how are you?" but immediately regretted it.

"How am I?" she scoffs. "I'm doing *good*, Isabelle!" I can't tell if she's yelling or just talking. Before I could apologise, she spoke, making me jump backwards. "Isn't that what you wanted to hear? Tell me! Aren't you also here because dad called you? Huh? You are, aren't you? He thinks I'm sick, you know. And now you're here thinking I'm sick too when you should be there, studying!" She raises her voice, each word louder than the previous as she makes her way towards me. I shudder when she is just about inches away.

My heart feels like it's exploding.

Please don't make this hard mummy. Please.

Chapter Fifteen

Little Things by One Direction

It's been three days since the day I got here and so far, and by 'so far' I mean the countless fights between my parents day and night, the house being turned upside down, the waking up in the middle of the night...

I would say things have been 'okay', but I'm not sure somebody else would say the same.

It's one in the afternoon and currently I locked myself up in my room to drown the maddening music mum's literally *blaring* from the speakers from the living room. I don't know what it is with her and music during times like this but it is agitating but then again, maybe if she enjoys it, she stays calm, and her staying calm keeps us calm.

"Isabelle!" I jump in my desk chair and almost scream at the sudden voice but then sigh.

"Yeah?" I call, while walking towards the door to unlock it.

"Why is the door locked?" She questions.

"Um, I was trying to do some work.." I say.

"Have you got exams for this semester? Have you already started studying for them? Or have you been wasting time on things like the crappy books you read?" She questions. I take a deep breath before *preparing* an answer for her.

"There's no exams this semester mummy. I haven't really got time to read these days so no," I answer, politely as possible.

"Has anyone touched you there?" She asks rather abruptly and I have to swallow my gasp.

"Of course not! Why would you say or even think that?" I ask, forgetting her condition at that moment.

"Are *you* actually asking me that?" She snaps.

"Wh-why wouldn't I mummy?" I ask her, taken aback when she laughs.

"You out of all people should know what I'm talking about *darling*." She says while I try to think why she's speaking that way until it hits when she says, "oh Isabelle, you naive girl. Of course as your mother I would ask that! You let your own *uncle* touch you while I was there, around, living... I wouldn't be surprised if you let someone else's hands on you without *me* being close to you." She spits, and yet again I have to swallow my cries and keep my tears under control.

"I never-is that what you think of me?" I squeak, not being able to find my voice.

"Of course! And even with *that* girl-" she starts.

"Please don't." I beg. She doesn't listen of course.

"You think you've changed but have you, Isabelle? Don't you still wish for that relationship? Don't you still think of her? Don't you still have her crappy notebook? Don't you still wish you were together even when she went behind your back!" I flinch away almost tripping over my own feet as her words sink in, like bullets, leaving me bleeding. "What was her name again?" I shut my eyes so hard that I wish she didn't remember. "Morghan was it?" She says seconds later and it feels like another bullet shot right through my heart.

"Please-"

"You must be still talking to her for all I care. What really happened between the both of you?" She suddenly asks and I tremble. I can't even find it in me to do anything because my body is frozen in place.

There's no turning back now. The wound that was only beginning to heal has been ripped open and probably will take forever to heal again.

"Isabelle-"

"Please stop," I beg and close the door, locking it.

I stare at the door for what feels like forever until she leaves. I can't even remember how long I've been standing because by the time I fall on the bed in a pool of tears, the sun's already setting.

The only thing that is running in my mind is Jeremiah. There's so much I want to text him, call him. I find myself wanting to hear his voice. Or to even text him and see him texting me back. I want to talk to him so bad, I'm crying as

I search through my Instagram right when the phone comes to life after turning it on after three whole days. I cry when his name comes up on the top when I type his name in the search bar. I click it and open his account. My finger touches the 'message' button and it opens a new chat because we've never really texted each other. Let alone calling each other.

Feeling defeated, I cry myself to sleep tracing his Instagram username for I don't know how long because sleep takes over in a matter of probably minutes.

Chapter Sixteen

No Tears Left To Cry by Ariana Grande

"That's the problem here. I should've thought first…I should've listened to you when you told me you'd be this way.. That would've saved so much of a disaster…" Daddy says walking away from mummy after probably the thousandth fight this week.

"That's why I'm trying to get divorced. Once you give me my money, I'll leave and poof, no more *disasters* George!" She says and I almost gasp. My dad doesn't even look surprised, like it's not the first time he's heard mummy bringing up getting divorced. I look at him, trying to find answers, I don't even know what to find but he just gives me a blank expression.

"Divorce?" My voice cracks as I approach my dad when mom isn't within earshot.

"Isabelle-" I raise my hands to stop him. I just need to know one thing.

"No, just please answer me honestly." I plead. "Do you want to get divorced?" I ask him plainly not ready for his answer.

"She wants it. I don't know what I want. You know I would never want that for both of you. I don't want us to be apart.. But if that's what she wants, I won't stop her..." he tells me just as a tear falls on my cheek. I wipe it away and just nod, speechless.

Selfishly, I don't want to say anything because I'm terrified. I'm terrified if I do say something it'll get worse and I don't want anything to get worse than this because I already feel parts of my body starting to break and something beyond this would completely shatter me...

I do realise I'm being self centred, but how else do you react when your parents are considering divorcing each other?

Pretending to be okay and just going with it is out of the question. I've done that one too many times to even count and I'm tired of it. I'm tired of just pretending everything is okay all the time.

What hurts more is how as a child I used to think no matter how broken we are, we get through these waves that come because they go eventually. But sometimes, the waves come and I don't think they go, they just pull you in deeper, deeper and deeper, day by day, slowly while you try with all your might to reach the surface.

* * * * *

"That's a nice song yeah," I smile as I agree, applying butter on the slices of bread.

"Play Ariana Grande's song." My mum says, more like demands but I laugh it off and do as she says.

"This one? *No Tears Left To Cry* right?" I play the song on my tab, setting it away from the appliances so food wouldn't get splashed on it as I make toast bread.

The evening so far has been alright compared to the past days. Mummy's been calm and quite happy. At least she looks like she is. I have no idea what has changed or that maybe she is getting back to her normal self. I'm forcing myself to not just have false hope about the second one, because it sucks. Waiting for mummy to get back to her normal-self. But tonight she is happy, playing music, dancing too, in the middle of the kitchen as I butter up the bread and toast them whilst making scrambled eggs.

Dinner goes by good. Mostly silent really but that is better than how the past days have been.

Little did I know, that didn't last too long as I thought it would.

"Mummy, you have to take the medicine…please don't make this hard." I take very small steps close to her.

"Who are you to give me that dirt? Now he's putting you up to give me medication?" She spits, making me bite my lip so hard, I can tell it's already starting to bleed.

"Nobody, but as your daughter, I want you to get better so please trust me on this," I say as softly as possible.

"Trust you? Do you know what you're saying Isabelle? Can't you see he's brainwashed you too?" She raises her voice, making me almost drop the glass of water. "Why on earth do I need medication huh? Look at me. Look at what those stupid, stupid drugs are doing to me." She gestures towards her body.

"I'm sorry mummy…"

"Those things are killing me everyday! They keep weakening me!"

"Catrina, we're not purposely doing this. Please darling, trust us on this." Daddy cuts in. I wince when he does.

"Trust you?" She flares up again, making me leave the pills and the glass water on the table and walk to my room, closing the door behind me letting them deal with figuring out a way to give the medicine.

"Oh gosh." I sigh as I sink onto the bed next to Merebelle who has her earphones on. "Can we watch a movie?" I ask her after tapping on her shoulder.

"Okay." She agrees and gets daddy's computer and sets it up on the bed. "Should we continue watching Riverdale maybe?" she suggests.

"Yeah, we should." I agree, laying on my stomach with my legs in the air. She sits similarly and presses 'play' just when the website loads.

"Gosh I don't know what to expect in season six." I mumble. She hums in response as the first episode starts playing.

Me and Merebelle have been watching Riverdale for months. We had to stop in between though when exams and assignments kept coming up but in between on long weekends mostly and times like these whenever we remember, we just put it up and binge-watch so many episodes until we get tired late in the night. That's literally one of the ways we cope when things at home are going rough.

I've realised when sometimes talking about your pain doesn't work, trying other ways, especially with someone going through the same thing, helps. It's also the best memories you have with your siblings. Times where you put the music all the way up and sing your lungs out with, watch funny YouTube shorts or scrolling through Instagram videos on your feed, talking about things that have nothing to do with what's happening. Those are what keeps each other going. Even if it's just a little.

* * * * *

"Oh my gosh it's raining so bad-I don't want to shower tonight!" Merebelle squeals, jumping on the bed. I fake-gag, she rolls her eyes while turning on the fan and getting under the covers.

It's past midnight and we're halfway done with the season but through to stop for today since it's late.

"You little pig." I mutter as I turn to face her. She giggles, making me laugh.

"Want to cuddle?" She asks suddenly.

"What?" I ask, even though I heard her already.

"Want to cuddle?" She repeats.

"Of course," I don't know why I feel emotional right now-that's just the sweetest thing ever!

"So, have you had any dreams of anyone lately?" She asks, making me laugh. Merebelle asking me if I've had 'dreams' of people is her way of asking, '*has anyone been occupying your mind lately?*'.

"I'll tell you but only if you tell me too." I came up with. She smirks.

"Fine." She mumbles. I mentally scream in victory.

"I'll go first." I start. "I'm not going to lie, but I've had this guy in my dreams for some time now. I keep playing our conversations or come up with my own conversations I wish I had with him in my head. It's dumb, pathetic really..."

"You like him, don't you?" She speaks for me. I just smile, answering her silently.

You have no idea Merebelle, no idea.

"It's crazy really. How can you like someone so fast?" I ask no one in particular.

"It's possible. The best relationships are like that. You know, when you know.. Something like that.." she says and I laugh at how cute that sounded coming from her.

"Since when did you start looking up relationship advice?" I laugh. She laughs too.

"You know, when you know." She repeats her words. "And to make things fair, I um..I talked to *him* at school..." she quietly says, fiddling with her fingers.

"Really? What'd he say?" I lift myself and lean my chin on my arm, giving her my attention.

"Nothing much really. He told me he wants to be a vet…" she smiles while saying. Merebelle also wants to be a vet.

"He did? Did you tell him that you also want to do the same thing?" I ask her while she turns towards me.

"I did. And we kind of made eye contact and I think it got a bit weird…" she tells me, sighing right after.

"What happened? Did one of his friends come or something?" I made a quick guess. She nods. I groan. "Urgh! Way to ruin a moment." I say, already annoyed at whoever it was that interrupted them.

"It's fine. Maybe we'll talk again soon.." she says. I hum.

"I miss him." I finally admit, feeling embarrassed.

"You'll see him soon." She assures me, planting a kiss on my temple and then yawns. I smile.

"Good night Merebelle." I kiss her forehead and let sleep take over my very much sleep-deprived body.

I miss you so much, Jeremiah. More than you know.

Chapter Seventeen

You know how when you're going through a lot all at once and in the *past* you would have cutting as your coping strategy? I used to hide a blade in my desk somewhere right at the back of where I keep my books. I remember at times when I really was struggling to find the blade with the amount of books burying it inside, I'll start scraping my wrists until I get a hold of the blade.

Well, in the present, a few months ago actually, I've decided not to make self-harm my coping strategy anymore because I was able to understand how that doesn't really benefit me but just destroys me. It's been months since the last time I've used a blade on my wrist but there were times when I thought of doing it. But thankfully, something in me stopped me from doing so.

For some reason, when things get overwhelming to the point where I've run out of tears, I run up to the balcony even when it's really sunny outside. I'd be burning but I'd still sit down and look up at the sky with closed eyes. It's not like it helped but being away sometimes helps.

"There you are," I gasp but sigh when I see daddy making his way towards me, looking hurt quite a bit. I hate that I have this annoying reflex in me that especially when

I'm alone or if I don't see anyone walking in the room, I gasp or scream. Even when it's just my family.

"Sorry,"

"It's fine. What are you doing out here? It's so hot here." he says as a matter of fact.

"Hmm. I just wanted to be alone.." I reply

"You've been coming out here a lot." He points out. I look away from him scared that he might read me.

"It's just peaceful..I guess," I half-lie. He doesn't buy it.

"You know Isabelle, just because you're hurting you don't have to punish yourself. Not like this." he says. "Come on, let's go down." he reaches for my hand.

"No daddy," I refuse, shaking my head stubbornly, tears running down.

"Isabelle," he says disappointedly, waiting for me to get up.

I sigh heavily at that and get up to my feet, following him inside.

Walking down the stairs midway I had to grip the railing hard as I stopped walking. I shut my eyes feeling a slight pain shoot through my head darkening my vision, my head spinning.

"Are you alright?" I hear my dad's voice from downstairs.

"Yeah, I'm good," I smile, taking small, slow steps down the stairs. I know what happened. I was having probably the hundredth blackout this year. I've never told my parents I've been having them, sometimes often but sometimes it comes once in a while because I have a feeling they'd want to see a doctor. I don't want that obviously.

* * * * *

It's ten minutes to twelve at night and I'm the only one awake, staring at the ceiling, watching the fan rotate over and over again. Approximately hundred and ninety eight times. I counted. I've tried forcing myself to fall asleep, but no matter what, I wasn't feeling sleepy for some reason. I lay awake on the bed staring at nothing with open eyes until my eyes closed only to open again with tears rolling down my face, drenching the pillow. I don't even know why I'm crying at this point.

I try closing my eyes and as soon as I do, I scream into the pillow when the nightmares I *used* to suffer going through every night at a point start to kick in. *Oh, God, PLEASE no.*

But, nobody hears me.

Because for the next several minutes, all I see is,

Fire planting itself everywhere. Me being locked up with all these men circling around me with bloody weapons.

Another scene comes up where I'm stranded in a very scary forest-like place. Woods really. Wild and full of mist covering the whole area. I keep running through the mist-covered surroundings only to meet with a ghost. An evil ghost. I don't even believe in them to begin with but the settings feel so real making me feel all those horrible emotions. Being chased by some evil non-existent ghost.

Being tied up on a bed. A steel bed. Maybe metal. Being stripped in a smoke filled room with strangers.

"Isa-"

I literally scream my lungs out. Turning into a panting mess a millisecond later. Eyes wide, I see my sister, looking shocked, worried, her face turning into a deep frown.

"N-not-a-word. T-to d-daddy.." I manage to mutter between heavy breaths. I feel like I'm about to explode just by my deranged breathing and now how much I'm sweating even with the fan right in front of us, hovering over us.

She nods with tears in her eyes before jumping on the bed next to me and holding me close to her while I cry myself to sleep.

Chapter Eighteen

Imagination by Shawn Mendes

It's been two days since the nightmares kicked in and ever since, Merebelle, yes she has kept her mouth quiet *but* she has been on top of me everytime I move an inch. She figured out about my blackouts. She knows about the nightmares. She knows about Jeremiah. She knows everything-to be frank. *Everything!*

"You're sure you don't have to see a doctor?" Merebelle whispers when daddy wasn't within earshot. I sigh, not annoyed at all but just upset that she won't stop convincing me to see a doctor.

"Yes. I'm very sure. I'm really fine." I smile to soften my flat answer. She sighs and then nods.

"Okay. Just please tell me if you don't feel good, okay? I need to know immediately." She says for the tenth time today and like always, I smile, sort of and then nod.

"Well, have a good day at school, you." I laugh to lighten the mood but fail miserably, but thankfully she smiles, saving me from another question.

"Thanks. I'll be back in the afternoon. Call me if anything happens." She says suddenly remembering her wrist watch and then after getting it she kisses my cheek goodbye and rushes out the front door and gets in the car with daddy and leaves.

For a change, I try to arrange the house even though there's really no point doing it because the next minute I do arrange the house, it's trashed. I still do though to keep my mind occupied.

I start at the front of the house, the living room, the upstairs and the big balcony there and back downstairs again.

"You're wasting your time." I jumped at the sudden voice that belonged to my mum.

"Uhh, sorry.. Just wanted to get the house in order since it's been a bit messy..." I kind of ramble. I really wish I wouldn't get nervous around her all the time. She's still my mother.

"Go find something useful to do, Isabelle. Stop wasting your time on house chores." She says, stricter, throwing me a little off guard. I oblige though.

I sweep the floor mess to a corner so it wouldn't fly all over the place and make my way to my room.

I sit on the floor in the middle of my room finding something to do when an idea pops into my head.

I pull my desk chair to a corner and start pulling out all the books, files, notebooks, textbooks, pen holders, boxes of different craft stuff, basically everything from my desk and set them all on the floor. I then grab a rag and wet it slightly and wipe the dust off my desk. I would say, giving my desk a wash by the way I was scrubbing on the surfaces around the hardwood. All edges, corners, flat surfaces, shelves all wiped clean and then wiped again with a dry cloth.

I then sit in the middle of all the things I pulled out from my table and start dusting them off and cleaning the objects and then re-placing them in their original places.

When I start arranging my notebooks, old journals and files filled with school past papers of different subjects, I come across an album book my mum made for me on my thirteenth birthday.

Happy 13th birthday darling!

The book's title read, making me smile at the memory.

I flip through the pages I haven't gone through in a while. I read through all the little notes *she* had written covering all the pages fully without a blank spot in sight. I flip through the photographs she's put in and laugh at some of the baby pictures of me with my fingers in my mouth or the picture where I have milk dripping down my mouth, having just burped. I was about five months old.

I trace my fingers across the cursive handwriting of my mum's on the notes. She really put in a lot of effort, making a whole album from my birth till becoming a teenager, making my eyes well up with heavy tears. I close the book immediately not wanting tears to smudge anything on the album's pages she's put so much effort into.

I place it on the shelf and then reach for my old journals I used as a kid growing up.

Strangely wanting to read through my old journals I take the first book from the stack of other books. It's a silver coloured one. It's like the 'sequel', as I'd like to call it, of my first journal which is old and doesn't even have the cover page on it. Just the written pages of years of worthwhile events that happened in my childhood.

I flip through pages and pages of detailed events and come to an abrupt stop at one page. It's a one-page entry. Just one full page. The shortest entry I've ever written.

Tears

Tears

Tears

And tears…

I seriously hate to repeat, writing what happened yesterday and today that's 6th April 2021. What's the point? Why can't I just DIE? Why? I have no words to say..to express.. It's like there's no life in me…but I'm living. That doesn't even make sense now does it?

I am pathetic, aren't I?

I don't know what to write to you!

I'm just-nevermind.

I want to hurt myself-I have no other option to get rid of this endless pain. It's worse than a freaking heartache. I can't even think clearly and that just is!

All I'm good at doing is freaking crying! In other words, I'm weak. I can't talk but cry. That's all I did today. Just cry.

I'm having a damn sore throat and that's been draining. Everything is so hard. I can't study. But I want to pass the exams which I know are highly impossible..unless God himself does it for me but obviously that won't happen 'cause I don't deserve it.

I want to be alone.

Have my own house,...phone,...car,... my own life... without all this unwanted mess!

I laugh at the last sentence. Is that even a sentence with all the dots in between?

Funny thing is, I can't even remember exactly what happened that night to get me to write so. So rushed? Like I was crying and out of words.

I usually skip writing in my journal when situations, days get too intense. Intense to a point to make me just cry a lot, so I avoid writing because when I do I end up with smudged ink splattered all over the pages instead of actual writing on it. But as a matter of fact, there have been times where I've still written, more like scribbled a bunch of sentences on paper.

I do that so I don't let myself be tempted to think the worst.

I turn the pages even more seeing the different entries being written in various amounts of colours. I used colours to make my entries appear 'happy'. I didn't want my journal just to be a book full of dreary writings on the worst days of my entire life. I wanted to include the happy memories too. Especially in times like this to read through. I enjoy doing that for some reason.

Dear...no one,

I know I'm weird because I've just had the craziest thought, well, BUNCH of thoughts I've ever had in my fifteen years of life. Not to be too dramatic...but what my green pen is about to throw up next is a whole load of craziness. Get ready haha.

Wouldn't it be fun to go to a library and read a book together with someone (I'm not sure who), share our thoughts about the book together?? And then maybe go to a park and play hide and seek (yes, hide and seek!) or something.. Oh! Oh! Play cards! UNO! Or even I spy and then listen to music together and have some ice cream. And then go for lunch-oh wait before that, go shopping and buy something together! (I don't know what; maybe like a key chain or something) Maybe throw a mini fashion show haha!! It would be fun-like to wear two or three outfits and walk the 'cat-walk' thing for the fun of it. (oh lord where did all this come from?) Have lunch somewhere nice and then go to the B-E-A-C-H!! Sing songs! Play in the water for a bit (maybe not too much). Collect shells! And then relax on a blanket or whatever and compliment each other. Maybe play like a crazy 'pick-up line' game. Or crack jokes!! Make the other smile.

Okay I know, I know. It's a STUPID idea, I know. It's juvenile to say the least haha.

It's probably not going to ever happen, but I don't know why but part of me has hope (very little) that maybe I'll get to do all those things or better things with someone special.

"Silly me." I chuckle to myself, letting out a deep sigh after reading that very page.

My mind drifts to the few days I spent with Jeremiah to cross out things on my bucket list and I smile and I think it's the first ever real smile I've smiled since the first day I landed here.

* * * * *

"Hey," I greet Merebelle once she walks through the sandy floor I just swept two hours ago. I sigh.

"Heyy, you look in better spirits." She tries to smile but she is hesitant. Like she doesn't want to offend me. So I smile.

"Yeah. I arranged my table." I tell her as we both walk to our sort of shared room after she lands her school bag in her room and then walks into mine sitting on my desk chair.

"The place does look good," she says, running her eyes around my very tidied up table. I smile, silently agreeing with her.

"You go have a bath. I'll get lunch ready." I tell her and walk out of the room to the kitchen and heat up yesterday's food.

It was just me and Merebelle at the dining table eating lunch. Mummy barely eats these days. She has her times. Moods, actually.

We keep conversation light, not talking like we'd usually do just to avoid unwanted trouble. Merebelle takes the lead in holding conversations. She starts them, and mostly ends them, moving to new subjects every few minutes with me only nodding and humming with short responses.

That evening goes by me whiling away time in my room like always searching for something to do but there's literally nothing to do. Nothing comes to my head and it sucks to be so jobless.

Why didn't I think to bring any of my books?

I open my phone for the first time today and open up Wattpad just when the power goes off, making me exclaim,

"Really!?" Frustrated, I groan. I try to focus on the screen in my hands and try to read a book from the hundreds of other books I've saved in the library over the past year.

After what feels like minutes, I feel a torch light shine in the doorway of my room, daddy's shadow prominent in the darkness. I mentally groan knowing already what he's about to tell me.

"Isabelle, c'mon. How many times have we been through this?" He says, disappointed, no doubt.

"What? I'm just reading" I play dump.

"It's dark. Too dark to be reading. Come out to the living room without being alone here," he says, well silently demanding. I groan.

"I don't want to come out there." I say.

"Well, you have to. It's dark and I don't want you to be alone here." he says again. I sigh and follow him out of my dark room and to the living room where mummy is seated on the far end of the three-seater sofa, Merebelle seated on the single sofa. I sit on the two-seater sofa across from both of them silently.

"Aren't you using your phone these days?" My head snapped up to look at my mum's direction, not sure who she was talking to. She is looking at me.

"Um, not much," I say.

"Really? Why Isabelle? Don't you have someone to talk to? Or people to talk to?" She asks, her voice displaying something that sounds odd. Strange. It makes me shiver.

"I don't know what you mean." I say once I clear my throat. She laughs.

"You can drop the act now Isabelle. Why would you hide something, sorry, *someone* anyway? And if that particular someone has to come up at some point." I can't tell if my mum is smirking or smiling at this point. She is unpredictable.

"I don't know what you're talking about," I say softly.

"You mean you don't know *who* you're talking about. Come on, tell us." She urges but why? I don't understand. I look over at Merebelle. Did she tell mum about Jeremiah? As if Merebelle read my thoughts, she frantically shakes her head no.

"I don't know what you're talking about." I say again, really confused.

"You have a boyfriend don't you?" She now spits, as if saying that sentence disgusted her. I almost choke on my own breath.

"No! I mean, no. I don't." I say, more than surprised at her assumption. How did she even come up with something like that? I've barely touched my phone the last couple of days.

"So you're letting history repeat itself then?" I don't even look at her at this point, scared. Scared of what will happen and of where this is going. "Like what happened with Riley. Do you two still talk? He should know better than to talk to a whore like you anyway.." she says, I gasp. I forget to hide how she is affecting me right now. "What, surprised? I was actually very surprised by your picture-perfectly put together crappy story Isabelle. Did you really think I believed all your lies? It was *you* who took advantage of that boy! You're just nothing but a self observant whore!" She spits like the words she's saying are nothing while I'm shaking in my seat. "And do I have to remind you again of the kind of thoughts that run in your filthy mind?" She shouts. "Or why don't you just open that filthy mouth of yours instead?" She is staring at me with this look that is scaring me more than ever. I never wanted to admit this but right now, I'm more than *scared* of my mother.

"What-what are you talking about?" I don't even try to hide how much I'm trembling right now.

"Oh honey." She says '*honey*' with revolution as she cuts her eyes to me. "Do you remember the kinds of rubbish you used to tell me?" She laughs mockingly.

"Whatt?" I get out. Everything I have ever told her from the past was the truth.

"Oh so you don't remember telling me you slept with that guy from some club? What's his name again? Freddie or something? You let someone touch you at sixteen! And God knows what you must be still doing in freaking London.." my head gets fuzzy, from all the words that leave her mouth, again, like bullets shooting through my already shot body, not giving a chance for the wounds to heal.

"I-" I feel that familiar black fog making its way in and clouding my head, making me feel ten times weaker than I probably should.

"Can't deny it, can you?" I look up at her, regretting it as soon as her eyes stare into mine.

"Th-those…were..n-nightmares.." I choke out. All the air in my system suddenly disappears while my strength slowly decreases and my composure slowly starts to sway.

"Nightmares, really?" She mocks. Then laughs. Really laughs. "You want me to believe that story? You had '*nightmares*' of guys doing things to you?" Her words implement all the previous sentences all in just one word.

"It's the truth…" I say just as the first tear makes its way down my cheek. I wipe it away quickly.

"No one would believe that, honey." She hisses. "We all know why..why you turned into this-this slut! All you cared about was getting pleasure…" she walks towards me now, my body stays frozen on the sofa. "You're nothing but a slut Isabelle! All you ever do is that. That's who you are." She grabs my chin, squeezing it between her fingers as she shouts right in my face making me flinch praying that this is just a nightmare, that I'll soon get up panting from the dream.

But it *wasn't* a dream at all.

"Catrina enough!" My dad pulls my mum but just a second after she pushes me, her force enough to push me backwards hitting the wall but not hard enough to knock me out of consciousness. I wish it did though.

My mum looks right at me, anger clear in her eyes while I take this as an opportunity to sprint up the stairs leading to the balcony, tripping on a few steps, hitting my thighs but that pain is the least of my worries at this point.

The first shower of salty tears stream down uncontrollably down my cheeks like a never ending waterfall as I fall to my knees on the hard surface breaking into sobs.

"If only you were here..." I say looking at the dark sky, stars littering the sky.

"Issa," I flinch. When I look up, I see Merebelle entering the balcony, locking the door behind her and taking longer strides towards me and kneeling down to her knees in front of me. "I'm so sorry.." she whispers as she holds my face in her soft hands. I break into an ugly sob. She pulls me to her, wrapping her arms around my back, letting me drench her t-shirt as I bawl my eyes out on her thin shoulder.

I felt my body relax under the comfort of my sister's embracing arms around me. I have never cried so much in my entire life for so many things all at once. I never expected anyone to come to the balcony to see if I was okay but *she* did.

She came for me when I really needed someone.

The moment she pulled me into her embrace, I wasn't only crying because of what happened earlier with mummy, I was also crying because I have never felt like this ever before. I didn't know I was needing someone right now to hold me until she came in. She knew exactly what I wanted even though she isn't a comfort person herself.

Merebelle was *everything* I needed at that moment.

Part of me was still finding it hard to grasp in my head that this was happening because never in a million years

I would've known I would experience something like this. It was all happening though! This moment with her.

I can't put into words how *happy* I am in this moment despite what just happened only minutes ago.

I felt that invisible barrier between us slowly breaking down silently as we held each other as I cried until I was out of breath, breathing sharply for air as I still cried on her shoulder finding it oddly comfortable.

"Let it all out, I'm here. I'm here now." I felt her give my hand a little squeeze and that was all it took for me to completely let it *all* out.

Chapter Nineteen

Begin Again by Taylor Swift

"Thanks." I give the cab driver a small smile before paying him and grabbing my duffel bag, throwing it over my shoulder and making my way towards the apartment building at exactly two-fifty-seven in the morning.

I walk through the entrance doors and towards the lift where I drop my duffel bag on the floor of the lift after pressing the floor button and letting out the loudest most exhausted sigh I have ever exhaled.

The lift dings, letting me know I've reached my floor. I sigh again tiredly before dragging my duffel bag all the way to my door, collapsing right next to the door on the floor.

Reached safely. Have a good day daddy. Miss you!

I sent the text to daddy before tossing my phone next to the duffel bag, too tired to be bothered to put it inside instead. I don't think I was able to do anything besides just lie there on the floor staring into thin air and very slowly drifting to deep slumber.

* * * * *

"Isabelle. You awake?" Why would someone ask someone if they were awake when clearly they're asleep? I hum nonetheless but don't open my eyes. "Isabelle…" that voice registers and I want to so badly open my eyes but I can't because I'm out of energy to even lift my hand up. I'm that drained.

"I can't.." I think I say. It's silent after that. Until it's not.

I'm not going to lie, there have been moments I've thought back to the day Jeremiah carried me up so many floors up to my apartment after finding out I sprained my ankle and yes, I've wanted to be held like that again, not once but so many times. I've wanted to go back in time just to experience that moment again.

"I'm carrying you up. You can't even move." I vaguely hear him say and a second later I'm being lifted in his arms. I don't even have the energy to wrap my arms around him or look at him or say so many things I've wanted to say to him.

"I've missed this.." I don't know who said it but before I could even say anything else, my body decided to shut down.

* * * * *

The first thing I notice when my eyes finally open is that I'm on my bed when I clearly remember I ended up on the floor next to my door. Or was that just a crazy dream?

I turn towards the corner of my room to see my duffel bag by the side of my dresser and my phone resting on my dresser.

Confused, I get out of bed seeing I'm in the same jeans and t-shirt I was in yesterday, well this morning. I glance at the clock and see that it's past twelve o'clock in the afternoon and then proceed to walk to the living room, stopping in my tracks.

You've got to be kidding me right now!

There, on the sofa is Jeremiah lying peacefully, his feet dangling at the edge of the sofa, making me smile at the sight. I grab my blanket from my bed and cover him with it before snapping a picture of him and then going to the kitchen to make coffee.

I didn't even notice the tear drops on the counter while boiling the water on the kettle after seeing *him* asleep on my sofa. Was he the one who got me to bed? Was he there the entire time?

I grab two mugs, wash them and set them on the counter, just when I feel his presence in the room, halting my actions.

"Hey," he says, softly.

It is taking everything in me not to let the new tears forming to let go by just hearing his voice. It feels like ages since I last heard his voice when it was only about two weeks ago or so. I don't turn away because I don't think I can, knowing I'll have to face him.

"Hey," I say quietly, still not facing him but now pouring the boiled water in the jug I put two and half spoons of coffee powder in.

I hate that it's awkward when it shouldn't be. There's no reason for things to be awkward. Nothing happened. Nothing between us, at least.

"I'm sorry-I-don't mean to be awkward.." I say, just above a whisper, finally turning around to face him. Luckily, my tears are cooperating right now because not a single one fell even though I felt it forming in my eyes.

"Don't be," he smiles softly, walking closer. *He shouldn't have done that.* "You got a haircut?" He asks, and freely runs his fingers in my now short hair making me hold my breath at the gesture.

Gosh Heart! Get yourself together!

"Yeah," I smile, slightly embarrassed.

"It looks nice," he compliments. I didn't think I'd even get a compliment on it because I didn't get my hair done in a salon or by a professional. *I* cut my hair all by myself. Alone in the bathroom late at night, my face soaked with tears is how I cut my hair.

"You don't have to…I know it doesn't look nice.." I mumble, taking a seat on one of the stools, hugging the coffee mug with my palms.

"Isabelle, it does look nice." He says, looking straight at me. "Why wouldn't you let me compliment you?" He smiles, the familiar cheekiness making an appearance. I smile to myself.

"I did it." I say this for the first time. "I cut my hair." I say, making it clear to him.

He stays silent for about ten seconds until he says,

"I like it."

"Why?" I couldn't help but ask.

"I just do," he says and then takes a seat on the barstool next to me.

"I missed you." I whisper the locked up truth. I feel like an idiot for admitting it in front of him-

"*Isabelle,*" he says, pulling me to him in *his* embrace, the one I've wanted so much for the past two weeks. God, I've missed him so much. "I missed you too." He answers me, kissing my forehead, making me freeze at the contact. My heartbeat starts picking up just by that and I'm struggling to compose myself at this point because I just feel the tears only filling even more.

"I never got to go shopping for the apartment." He says in my hair. I pull away slightly, not fully though. I love that he is not dwelling on the situation on how I suddenly disappeared without an explanation. That just shows how perfect he is. Like he knows when I don't, well, *can't* talk about what happened the past two weeks. I love that about him.

"What do you mean?" I ask but then slowly understand just by the way he's looking at me. "You..waited..for..me?" I whisper in disbelief. He nods, smiling, but also looking serious. "Why?" I ask, wondering why he couldn't just do the shopping himself.

"Why? I didn't want to go without you. So I waited." He says quietly, tears blurring my vision, ready to fall anytime now.

"Jeremiah.." I exhale, hugging him. I didn't know what to think or say about what he said. I wonder what he would have done if I never got to come back to London. What if I had to stay in San Diego for much longer? What if I never came back? Would he have still waited for me?

"Why didn't you call or do anything to reach me?" He whispered just as the first tears made their way down my cheeks and to his shoulder, staining his white t-shirt.

"I wanted to. So many times. I just-I didn't know what to say.. I was scared. I didn't want to-"

"Please don't say 'bother you'," he says the two words I was just about to say. When I don't say anything, he sighs. "Isabelle, how many times have I told you that you're not a bother?" I cry on his shoulder, holding him tighter. His shirt squeezed in my fist. I hug him tighter than I've ever let myself to.

I don't think I've ever needed someone so much but now just by being in his arms. I've always made myself, or rather, forced myself to believe that needing someone is a weakness.

Again, I was and am wrong.

Everybody needs someone. Even the strongest of people need someone, anybody. And that's okay. It's okay to not be strong sometimes. It's okay to have to depend on someone to hold yourself together. It's okay to bawl your eyes out because I've come to learn that not everybody has the strength to do even that.

It's okay to let go and be weak! We're human, we don't have to always be strong. It's okay.

Chapter Twenty

It Is What It Is by James Miller

'It Is What It Is' by Jamie Miller plays in the background while I dance my way through the floors of Jeremiah's apartment, arranging all the new products we bought for his apartment.

"Oh my gosh Jeremiah you're such a slob!" I giggle, messing his hair and then running to get one of the paintings we bought earlier today in the store.

"Excuse me?" he says, I smirk.

"You're excused, *slob.*" I say with a mischievous grin. He shakes his head to himself before making his way to me with an even more evil grin. "Whoops," I say when he is just inches away from me, towering over me. Damn his height. Without another word, I'm thrown over his shoulder as he walks back to his sofa, tossing me on it and doing the most unexpected thing I've ever expected him to do.

He.

Frikin'.

Tickles.

Me.

"S-t-o-p," I try to say between my loud giggles.

"You wish!" he says, smirking as I scream, laugh, squeal.. you name it. I'm trying to get out of his hold but of course I fail.

"Jeremiah! I. Have. To. Breathe!" I scream through giggles, gasping for breath. He stops abruptly making me sigh in relief. "Meanie," I scowl like Addy would. He laughs looking at me. "Gosh, my stomach hurts." I groaned, rubbing my hand up and down on my stomach.

"You called me a slob." He defends. I laugh.

"Aww poor baby," I playfully roll my eyes while sitting up only to have to be pushed again on the sofa as Jeremiah begins another tickle match. "JEREMIAH!" I scream so loud that I think I lost my voice, getting him to stop.

"Sorry, you're just *so* ticklish," he smirks. I laugh, shaking my head, standing up to finish what we started. I grab the painting I was having earlier, looking for a perfect spot to hang it on.

"Where would you like to have this hung?" I ask Jeremiah, not facing him full-on.

"You're the boss, you tell me," he says with a smirk, leaning on the wall staring at me when I face him, a cheeky grin plastered on his pink lips.

"You're ridiculous." I mutter, standing on my tippy toes placing the canvas board on the wall the sofa's against. "Here? A bit higher though" I ask, facing Jeremiah halfway.

"Looks good. Maybe in the middle a bit…yeah?" He suggests.

"That actually does look good." I say and step up on the sofa, easily holding the painting in the middle of the wall. "Okay." I exhale, jumping down from the sofa on the floor. "Curtains next," I announce, pulling the big shopping bag that has the beige curtains we bought. "How are we going to do this?" I ask no one in particular.

"Easy. I carry you. You hang them." He says, like it's simple.

"Yeah right." I mumble. "How's that easy?" I ask.

"Why not?" He questions back.

"Well, for starters, you'd have to carry me for who knows how long until I get all the hooks done on the curtain. Doesn't that sound a little I don't know.. Doesn't that sound like a lot, Remy?" I asked him, who seemed to find what I just said amusing.

"Not at all." He says casually and proceeds to get the rest of the curtains out of the bag, laying it on the floor.

Once both of us hook the curtains with the wooden circles, I get a blanket from the sofa and lay it on the floor by the sliding glass doors.

"Okay, let's do this!" I sort of cheer with a laugh getting one end of the curtain as Jeremiah walks towards me.

"How do you want me to carry you?" He asks. Good question actually. I look at him and the curtain top wall a few times before deciding.

“Shoulders?” He nods, squatting down so I could climb on his shoulders. “Okay,” I say, holding tight onto his head squeezing my eyes shut as he slowly stands tall to his feet.

“Phew. Now that wasn’t hard was it?” He says with a chuckle, holding my legs in his hands. I’m praying he doesn’t decide to tickle my feet.

“Just try not to drop me,” *and tickle me.* I mumble, not bothering to look down but proceed to connect the hooks on the curtain pole. “Can you walk a little to the right?” He moves to the right as I keep hooking the circles onto the rest of the pole for the next several minutes until I say, “Andddd, done!”

“Awesome! Wanna get down? Or are you liking it up there?” He jokes, making me close his eyes with my hands. He laughs just standing in the same spot as I run my hands in his hair involuntarily in silence.

“Okay, please get me down.” I request and hold onto his shoulders so tight I think I left a fingerprint on him, as he slowly gets me down to my own feet. “Thank you.” I breathe. He nods, like it was nothing.

I take a moment to look around at the new additions we made to the place and silently admire what we’ve done to the place. My eyes catch the small photo frames Jeremiah added onto the shelf on the wall just above the sofa in his living room. Each frame is a memory that already is imprinted in my head and seeing him having the memory displayed in his apartment makes me happy for some reason.

"You've got a beautiful smile Bells," I smile, not looking at him as he says that.

"You've gotta stop with the compliments, Remy..." I smile as I say.

"Make me." He teases. I laugh. He really should find someone else, and not me. I don't deserve him. He deserves better. I don't know why he can't see that.

That night after adding all the new accessories and belongings to his apartment we ended up having pizza over watching The Vow.

Who knew your neighbour was a secret sucker for romance?

Like the saying, '*people are interesting at night*', or maybe that's something I came up with after the so many nights I've spent with Jeremiah. That's what I thought while listening to Jeremiah talk.

The night didn't end for us. Even after the two-hour movie, we kept talking about so many things I never thought I'd talk about to anyone. All those locked up conversations inside me suddenly were all out in the open. All those stories I've been saving up in folders in my head were all out and spoken openly to him.

"What?" I smile when I find him staring at me, smiling.

"You're beautiful, you know." He says, still smiling and I wonder if I'm dreaming things. "You don't believe me, do you?" He says, again reading me. I just shake my head, sighing softly. "Why?" I hear him whisper even though it's just us and mindless TV running in the room.

"I don't know. I could never call myself that. It just doesn't fit. It doesn't go together-"

"Stop. Stop, okay? You need to stop thinking so low of yourself. You need to believe in yourself, Bells. There's only *one* you in this whole world, no one else like you. Just you. And with everything I know about you, I think you're one of the most beautiful people I've ever met." I shake my head at that, making him abruptly stop and stop me. "*Stop.*" I shake away my tears forming in my eyes, or at least try to before he notices but he does.

"Sometimes, the stuff that happens in your life gets engraved automatically and that influences you… leaving you with only those moments to haunt you for the rest of your life." I have no idea how that came out of my mouth but that just made me realise how broken I am. How broken I'll always be.

I thought I could be someone better, someone *good* for him, but I don't think I ever could.

"I want to tell you something, okay? And I want you to shut up until after I finish, okay?" He swiftly takes my hands into his and places a kiss on my knuckles before saying the most intimate words he's ever told me. "You said you like butterflies right?" I nod, impressed that he remembers even the littlest details like my liking towards butterflies. "I don't know if you ever realised this, but butterflies don't even know how beautiful they are. You're like that. You're so oblivious to how beautiful you are as a person, a woman but to everybody else you are so beautiful, like a butterfly. *A beautiful butterfly.*"

Chapter Twenty One

Falling Like The Stars by James Arthur

I know it's probably not healthy to spend a lot of time with someone you have crazy feelings for but what happens when your whole body wants what your heart wants? There's literally no going back now. I'm in too deep and I have no idea how to just stop. I'm not sure I can stop. Not when I'm fully aware of my feelings for him. Not when my whole body knows thoroughly I'm madly in love with my neighbour who also happens to be my personal therapist for the past couple of months.

"So, will you tell him soon?"

Today's the seventh of August and it's the first time I'm not home celebrating my sister's birthday. But here she is, advising me on my personal life while I'm on my way to work. Every part of me is literally yelling 'man, how the tables have turned', making me laugh.

"You know I won't." I sigh, sipping the fifth mug of coffee for the day now.

"Hmm I realised. Where is my sister who had her guts on twenty-four-seven?" I laugh.

"She's long gone," I dryly murmur.

"Nope, she's still alive in the present," Merebelle says. I smile. "Talk to him. There's only so long you can hide it. Life's too short to hide things especially from the ones you *love*. Am I right sissy?" I can already sense her you-know-I'm–right-smile on.

"You know you are." I sigh, gripping the coffee mug in both my hands contemplating the pros and cons of really telling him about how I feel.

"Well then, Im'ma gonna leave you to it." She says quite enthusiastically before we exchange 'I love you's and hang up.

"God, why does love have to be so hard?" I whisper to myself.

I get out of the car after taking the deepest breath I have in my entire life and make my way towards the entrance of the huge building. I keep my face focused on the floor as I walk past the lobby and towards the lift quietly. I enter the vacant lift and press the 10th floor button, leaning against the back wall of the lift thinking of the many ways today's day might go.

"Good morning Isabelle," I gasp loudly, my hands landing on my chest feeling the sudden increase in pace my heart was beating.

"Jeremiah." I sigh, a little relieved it was just him.

"Sorry. I didn't mean to scare you," he says genuinely looking concerned. He always does. And I mentally scold myself everytime this happens.

“Oh, don’t worry. I’m sorry I didn’t see you..” I tried to come up with an apology but once my eyes landed on his, it kind of seemed impossible to process anything right now.

“Where are you headed?” He asks and I mentally thank him because I don’t think I would’ve stopped staring at him if he didn’t say anything.

“My office. I’ve got to finish a manuscript today. What about you?”

“I came to submit the manuscripts I’ve been working on actually. And got a couple of meetings to join today so yeah…” he explains. “You look nice today.” He says, looking me up and down. I have no clue why my body just decided to shut down just by his very words. It was just a compliment, so why all the dramatic actions? “Isabelle, you really need to learn to take compliments.” He says with a grin, walking out of the lift just as it dings, leaving me alone to deal with my stupid emotions.

Once I settle in my office I get straight to work without wasting another minute to let my thoughts drift away.

* * * * *

“Come in!” I call, not moving my eyes away from the manuscript.

“You do know that it’s past your work-time, young lady,” the familiar British accent says, my focus still on the last page knowing all too well that the accent belongs to no one but Jeremiah.

"I'm aware. Why are you here?" I ask, now finding it hard to focus on reading. "No, don't tell me yet..." I quickly said before he could say anything trying my best to finish reading the last page.

Five minutes pass.

Three minutes.

Two minutes.

Sixty seconds.

"Unbelievable," I say, completely shattered by just a page from a manuscript. "Unbelievable." I say again, unable to grasp the climax of the story as I exhale a breath, finally looking at Jeremiah staring at me. I almost forgot that he was in the room. "You..you're still here…" I mumble. He smiles. "Sorry about that-I just-the book-it's amazing really-just never expected that ending." I ramble. He nods with that same smile. "Wow, what time is it?" I ask finally.

"It's a little past nine," he says, looking at his watch. Wow. I usually leave work around six.

"Did you just finish your meetings or?"

"Or." He answers, making me furrow my brows in confusion before understanding what he meant, making my eyes go wide. *He did not.* And the fact that he chooses 'or' and always ends up being the exact same thing I thought about is comfortingly scary.

"Why did you wait for me?" I couldn't help but ask before my brain starts making up assumptions that for sure will start bugging me forever.

"I don't know. I just wanted to." He says, avoiding my gaze. I didn't know how to feel about that so I just started packing up my things.

"Let's go." I say, leading the way out of my office and towards the lift.

We both stayed silent the whole journey from the tenth floor to the ground floor, the lobby which is pretty unusual for both of us since we normally make conversation if we met in the lift.

Once we reached the almost empty lobby, we both walked out of the building to be invited with piercing rain literally making my sides vibrate, goosebumps already forming on my hands at how cold it is outside.

As much as I hate how cold it is, I am incredibly in love with the rain and especially when it's heavy. I've always loved dancing in the rain or just walking quietly in the rain whenever possible even though there's high chances of getting sick which to me didn't really matter because there's only so many times it'll rain in a year and I want to make the maximum out of it.

Life's too short to overthink! So just THINK-OVER!!

My adrenaline suddenly gets on its high side, literally convincing me to put myself out there without overthinking so much.

And just like that, without a second thought I jump on the gravel road of the car park, pouncing on a water puddle making water splash in different directions making me giggle at the sight while getting soaked by the second.

"Now *that* was freakin' spontaneous!" I hear Jeremiah's voice over the thumping rain, making me grin.

"What would be even more *spontaneous* is if you'd join me!" I say, eyes focusing on him. He smirks. That can only mean one thing. I smile in the rain watching him as he makes his way towards me, getting soaked.

"Hi," he says, I giggle once he's so close to me, towering over me making me have to look up at him.

"Hi," I smile.

"Didn't peg you as a *spontaneous* person," my mouth drops dramatically, pretending to be offended. He laughs.

"Spontaneous may not be my forte, but it definitely is there somewhere." I say before I could stop myself.

"I'm starting to see that," he replies. When I look up at him, he's already looking down at me. I smile, pretty sure I'm blushing by how close we are to each other.

Just by looking at him something sparks inside me, consuming me entirely. It's like I've become this whole new person because of him these past few months. I feel I've gotten to know the best version of myself the past few months because of him. And because of him, I've learnt to accept everything that comes with life, good or bad. I'm learning to accept that everything happens for a reason. Just a bit confused about what I've been feeling lately though.

Suddenly, like a light bulb going off, an idea pops into my head. My mind goes to all the times I used to purposely dream dreams involving Jeremiah and I in it. Pretty cliché, I know but hey, at least I didn't scribble hundreds of pages about it. Yet. There's this particular one of a kind dream that is so different to all the other infinitely many dreams I've ever had.

And that's what I do. I *relive* that dream.

"I'm going to ask you something I've been wanting to do for some time now. Is that alright?" I ask, my body shivering, not at all because of the rain. He takes a second to process my words before nodding his head. "Okay." I let out a somewhat relieved sigh and tried to shake away my nerves before smiling up at him. "Do you-"

"Dance?" He finishes my question, like he's just been reading my mind all along. I smile as I nod. "Nope," he says shortly and I almost pout. "You can still ask, you know." He says seconds later, which could easily go unheard with the throbbing rain but I hear him.

"Would you like to dance, Jeremiah?" I smile ridiculously too much. Why am I smiling so much? I thought I was nervous a second ago?

"Sure, Isabelle," he smiles as he says my name. It's my favourite thing about him. Him saying my name paired with smiling.

My hands start shaking when I pull my phone out of my back pocket and open my music app. I open the playlist that just has one song, *'Falling Like The Stars'* by James Arthur in it, clicking play just as my heart beats faster than it ever has.

I didn't have to tell Jeremiah to position himself and place his hands on my waist while I placed mine around his neck, almost touching his hair. He positions his hands gently and slowly like it's the most intimate thing he's ever done.

He sways along to the music like I do and keeps his eyes pouring on mine. I have to keep telling myself to snap out of it but him looking at me like this for too long is making it difficult to 'think wisely'.

I lean the side of my head in his chest, listening to his heartbeat as we continue swaying in the rain, almost like just holding each other. I mentally laugh at myself for picking such an obvious song but also thankful because maybe the song will speak way better than I ever could.

"Tell me something you want me to know about you." I say the first thing that comes to my head.

"No one has…asked me that before.." he says but I get the feeling he didn't mean to say it out loud. I smile.

"Maybe because it *needs* to be asked." I smiled up at him, quoting words he once said to me not very long ago.

He doesn't smile like he usually does, which makes me worry.

"You okay?" I ask softly, without even realising, my hands suddenly cupping his cheeks.

“Isabelle,” when his eyes meet mine, his pupils are dilating profusely. “Heathers,”

“Jeremiah..” I giggle softly. “I don’t know your middle name-”

“I would be lying to myself if I didn’t say I’m so in love with you,” he breathes, cutting me off just as the song ends. “I’ve grown a thing for you the past couple of months-basically since the day you moved in across from my flat,” he chuckles but continues.

“‘Grown a thing’.” I repeat his words, finding it hard to believe him.

“I love you, Isabelle.” He says, making my heart just stop. “I don’t think I could ever stop loving you or to even think of a day where I won’t get to love you-that’s just impossible. I can’t remember how it happened, it just did and I’m sorry I fell for you. I’m sorry not sorry I love you..” he says making me laugh with tears in my eyes. “I’m sorry. I didn’t mean to make you cry,” he says softly, gently wiping my cheeks with his thumbs. I hold his hands that are cupping my cheeks now.

“I’m sorry,” I say after catching my breath without sounding like I’m crying like a baby. This feels so surreal. I’m surprised I never dreamed of him saying anything like *this* in my absurd dreams.

“For what?” he strokes his thumb on my cheek.

“For crying,” I mumble, looking at him but avoiding his gaze.

"You're apologising for crying?" He asks incredulously, his voice incredibly soft. I look up at him, finally to his eyes. It's so green and so up close that I see a few golden lines in them that I didn't see before. It's like his eyes just got a lot greener than they already are.

"Tell me something you want me to know about you." He repeats the same question I asked him before. I smile. He's *good.*

"I think I've 'grown a thing' for you too." I quote him as I say but mean everything I've been feeling towards him.

"Have you now?" He teases and abruptly tickles my sides making me jump and erupt into a fit of giggles. He uses that as an opportunity to wrap his hands around my mid thighs and lift me so we're both eye level and I don't have to look up at him anymore. I wrap my legs tightly around him more than surprised at how my body just reacted to him so fast.

When we look at each other, I find myself playing with Jeremiah's hair, where my hands are wrapped around his neck. Standing and having to look up at him seems much better because I can't look away from his face now that our faces are basically centimetres away. He's made it hard for me to look away.

"I'm madly in love with you Jeremiah." I say the most naked truth I've ever said just before kissing his wet plump lips in the rain. Mentally, my mind checks out the last task on the bucket list I wrote not so long ago.

- ~~*Love somebody.*~~

He opens his mouth almost immediately like he's been *waiting* for me to kiss him. His hands bring me even closer to him while holding me securely while my hands get lost in his brown locks as we kiss, savouring the moment, like it's just us in the vacant car park and nobody else around.

He

Kissed

Me

With

Love.

Epilogue

Flightless Bird, American Mouth by Iron & Wine

Two Years Later

I never thought I'd ever get up from bed with a huge smile on my face, excited for the day. The feeling almost felt strange, to be happy even before starting the day, I mean, honestly, I haven't ever started a day with feeling anything except for the times where the previous night consisted of something so haunting that I'd wake up in the morning remembering whatever happened like it happened just a second ago.

But today, I was happy without even putting effort.

The past so many months have been the most eventful months I've ever lived through but I'm not complaining one bit because I wouldn't even think of trading those months for anything in the world.

I never thought I would ever find love let alone experience falling tremendously in love with someone. I may have had a couple of crushes here and there, yes but I never was fully able to give my entire tortuous-self to somebody. I never thought I'd be loved ever by someone the same way I loved them.

It's dreamlike how you could have someone to unconditionally love you with all of your imperfect flaws and fully accept you just the way you are no matter how messed up your life has been and to have the privilege of loving that person with everything you are.

I can never say I deserved Him no matter how my life turned out to be but I will always be forever grateful to Him for being a part of my life through everything and eagerly wanting to spend his forever with mine.

"Dear Isabelle Heathers,

Writing vows was something I never thought I would do at the age of twenty-four. I thought I had had my whole life planned out until you came along and proved me so wrong and made me see what more life is about than just living for the sake of living. How life could have a purpose. How there's more to life than this world could ever give. To me, marriage isn't something I was hoping for or thinking of even accomplishing because I never really believed that true marriages exist in a world we live in. Most marriages end up in divorce or separations. I don't see people finding other solutions to amending a broken marriage. That made me believe that there's no point to marrying someone and vowing to love them forever.

But,

I would do it for you. I want to say that you were always capable of bringing out that positive side of me no one else could ever bring out. You made me want to do things. Things like wanting to get married at twenty-four. Things like writing a three page vow." The crowd laughed a little at that and so did I but that just made my tears fall even faster. I can't believe he's doing this. For me.

"But baby, words cannot describe how much I've waited for this day to happen ever since I realised I loved you and I don't want to waste another minute without letting you know my forever is to be spent with only you. The very first day I met you, something sparked. People call that fireworks or the obvious, butterflies. I call it *hope*. Hope because you being put in my life brought so much hope too and that changed how I look at things. You brought hope into my life. You showed me how having hope could take you places faraway. You showed me how having hope would lead you to not give up on life even when it gets you down. We didn't need a year to figure ourselves out together, we just needed couple of months and in those few months I never thought I'd be able to experience all those precious moments I experienced with anybody but experiencing all of them with you is the one of the many amazing things that has made me this man I am today. I'd even say it's one of the reasons I'm here today. Nothing could ever change the way I feel about you. No matter what flaw, what wrong, I'll still love you because you were meant to be mine. Just like I am meant to be *yours*, you're *mine*. You were specifically made for me and I have no doubt that after today, our journey together, even years from now don't go the same, I'll still know that we'll still be together. Because I once thought I lost you forever but you came back. We'll come back for each other, that I'll know for sure because like I said, we were made for each other. Nothing can change that. You say you don't deserve to be loved. From now on, I want you to trust that you do.

So much. Because it's the ones who are lowly and think they aren't worth it should be loved the most. And Isabelle, I love you so much for all that you are. Nothing could ever make me change my mind because I was made for loving just you. No one else. I want you to know that, from this point forward, everything we are going to face, we face it together. It's us now, you and me, Isabelle. Can I say that again? It's you and me." He reaches his hand to my cheek and caresses it. "In good times and bad, for richer or poorer, in sickness and in health, I vow to love you every single day and to cherish you, protect you, be there for you, to spend my forever with only you. I love you."

I didn't have to check my eyes to know that I'm crying at this point because my eyes were literally pouring every last bit of moisture there was left.

It's taking everything in me to not hug and kiss him so much because that's all I want to do, to say that I believe in him and that I'm with him from this point forward, together in everything we ever will do and of course that I love him so much and want to spend forever with only just him.

"You just blew my mind for the hundredth time Jeremiah Walker. The first time was when I first met you." I smile, dabbing under my eyes with the already wet tissue so I could ready myself for my turn.

"Knock em' dead Issa!" I hear Merebelle's voice from the crowd that just makes me burst out laughing, simultaneously shedding more tears.

"She already has and she doesn't even have to try," Jeremiah says just so I could hear. I couldn't help but smile at that. I squeeze his hand silently acknowledging him.

"My Jeremiah Walker,

First off, I can never top what you just did and besides you've always been so good with words and making my heart just melt all the time...but let me just say..." I take a deep breath, ignoring the fresh tears welling in my eyes.

"You just made me fall even more in love with you than I already am if that's even possible. You're making me experience things I never thought I'd get to experience but now, today it's all happening and it's all because of you. You have no idea how much of a lifesaver you are. You were put in my life at exactly the right moment. And in such impeccable timing. I like how you said you were made for loving me because that's so true. I didn't know the first thing about true love until I met you. You showed me how loving somebody is putting their needs first before your own and Remy, you did that and not once, but so many times you've had to do that for me and I can't thank you enough. I still think I don't deserve you because for being a flawed human being, I deserve death and all the worst possible punishments a person could ever get but then you came along and just gave me hope. *You* are my hope. And the best thing that has ever happened to me. I've always wondered how my life would be if I had someone who would love me in and out. I used to *dream* of someone to love me for who I am until you. You chose me out of so many. I can't thank you enough for the infinite amount of love you've shown me, for loving me even with all of my flaws, accepting me, cherishing me, making me feel special every single day, and for all those moments only we get to share! Thank you for being my personal therapist even to this day. I'd always look up to you anyway and just realise how after today, I get you all to myself for free! You make me feel so lucky!"

I dab my eyes one more time before mustering up every little bit of strength to say the next statement.

"It's still so very strange just seeing how my life turned around after you. How my life changed *after* I met you. And now I can't wait to spend every second of my life with you. I vow to be the woman you want me to be for the rest of my life and I vow to forever love you with everything I am. I love you."

I couldn't stop smiling. It was all I could ever do at this point, by just seeing him, standing so beautiful in his tux, eyes never leaving mine, tears pooling at the edge of his eyes making his eyes glisten but not letting them fall. Gosh he looks incredibly beautiful. And he's all mine.

My mind is racing to the point where my ears have shut out every sound around us, but only listening to the little sounds of him. His gentle strokes on my hands. His hair tugged at his collar. His way of scrunching up his nose a little. His breathing...

"...and by the power vested in me, I now pronounce you husband and wife. You may kiss-"

"About time!" Jeremiah interrupts before the priest could even finish his sentence, making everybody laugh as he closes the gap between us, cupping my tear-stained cheeks and finally leaning down and kissing me oh so passionately.

"I love you," we both say at the same time, making us both smile at the moment.

"We did it," I smile, when he pulls me in for a hug after kissing me on my forehead.

"Together." He adds, completing the sentence sealing it with another kiss on my neck.

Jeremiah then surprises not only me but the entire crowd by carrying me bridal style. I didn't even have time to scream because my mind still hasn't registered him carrying me. But when it does I can't help but kiss him which makes him stop walking halfway down the aisle making the whole crowd applaud louder and some even whistle and whoop!

Life after you has just begun and will always be the best thing that has ever, ever, ever happened to me and I can't wait to get to spend it with you.

THE END.

Note from the Author

It is recommended that this part be read after reading the book, as it may contain spoilers.

* * * * *

I never thought I would ever publish something, let alone write something personal from my life.

I guess this was a way of sharing my story to the outside world, to those who I will meet in the future and to also to those who I will never get to meet. Writing my story the way I did was not an accident but something I had been contemplating for a while, until I started writing plots inspired by my own life events and experiences.

Choosing God during the year I decided I wanted him to be a part of my life and not someone just on the surface was something I personally think I never would have done as a person. With everything happening that year, I was still a kid and figuring out life as a teenager and was in this stage of wanting to be independent.

Nothing helped me see how God's love was surrounding me until he himself revealed himself fully to me. No words, nothing was needed to help me. Just him. And *voila*, here I am.

It's never too late to start seeking Him. That's what I want people around me, all over this planet to know. It's never too late to let him in your life. His love is always going to be the same for every one of us and that's never going to change no matter what we do. That's something I learnt through my journey, seeking God, no matter how much I still keep failing him almost every single day, his love for me is still the same not just from the day I made him my Lord and Saviour but way before, from the day I was brought out to this world.

My God has always been the same to me, no matter how big, how small I sin, he always has his arms stretched open for me when I return to him. It was never easy for me to let God work in my life until recently, two years ago to be exact. I knew he was there but I have always been hesitant to trust in him. But now, I want to trust him because he has brought me so far and I know for a fact that none of that had anything to do with me, but everything to do with how he worked through my life.

Something I'm learning and experiencing these days is how God makes me feel when I choose him. Choosing him through everything I do, my actions, my words, the way I do things. Just making sure I make him happy with whatever I do. It's not easy but it's definitely satisfying to see the results of that little effort. Because just think about it, he doesn't even expect a lot from us, he just wants us to put a little effort to draw closer to him, and for what? For our betterment. And what does he get? Nothing. Just realising how much he has given and done for me, and comparing that to what I've done for him, which obviously doesn't even come close just makes me feel so sad because he didn't deserve the cross. He didn't deserve that pain. But he wanted to go through it just for us, so that we would have an opportunity with him. So we could have forever with him.

I may have said a lot of things, words that honestly I still to this day struggle to follow, but I still try and continue wanting to do because He is worth all that I could give him.

Life After You is basically my life after I let God in my life. He was my Jeremiah and I was his Isabelle. I think that sums up the truth of how I began writing this story.

Acknowledgements

I'm just going to start by saying Life After You would never be here if it weren't for any of you.

The very first person I'd like to thank is my Father of course. No, not my father, meaning biological father but my- I'd like to call him my Forever-Father because he's my father not just for who knows how many years I'd get to live on earth but past that, even after I leave this earth. You Father is the reason this book is here, written to begin with. As some of you may know, this book basically is my life *after* finding my Father. It's the life after Him. So, thank YOU for giving me yet another opportunity to write *something* this year and for it being mainly about you. I hope you understand my twisted way of putting our relationship into a story. The bottomline of the entire twenty one chapters plus the epilogue is just how in debt I am of you. I want this book to be one of the many reminders of all the infinite amount of amazing things you've done and keep doing just for me. And this book is always going to be a weird little portrait of me admitting that I'm madly in love with you Father and I *want* to indulge in that phrase, you, forever.

I want to thank my beautiful family for sticking by me through thick and thin and accepting me for who I am and loving me even when I don't add up to a daughter and sister they deserve. Mummy and Daddy, if you're reading this, know that no matter what, the bad and good, I will always love you guys so much because you both are God-given and there's no way I'll let a day pass without letting you guys know that you both mean so much more than words could ever say. Thank you for supporting me and being the amazing parents you both are. And my darling Maveesha, you have no idea how much I've come to see the progress we've both made in the past couple of years and even if it's just a little progress, I value that so much. I'm sorry I don't treat you like I should everyday and I know I haven't been the best person to deal with but, I hope you know that I love you with all my heart darling and nothing can change that. Akki is so honoured to have you as her sister and will always be because you too are a precious gift from God. He wouldn't have chosen a better person but you for me, because you're *perfect.*

My dear Mama, oh how I wish selfishly for you to miraculously appear even if it's just for a few minutes to get to read my book. You were the first to read 'Meriliya Sanchez' and you were the first person I ever showed my work to. You were my biggest fan. Maveesha is now, but you were my first and I miss the times we'd stay up late just reading my work in bed till we fell asleep. I never got to say this to you but I hope you know that I love you so much and thank you for being my first biggest fan!

I also want to thank my beautifully amazing sisters in Christ for always being so adorably enthusiastic whenever I drop an announcement about either an upcoming book or whatever it is, being excited for me and supporting me all the way. It doesn't end just there because you guys helped me to come to know the amazing God we worship and I can't thank you guys enough for being there through my journey of seeking God and always being there to help me out. I love you guys so much.

I'd also thank this amazing 'Special Someone' for just being his own amazing self. Thank you for the hundredth time for being there all those countless times I needed someone. This book does have a little bit of you in it, I did have about two whole chapters initially but then I wasn't sure if it was right to do that without your permission even though I wanted it to be a surprise because who knows if the whole world gets to read them right? Plus those are special moments. Maybe it shouldn't have to be shared with the whole world haha. Thank you for supporting me in so many ways but especially being available when I need someone to talk to. Thank you for being such a kind friend to me and like I said, supporting me. Isabelle and Jeremiah appreciate all of your support right from the start.

I also want to thank this other special person. Dear Bambi, have you ever wondered why I call you 'Bambi'? This is why. Bold, you're pretty bold for your age. I would've said brave but that's a common word and you probably know that already so I picked bold instead because that just describes you. Amazing, I honestly couldn't come up with a different a-word besides, you are an amazing person, to me at least for the month's time I've gotten to know you. Mystery. You're still sometimes a mystery to me. You're very hard to figure out sometimes, I'd have to ponder so hard to understand the things you say sometimes. But overall I think we all are mysteries of different kinds. Brilliant. Do you know how brilliant you are? Well, you are. And not just in studies but mostly in everything else too. I can't really explain how brilliant you are because you so damn are. Lastly, sorry but you're an idiot sometimes. Now, don't be mad at me, or come at me after this because you must know that I meant that in the nicest way possible. Now, getting to the point, I want to also thank you for being an amazing friend to me. You've been there in ways you might not realise but you have, so thank you. And of course, this book wouldn't be here if it weren't for your tiny push the other day. So thank you again.

Last but not least, I'd like to thank my readers for being so supportive and loving towards my work since I started writing. You guys mean so much to me too and I can't thank you guys enough for showing so much love and support to me since day one.

Thank you!

www.ingramcontent.com/pod-product-compliance
Lightning Source LLC
La Vergne TN
LVHW041212150826
845673LV00001B/371

* 9 7 9 8 8 9 0 6 7 7 8 5 3 *